Dying Is the Easy Part

Dying Is the Easy Part

William J. Jefferson

Dying Is the Easy Part

Published by Wheatmark™
610 East Delano Street, Suite 104
Tucson, Arizona 85705 U.S.A.
www.wheatmark.com

Publisher's Cataloging-In-Publication Data

Jefferson, William J., 1947-
   Dying is the easy part / William J. Jefferson.

      p. ; cm.

   ISBN: 978-1-58736-951-3

   1. Family--Louisiana--20th century--Fiction.   2. African American men--Louisiana--20th century--Fiction. 3. Rural life--Louisiana--20th century--Fiction. 4. Spiritual life--Fiction. I. Title.

PS3610.E34 D95 2007
813/.6   2007935002

Dedication

THIS BOOK IS DEDICATED to my parents, Mose and Angeline Jefferson, to the parents of my wife, Herman and Bernice Green, and to my grandparents, Mama Matt and PaPa, who you will meet in the book, the people who had the most to do with raising us. To these I add my eldest sisters, Barbara, Betty and Alice, and my eldest brother, Mose--each of whom had a significant hand in my upbringing.

Contents

Introduction

I AM A SOUTHERNER. Race and poverty have always been integral parts of Southern life. African American and white Southerners, mostly, have been affected by and have seen these issues differently. Family life has also always been paramount in the South. And, like anywhere else, we mostly become the people who raise us. If our parents are kind, we children want to please them and to be like them.

My parents were deeply religious. They interpreted the events in their lives and mine principally through the prism of religious faith and Christian values. Against the backdrop of race consciousness, discrimination, poverty, and oppression in Southern life, religion provided an ark of peace for us that did not depend upon an understanding of our circumstances.

For all that I thought I knew about faith, it took a church service in Cameroon, Africa, to provide the ultimate understanding. The service was a raucous, Pentecostal-style, fever-pitch experience. But it wasn't the spirited drum beating, the incessant congregational participation, the call and response, or the vigorous dancing and urgent prayer chants that clarified things. It was bearing witness to the honest, joyous celebration of the congregation's faith and love for God. The service was not about asking God for prosperity, good health, favor, or family or world peace. No one seemed to be praying for anything to meet a personal need. It was not about bargaining with God—*in return for my obedience and service to you, God, grant me my wants and needs.* There was not even an emphasis on praying to God to deliver some other person from sickness or some other unwelcome condition. It was pure worship. The congregants were simply asking God to grant them a relationship with Him. It was as if you were approaching the King and asking Him, purely because of His greatness, if He would let you know, even if He didn't tell it to anyone else, that He knows you and cares about you as an individual saying to Him that you would be satisfied with that alone. The chorus, "*Fait quelque chose dans ma vie, Seigneur,*" was sung throughout the night, after prayers, after preaching, after testimony. Translated, the message to God was, "Do something in my life." Whatever you will, God, in and through our lives, it means. But please acknowledge a relationship with us by doing something—anything—so long as it is You doing it. It can be something marvelous, something excellent, something good or just a touch. Even if it is suffering, just let me know that you permitted it, God, and You are with me as I go through it, and it'll be all right, they were saying. It is this striving, imperfectly, for this most perfect expression of an all-trusting Christian faith in God that has inspired my life, that has kept me, and that has enabled me to fight on in times of trouble and despite my own imperfections. This is the enduring legacy of my parents.

The stories told here are about the people, the surroundings, the difficulties, and the triumphs of my life. That they deal with racial clashes, rural poverty, humor, family challenges, and consuming faith is not for dramatic effect. They are simply the stories that I grew up with, the stories that I continue to live with, the stories I know. I have become what my parents and what a few other folks who had some real say in my life were. I believe in fighting to keep families together, refusing to accept externally or internally imposed racial limitations, winning in spite of poverty and disadvantage, and finding humor in life. But through everything, I believe in praying hard for God just to be with me and in trusting Him enough to leave my life in His hands. This is what happened to me. I hope, through the stories that follow, that something similar will happen to you as well.

Name It and Claim It

MY PARENTS USED TO tell me that I was born on the same date as Albert Einstein.

This attempt at comparing me to Einstein may seem unreasonable to the rest of the intelligent world, but my mother and father saw it as squarely applicable. They told me that I was as smart as Einstein, which was the whole point of their March 14 birth date analogy. And they told me often enough and early enough in my life that I didn't know enough not to let it have an effect on me. It was not the effect produced by misplaced pride or foolish pressure, but rather one that generated hope in a young heart and encouraged the thought of rising beyond one's circumstances.

The year of my birth, 1947, was also the year that Jackie Robinson broke the color line in baseball. Reading this fact as a predictor of my future prowess in sports proved even less prophetic than my shared birth date with Einstein was of my brain power. Holding Mr. Robinson's and Mr. Einstein's accomplishments out as beacons kept me aiming for trophies and sheepskins. And Jackie Robinson's courageous and graceful daily battle against racial injustice had the additional good consequence of focusing our family's thoughts on the long overdue changes that had to be made in the South, which became a matter of special commitment to us in the years that followed.

Fortunately, no one named me Einstein or Robinson. But there was a prescient guest who visited our humble home on the date of my birth, in my parents' bedroom where I was born, who would figure prominently in what I would be called, and, more importantly, in who I would become.

Mrs. Mary D. Shorter, who later became my fifth-grade teacher, also shared my birth date with Mr. Einstein. In her classroom, however, we were more kindred spirits with each other than with this great scientist, for we disfavored math and science for the happier pursuits of word merchants. The early seeds my mother had planted in me in reading and spelling, through her unvarying weekly treks to the East Carroll Parish Colored Library, blossomed under Mrs. Shorter's tutelage, filling my every interest. Mrs. Shorter also apportioned a share of her deep appreciation of history and her love of God and scriptural quotes to me. We in her class appreciated most of her Bible references, except the too-often-quoted passage having to do with "sparing the rod and spoiling the child," which she used to justify whipping us into obedience.

But it was in another, less academic, but more practical area that she made an equally enduring impression. It was also a dangerous place for her and us to explore. It was the world of politics.

In 1957, in rigidly segregated East Carroll Parish, when I was in the fifth grade, Mrs. Mary Shorter, in violation of every Jim Crow law on the books of our state, talked about politics. She was not teaching us sterile civics lessons about how government works, but the explosive ones about how and why it wasn't working for our people. We couldn't vote, and we had to get an education to change things, she pleaded. "They can take your land or your house or your car, but if you have an education, they can't take that away from you. Look at Dr. King, how smart he is," she preached. She talked about this to kids whose parents could not vote; and whose parents would have been deathly afraid for her and us if they had heard her talk about Black folks and Southern politics all running together. For us, nothing was more relevant than Dr. King and the struggle for civil rights that was then captivating the country. To us, then, there was no one more important than Mrs. Shorter since she explained, supported, and taught us lessons from his every action. Nothing made me more interested in learning. It also brought about my fascination with politics.

Black history rolled from her tongue in real life terms, too. When a girl in our class brought a white baby doll to school, Mrs. Shorter became outraged. "Don't bring that white baby in here," she scolded my terrified classmate. "We don't have to do that anymore, child."

But these classroom experiences were all in my future when Mrs. Shorter appeared at our front door to see Angie's and Moses's new baby boy, born on her birth date.

Mrs. Shorter was not one of my parents' closest friends. She was, however, one of their most respected. No one was more revered in the Black community than a schoolteacher or a preacher. Mrs. Shorter was not only a school teacher, but a Sunday school teacher as well, and a member of the church's choir. This put her awfully close to claiming a position in both professions. On Sunday mornings at church and Sunday school, on Tuesdays at prayer meetings, and on Wednesdays at choir rehearsal, she was right there with them, my parents and the other everyday Black people, singing and shouting, teaching and praising and speaking out. So her influence was powerful. When my father opened the door of our home, and she explained that she had just been at the church, had heard about the birth of their new baby, and that God had led her to stop by, I can imagine the front door of our house opening up for her like the Red Sea for the children of Israel. To a family always hoping and praying for a spiritual revelation, I am sure this seemed like an irresistible, if not an unmistakable, one to my folks. She was ushered immediately into my parents' bedroom, where my mother was cuddling me. With just a nod to my mother, she extended her hands to receive her newborn, and my mother handed me over to her without a word. Mrs. Shorter, I am told, drew me close to her breast and held me there, hardly looking upon my face. And, she held me there for a while. Then, she spoke, with a question. "Does he have a name?" My mother had already picked out a name for me, but I would guess she wished she had not, so that she could take whatever was to be suggested by Mrs. Shorter. "I've decided to name him William, after my father's brother," my mother admitted in a quiet voice, almost sounding apologetic. Instead of a grimace or groan from Mrs. Shorter at this news, which I expect would have undone my parents, Mrs. Shorter extended me out from her chest, as far as her short arms would reach, took a good look at me, and exclaimed, "Hallelujah."

William Jennings Bryan was a radical economist. He argued, unsuccessfully, as a U.S. congressman and as a three-time presidential candidate for the silver standard over the gold standard to back our currency. Bryan defied his Democratic Party for his outspokenness on the silver issue, imperialism, prohibition, and other issues, leading to deep party divisions and his ostracism by party bosses. He was called the "Great Commoner" because of his fight against big banks and large special interests and because of his defense and advocacy for the average person. He was also a fundamentalist Christian who deplored Darwin's theory of human evolution and insisted upon the strict and singular account of the book of Genesis as the only explanation for human existence. He was lead counsel on the *Scopes* trial, which he won, contending that Scopes, a professor, was illegally teaching Darwinism rather than creationism to his students. Bryan died in 1925, a few days after his court victory in the *Scopes* trial, perhaps with the satisfaction that he had done the Lord's bidding as the final act of his long career on the public stage. Although the decision he won was short-lived, he had won the lasting admiration of serious Christians such as Mrs. Shorter. And she undoubtedly identified with his reputation for standing up for the little guy and for sticking with his convictions against stiff opposition, despite mounting losses, and in the face of ridicule. Her reaction to my mother naming me William, then, while I am sure it was befuddling to my parents, was confirmation for her that she was on a mission for the Holy One himself. "Hallelujah," she repeated.

Now Mrs. Shorter began acting in a very strange way—clutching me to her breast and extending me to the length of her arms, raising her glasses prescribed for her nearsightedness to get a better close-up view of me, while all the while praising God. My mother would later tell me that she was starting to lose her comfort level with Mrs. Shorter, beginning to worry that I might be mishandled, or dropped, or thrown up toward heaven, or something like that. Just as my mother was about to reach out to get me back, Mrs. Shorter addressed her for the second time, with another question. "Does he have a middle name?" My mother hurriedly deferred to my father to see if he had a middle name in mind, and being quickly assured by his look that he did not, said simply, "No, ma'am." An expression that was a mix of exhilaration and satisfaction came over Mrs. Shorter's face as she said, "I can see that he is going to be especially blessed and do some special things. Let me put something in his name!" And so I became William Jennings at the insistence and under the anointing of Mrs. Mary Shorter. "Hallelujah."

My life has been spent working under the burden and blessing of this prophecy. While my parents lived, at every accomplishment, we discussed whether this one was the fulfillment of this divine forecast or whether there was more. I have never really received any confirmation from God as to whether I have arrived at the place that was his highest destiny for me, so I know He continues to have a greater calling for my life. Perhaps it's not a position, or a title. Maybe it will just be a higher opportunity for service. I can say that the ever-conscious thought of this early prediction, repeatedly confirmed to me by Mrs. Shorter over the course of our relationship, has been a catalyst for my continuing to reach beyond my grasp. At every setback, I have always known I would overcome, because of God's blessing on my life. Of every foolish sidestep or misstep that I have made in my life, I have been able to persist and recover, knowing that if I seek God, He will forgive and renew His claim on me. Who would have predicted that a barefooted Black boy, born of terribly impoverished parents of limited education, to parents who could not even vote, into a large family, under the bitter burdens of segregation, would be raised by God and the prayers of his friends to the U.S. House of Representatives? Well, we believed, and we still trust God for an enlarged territory.

Of course, since he played such a prominent role in my naming from the start, I have spent considerable time getting acquainted with William Jennings Bryan. After a lifetime spent studying him, I finally got to meet him. It was in Statuary Hall at the U.S. Capitol on the day that I was sworn into the U.S. Congress, a cool day in January, 1991.

*And on my servants and on my handmaidens I will pour
out in those days of my spirit; and they shall prophesy.*

ACTS 2:181

Why Cars Had to Be Invented

HORSES ARE USUALLY DEPENDABLE animals. They are hearty. They
are equally rewarding as pets or as warrior steeds. They have revved
many an engine of commerce, and supported many a traveler and
sportsman. They helped to defeat the British and to win the west.
They have themselves been heroes and movie stars and have carried
many to stardom. They can be beautiful, trotting at a relaxed pace,
stretched out running in an open field or on a racetrack, or just
simply rearing up. But dogs need not worry. Horses will never be
man's best friends. For unlike dogs, horses don't keep secrets very
well. Not having his secrets kept can sometimes be the undoing of
a man.

My daddy had a horse he loved dearly. Her name was Tillie.
Tillie was a girl horse, but the point I wish to make has nothing
to do with gender. The breach of secrecy is common to mares and
stallions. Tillie was white and therefore struck a sharp contrast to
the roan, chestnut, black, and gray horses in our town. For a female
horse, she was big and muscular. And she had a distinctive gait,
almost a prance, as prideful a step as if she were adorned with roses
in a winner's circle, just beginning a victory lap. So Tillie stood
out among horses, especially in our small, rural town. Daddy was
justifiably proud of her.

I can still see my daddy on his brilliant mount, coming home from the saw mill, riding Tillie in sidesaddle fashion. It looked almost like a circus ride and Tillie like a huge white circus horse. He rode her without a saddle and without a bridle. He just had a rope lapped loosely around her neck, which was mostly used to tie her to a post while he worked or to regulate her speed when he rode. When Daddy said "whoa," Tillie stopped on a dime. She geed when he said gee, and she hawed when he commanded it. She was a horse of uncommon obedience, military-like discipline, and impeccable training. It was almost the same when she was hitched to a wagon. Of course, a trace or singletree was needed then, which attached to a harness and lines on one end and to a wagon on the other. Though this wouldn't allow her the freedom she had in a bareback ride, there was still no need to have a bit in her mouth. My father would just flick a feathery touch of the line on the left or right side as he hawed her left or geed her right, or whoa-d her to a standstill.

Tillie got so good at following commands that she started to anticipate them. If Daddy started out at six thirty in the morning, Tillie would head straight for the saw mill. When he mounted her at six o'clock in the evening, when his work was ended, she galloped toward home. When we got dressed up for church on Sunday, and Daddy hitched her up to the wagon, she lit out at a comfortable trot straight to the church house. And when she arrived home from work, or church, or a fun ride, or a wagon tow, and Daddy either dismounted or unhitched her from the wagon, she walked directly through the barn door into her stall. Tillie was proud of what she knew and proud to show it off. The Good Book says that "Pride goeth before destruction, and a haughty spirit before a fall." And so it was to come to pass for Tillie.

I agree that necessity is the mother of invention. But invention can also be born of another motive. Sometimes the motive is for good and sometimes it can be for evil, neither motive having little or nothing to do with necessity. Often, it may not even have anything to do with the search for a higher technology. For example, it is plain that, generally speaking, for transport usages, a car can do more than a horse. But sometimes a car may be more desirable than a horse because, in some other important respects, it can do less. In other words, invention may be driven by low motives. And it may be to cover bad habits, which are never necessary.

Cars have no personalities. If they are of the same make and model, they do everything exactly the same. They never learn anything. They neither love nor hate. They have no favorite things to do. They develop no habits. They start up only when the ignition is engaged or the crank is turned. They stop and stay only when you cut off the engine or apply the brakes. They go only when the accelerator is depressed. They do no more and go in no direction other than that to which they are steered by a driver. They have no memories of their own. They don't show off, because they have no pride. By contrast, horses do possess all of these qualities and can do more than cars in all of these regards. When you live in a small country town and have bad habits, these distinctions can make a lot of difference. But my daddy's case alone would not have justified the invention of cars. To understand what happened, you must multiply my daddy's case by many, many other men in many, many towns, large and small, across America and the world. Each of these men had something that they would just as soon have kept secret. Time has shown, however, that horses are no good for this purpose. Each of them is a virtual sieve when it comes to holding secrets. What's more, the better the horse the bigger the problem, with respect to secrecy, for the man who is involved with the horse.

Now you can be sure that if a man has a bad habit of taking one or two drinks too many, or losing a dollar or two too much at a friendly card game, or having a girlfriend too many, he would be an odd man indeed if he wanted it to get out. This goes double if the man is married and triple or worse if he's married and his problem is a girlfriend or girlfriends. Indeed, it is highly arguable that secrecy may be the most important ingredient in a marriage, perhaps even more than love. Think about it. How can you truly love someone about whom you know bad things? On the other hand if the bad thing or things of which one is guilty aren't known by a marriage partner, love can still flourish. The adage that "ig-norance is bliss" was probably first mentioned in relation to the marital estate. In any event, the marriage of my mother and father was apparently prospering on ignorance, mostly on my mother's part. Even though Mama was a strong woman, she was old school when it came to trying to control her husband. So she gave Daddy space. She was more of a homebody than was he, she reckoned, and it didn't bother her that most people, including Daddy, liked to get out more than did she. So she was caught off guard when the rumors came—rumors that Daddy had taken up with a young woman, a Miss Perle Jordan. She didn't know this Miss Perle, but people said that she had met Daddy on a trip he made to cut sweet wood in Alabama and that he was taken by this even sweeter and very attractive young woods dweller. They had struck up a romantic relationship, and this had led her to move to our area. Miss Perle was said to live way out in the woods, much farther into the coun-try than we did.

Daddy's distinctive horse was so well-known that he dared not stop around town someplace where he shouldn't have been, because he was sure to be found out. Thus, were he to fall into dallying with a young woman, it made sense that she should be a country girl living deep in the woods as Miss Perle was supposed to live. Mama tried to ignore the talk, but it started to hurt as she heard it over and over. Soon, she began to feel that all her women friends knew. She spoke to her sister, Gert, about it, and Gert advised her to leave it alone. With a house full of children, what was to be done but to let it pass? "You can't let what other people say ruin your life," she offered. "They'll be home with their husbands, and you and yours will be busted up." Gert's voice evinced the pain of experi-ence.

But try hard as she might to follow her sister's advice, Mama wasn't really the type to just let things pass. Finally, on a certain Sat-urday night, when Daddy came home late, she softly approached him. "Honey," she said sweetly, "folks been talkin' 'bout you and another woman. I don't like askin' you this, but, is it true?" She could have been less direct, but she wasn't used to asking this kind of a question. So she wanted to put it to him nicely and give him every chance to respond. Were it true, she figured, he would know that she was on to him, and therefore get rid of the problem. Were it not true, she thought, then he would just have to respect the fact that she cared enough to try and protect their relationship.

"Where you git that foolishness from, woman?" Daddy inquired demandingly. "You been talkin' to that busybody sister of yours again?" He scowled. "That's why she ain't got no husband today. She's always pickin' and pickin', and spreadin' lies. I ain't dealin' with this tonight. No, I ain't dealing with it ever. I'm tired and I'm goin' to bed, and I think it's best if you do the same," he said brusquely.

His answer and his attitude angered and disappointed Mama. Gert had never told her a thing about Daddy and another woman. There was a time when Gert used to gossip to her about this or that, but she had changed. Mama would have taken almost any answer from her husband if he had taken time with her, shown concern for her feelings, and told her not to worry. But now she was worried that there might be something to the rumors after all. That night she cried silently into her pillow. She couldn't sleep. If she really did have a problem, she needed to think hard about fixing it.

Next morning, Mama got her children up and rustled them some breakfast. She felt like going to church today more than ever. With everything else Mama was feeling that morning, for some strange reason, she was also feeling a little guilty. Maybe she shouldn't have brought up the talk about another woman at all. Maybe, like Gert had said, it was better not to trouble herself. At church, if it really were her fault for feeling the way she did, then she could seek forgiveness and start over with a new approach to handling her torment. Even if it weren't her fault, she was determined to ask God for the strength to forgive her husband and for answers to heal their marriage.

Daddy got the wagon ready for church and hooked up Tillie. He helped Mama to get aboard the wagon, and the rest of us children climbed in as best we could. Daddy called out to Tillie, "Git up," and Tillie made a beeline for church.

Mama didn't spend our ride on the way to church looking at Daddy like she usually did—admiring his dress, his handsome countenance, and feeling blessed to have him as her husband and the father of her children. She hardly looked at him at all, but not because she was angry with him. She just wanted to stay focused on the Lord. She wanted to go to church and pray her way through the quandary she faced. Daddy didn't say much either, but he had different motives. "Mornin'. Come on y'all, let's go," was about all he'd said that morning. Daddy had adopted a "don't ask me no questions" kind of an attitude and bearing, and he meant to have it sink in with our mama. He couldn't know it at the time, but he would have been a whole lot better off lightening up. Mama would have felt a lot better and been less inquisitive. And for sure she would not have invoked the Higher Power to help her solve the mysteries of Daddy's behavior as she was now doing. But she was all the way in the God zone now, having turned everything over to Him.

Fixing her mind on Jesus, focusing on the upcoming church service, her eyes directed forward, she suddenly noticed how elegant Tillie looked as she pranced and trotted her way to church. Her beautiful white mane was flowing, and she was moving easily with the breeze. The sun shone brightly on Tillie's coat, and it seemed to glow in an almost angelic whiteness. Mama even thought she saw something like a halo above Tillie's head, hovering over her flickering, attentive ears. What a spectacular creation, she thought. "Tillie's movin' us along like she's in charge of all of us, to deliver us where we need to go, like she knows what's best for us," she said to herself. "Surely, she was God's gift to us, a God-sent tool," Mama mused as she started to feel as if the very spirit of God had descended upon her. That morning, Tillie's magnificent performance and Mama's religious passion crossed paths and gave rise to an epiphany. Perhaps God was already answering Mama's prayers. She would have to wait to see exactly what His answer was.

Whatever it was, though, Mama was sure that it was wrapped up, tied up, and tangled up with Tillie.

From that day forward, Mama started paying close attention to Tillie, building a better relationship with her. How Tillie took Daddy to work, brought him home, and took herself to the barn, all became matters of obsession with her. Mama gave Tillie's nose an extra rub when she tossed her hay into her stall, and she took a moment to linger and talk to her like old neighbors or good friends visiting over a fence. Whenever Mama encountered Tillie on the way to church or just around the house, she would pet her up and speak gently to her. Mama watched when Tillie left with Daddy to take him where he said he needed to go. She noticed how Daddy directed her and talked to her. She just watched Daddy and Tillie all the time, as if God were leading her to do so. That is how she felt about it; that is how she felt guided to a way out of her pain.

It had been three weeks since the start of Mama's passionate relationship with Tillie. During this entire time, Mama prayed continuously for God to fix her problem. At about the end of this praying time, Daddy announced that he was going on a deer-hunting trip with his friends. The trip would cover two days, Saturday and Sunday, with the actual hunting taking place on Saturday evening and Sunday morning and evening. Daddy would return home late Sunday night. This being the Friday night prior to the upcoming Saturday and Sunday of the hunt, Mama followed her usual pattern. She dutifully packed Daddy's hunting clothes, got his boots out, and made him a meal for his trip. Mama slept lightly the whole night, as if she were anticipating a big test to soon come. Mama didn't know what this feeling meant, but she felt sure that God was stirring things up, causing her to feel this mix inside.

It wasn't until Daddy had gotten well off on his hunting trip that Mama got up. She spent her morning dusting and reading her Bible. So it wasn't until around two thirty that afternoon, as she began doing the family laundry, that Mama began to feel that something dramatic and special was going to happen between her and her God that day. After washing her clothes, Mama wrung them out, then took them outside to hang them out to dry. Then, the miracles started to happen. As she hung out the last of her laundry on the clothesline, she spontaneously burst into a ringing rendition of "Swing Low, Sweet Chariot." Still humming this hymn, she came back inside to wait for the sun to do its job and dry her clothes, and she wondered what her singing was all about. Mama sat down to cool herself, and quickly fell off into a late afternoon nap. As she dozed, she dreamt a strange dream that seemed to portend a prophecy. There she was, in her dream, riding on horseback in a massive sea of other women riding their horses with her. Some were sobbing, some had their fists hoisted in a defiant gesture, and some just looked grim and stone-faced. She woke up in a cold sweat. What did all of this mean?

It was now five thirty, and Mama shook herself out of her dream. It was getting late, and she knew she couldn't leave her clothes on the line till morning when the dew would wet them all over again. She rushed back outside to take in her laundry. But when she got to the clothesline, the meaning of her dream started to seep through. It came upon her as a fog, a kind of mist that surrounded her. And in the midst of this fog, she saw Tillie prancing away from her and then returning to her. "Does she want to give me a ride? Does she want me to follow her somewhere?" Mama wondered. It didn't make much sense to Mama, but the powerful pull of this recurring mental picture compelled her to a course of action. All of a sudden, something told Mama to let go of her laundry basket and get moving in Tillie's direction. So Mama set her basket down and with a dreamy-eyed look on her face, dropped her apron and made her way straight toward Tillie's stall. Even then, she wasn't sure why. A voice seemed to be telling her, "Go with Tillie. Go with Tillie." But where? How? Mama had never ridden or driven Tillie. But some special power seemed to have a hold on Mama, and she just kept on walking toward Tillie. As she neared the door of the barn that housed Tillie's stall, Mama spotted the wagon that Daddy used to drive us to church on Sundays. "Yet another sign from God," she thought. Then, instantly, she knew precisely what to do. The wagon itself seemed transformed. Mama was going to hitch Tillie, not just to a lowly wooden wagon, but to now what appeared to her to be God's own chariot. Yes, somehow, some way, she was going to hitch Tillie up to God's sweet chariot and ride.

Mama had closely watched Daddy hitch Tillie to our wagon over the past three Sundays, and she had a pretty good idea of what to do. Tillie didn't take much tying up, she knew, just the easiest hitches. Tillie was so good, she'd seen, that she would just back up into the traces, up to the singletree, once it was presented to her.

Mama went to the barn and got Tillie out of her stall. She walked Tillie over to the wagon and showed her the singletree. Tillie backed up to the wagon and stood there waiting patiently for the rest of her gear. Mama slipped the collar over her neck and hooked the lines and leads onto it. She hitched the wagon to the singletree.

At about six o'clock at night, all was ready. This was around the time on Saturday nights that Daddy usually left to visit with his friends, play cooncan, or do whatever else he said he did. Mama got into the wagon. She took a deep breath. "Git up," she gently ordered, and Tillie pranced away. Mama gave Tillie her head. She just flicked the leads in the feathery way that she had seen Daddy do as a signal for Tillie to keep going. And that she did. From our house, she rode Mama on the road toward town, and then she abruptly cut through a path in a field of corn that led to a road that headed away from town. It ran along a tree line and straight toward the deep woods. The road narrowed into little more than a not-so-well-traveled, bumpy path. On and on, Tillie trotted, with Mama talking to her in the same friendly, familiar tones that she heard Daddy use. "Good girl. That's the way, girl. Good girl." Tillie trotted along this way for nearly twenty minutes, and then she started to slow, until she came to a walk. Off the road she went, pulling up under a clump of trees and bushes and stopping there. *Where in the world was this?* Mama thought. Had this horse gotten her lost out in the middle of nowhere? She didn't see anything. She looked around again, this time a lot harder. Then, way to her right, she saw a flicker of light, like from a weakly lit lamp or a candle. That was all she could see through the trees. It was too dark to see even the outline of a building or anything from where she sat. "Git up, Tillie," she said softly. But the horse didn't move a muscle. There had to be some other explanation.

Mama alighted the wagon, and walked gingerly in the country darkness toward the light. She wasn't afraid of the darkness, for she had lived with pitch-black country nights all of her days. But her heart was troubled tonight, and she was afraid—afraid of what she might find out there in the darkness. She wandered, almost tiptoeing the better part of two hundred yards down this wooded road, until finally she came to a path that led to what appeared to her to be a tiny cottage. She could barely make it out in the darkness, even though it was a moonlit night. She turned into the path, and walked down it only a few steps when she gasped at what she saw. On the newly painted mailbox, written in juvenile scribble, were these words: "Perle Marie Jordan, Route 5 box 26." Her heart sank. Mama plodded her way back to the wagon. Her knees wobbly, she had to try two or three times before she was able to lift herself back onto the wagon. She sat down heavily. She turned Tillie around. Sobbing softly, she said in a quiet, exasperated voice, "Git up, Tillie, git up. Take me home." And home Tillie trotted.

Daddy came into our house from his hunting trip to a big surprise. Mama was sitting there to face him. She was no longer crying, and her mind was made up. She was not deferring to Daddy on this Ms. Perle thing any longer. She told Daddy what she knew. He sat silently, biting his lips as if to hold back tears, and dying inside.

"I didn't know how to tell you about her, Mama," Daddy said in a low voice. "But she's mine."

Mama couldn't believe Daddy's brazen admission. "Yours?" she said. "What about me, what about us?" Mama was trying hard not to lose her religion.

"She's my girl, my baby," Daddy said.

He's getting in deeper and deeper, Mama thought, *using sweet eyes to punctuate his words as he talked about Perle.*

"She's my daughter," he said, sighing with relief. "I should have told you. But it was a long time ago, before us, and I just didn't know how to. Her mama died and, well, now she's here. Forgive me."

So Mama and Daddy got back straight again, no thanks to Tillie. And Daddy knew that after that, he and Tillie would never be the same.

But Daddy got a measure of revenge. He sold Tillie. He sold her for little or nothing. He sold her without telling Mama. He couldn't take the chance that Tillie might reveal something else he didn't want Mama to know. Tillie's sale was her punishment for betraying him. "After everything I've done for Tillie. After all we've been through together," he found himself repeatedly muttering to himself, "She gave me up!"

It is for reasons like this, when horses have given men up, that in households across the country and the world, men have been found out by their wives and girlfriends as gamblers, liars, cheats, or womanizers, or guilty of a myriad of bad secrets. In every town and hamlet in America and abroad, women mounted horses and wagons and rode or drove them into new revelations and understandings of their husbands' shortcomings. Horses simply grow familiar with the ways and routes of men, and men grow close and dependent upon horses and let them in on everything they do and everywhere they go. Men discovered that alliances with horses can lead to great disappointment, for a horse is liable to tell everything it knows about the relationship to anybody—a stranger or, worse still, even a wife or a close friend. Therefore, men clamored for change, and the invention of the automobile was the natural consequence. They wanted something hard, and inanimate. Their hearts had grown cold toward horses as daily companions. Most of all, they wanted to ride and go places on something that wouldn't tell where they had been. Therefore, those who believe that Henry

Ford invented the car in order to harness more horsepower are terribly misled and uninformed. Quite the opposite is true. Cars were invented at the behest of wayward men who wanted less, not more, horsepower.

If ye then, being evil, know how to give good gifts unto your children, how much more shall your Father which is in heaven give good things to them that ask Him.

MATTHEW 7:11

Learning to Pray

I HAD WALKED TO the little corner grocery store a few times before. Everything had gone just fine, so Grandma Matt had no reason to expect that anything bad would happen to me when she gave me permission to go to the store that morning. The store was just two blocks away from her house, and if she wanted to, she could watch me from her front room window, all the way there and all the way back. I was seven years old, and that was big enough to do a full day's work in the cotton fields, so walking by myself to the store wasn't anything. "You're an apt little boy," Grandma had told me. "You can count your change better than a lot of grown folks 'round here can." I had asked her if I could get some Happy Jack Wagon Wheel Cookies from the store, and she had said I could. They were my favorites, and I was grinning from ear to ear like Happy Jack, thinking about getting a stack of them. They were two for a penny. Grandma gave me fifteen cents. She said that would buy me more cookies than I could eat. I told her I wouldn't spend all of the money. I would just get twenty cookies and keep the five cents change for another day. She was so proud. "That's Grandma's man, Billy," she crowed. "That's Grandma's little man." And she smacked her snuff-filled, juicy-lipped kiss hard against my face.

Life didn't get any better than staying uptown at Grandma's, all by myself without any of my brothers and sisters. And I was away from our farm way out in the country for a day or two, leaving my daily chores to someone else. But I would have worked hard just for the chance to stay with her. She was the best cook in the world, and God, did she ever fuss over me. This morning was no different. Before she let me go to the store, she made sure my shoes were cleaned up and tied just right; that my belt was fastened in the right hole; and that my shirt was tucked in. She rubbed some pomade on my kinks, and brushed them with her warm, smooth, trembling hands. Then she stood back to study how I looked and nodded and winked her approval. "Looking good," she announced. "All ready?"

I stood straight up. "Yes, ma'am," I said.

"Don't tarry now, and I'll see you in a few shakes … a few shakes of a rabbit's tail." Grandma smiled. Then she laughed her catchy laugh, and I laughed, too. I knew that a rabbit had a real short tail, and I'd have to hurry back. Then she gave me a big, squeezy, squeezy hug and another snuff-filled, juicy-lipped kiss and pushed open her screen door. I skipped out. At that moment, I doubt whether any boy, anywhere, had ever had a happier send-off to any place.

On my way to the grocery store, I must have skipped the fastest I have ever skipped, because it seemed like I got there in no time. Mr. Charlie Sansonne, who owned the store, was a big, burly man with dark hair and dark eyes, and his look frightened me when I first met him. But he always seemed real friendly toward me, probably because Grandma bought all her food from him, and he knew I was her grandson.

"How's Matt this morning, boy?" he asked with a big grin. "You tell her I got some fresh neck bones and some pickled pig feet that'll go real good with that mess of greens she just bought. Tell her to come and get her some."

"Yes, sir, Mr. Charlie, I sure will," I said.

"You come for the same thing you came here for a few days ago, boy?" he asked.

"Yes, sir," I said, "the very same."

"How much you want this time, son, another nickel's worth?"

"No sir," I said a little self-importantly, "I want a whole dime's worth today!"

"Your grandma must have come into some big money, boy," he teased, "but all right, if that's what she wants you to have." Mr. Charlie dug his big hands into his cookie jar and counted out twenty Happy Jack Cookies. He put them in a brown bag, folded the top over to close it up, and handed my precious cookies over to me. "Sure you don't want one of them pickles in that jar over here, just cost you another two pennies?" Mr. Charlie asked. I think Mr. Charlie left his pickle jar open so the smell of his pickles could waft out just to entice folks like me.

"No, sir, not today," I said. "Maybe tomorrow." I really felt good about not giving in to my pickle itch, and I knew Grandma would be real happy about it too. I skipped out of the store, with visions of Grandma hugging me for being so good and visions of me biting down into my delicious snack. I was as happy as a creepy-crawly bug snug in a rug, and I was sure that my skipping back was gonna be as quick as two shakes of a rabbit's tail.

My spirits were so high and my thoughts so giddy that I never noticed that a bunch of little white kids, little like me, had started to throw rocks at me. Until one of the rocks they were hurling hit me in the knee, I hadn't even looked those kids' way. That hit mostly startled me.

Then, *crack,* another one hit me, this time in the side of my head, and I screamed out in fright and in pain. What was going on? Why were these kids hitting me with rocks and stones? What did I do to them? The hail of rocks kept coming and I started running as fast as I could. Then a rock stung me, *smack,* on my right hand, and the pain was so sharp that before I knew it I had dropped my bag of cookies. Now I really bellowed. And, they were yelling at me, "N——, n——, n——!" What were they talking about? "N——, go home! N——, go home! Run, n——, run!" And they laughed as I left the flying rocks and the mean shouts, and, worst of all, my beloved cookies in the distance.

When I got to the front door of Grandma's house, it was already standing open and she had her arms flung wide open to receive me. She wrapped me up with her flabby arms, buried my face into her pillowed breasts, and hugged me as tightly as she could. "Now, Billy," she consoled me. "Now, Billy, don't cry."

"But, why did they hit me, Grandma, and why did they call me names, and why did they take my cookies?" I blurted out breathlessly through a river of tears.

"It'll be okay, Billy," she said. "It'll be all right. Don't you worry about them. You're here with Grandma now. It'll be all right."

"What is a n——, Grandma, and why did they call me that?"

"Because they're trying to make you feel less than them, and that's a name that's supposed to make you feel ashamed of being colored. But, that's for them to worry with, not you. It don't matter what nobody calls you, all that matters is what you answer to. You ain't less than nobody, Billy; you're good as anybody in the whole wide world. Don't worry yourself no more with it, son. It'll be all right."

That's all she said to me—no why or wherefore; no promise to whip them for hurting me, and not even the mention of a plan to get my cookies back, either. Nothing! I got real confused about Grandma. I even thought in that moment that I didn't like her as much as I used to, just a few minutes ago. It was all so bewildering. I didn't know how I felt about her. I didn't know what was going on. "Grandma," I pleaded, "what are we going to do to them?" I looked into her eyes, and she looked so miserable, almost like she was going to cry. And, then, I really felt helpless. What was happening? I didn't know why Grandma looked so sad. My mind drifted off. I couldn't focus on Grandma. Nobody had ever talked to me about racial hate. I didn't know anything about it, and it was making my head hurt.

Suddenly, Grandma grabbed my arm. It shook me. Something seemed to come over her. Her face turned sunny. She smiled at me. Then she laughed aloud. "Look at you," she said. "All ready to get at somebody for doing you wrong? Well, that ain't your business, boy, ain't none of your business. White folks been treating us bad for years and years, and ain't nobody got no answer to it yet. But, one day, son, there's gonna be an answer—yeah, there'll be an answer, all right. But it ain't gonna come from no angry colored boy with his fist balled up, and not from some mad old lady either. It ain't gonna come about that way. You know why it ain't gonna happen like that? 'Cause it's not God's way. And 'cause we ain't in charge, son. We ain't in charge. But, you know what? These white folks who are mean to us ain't in charge either. Oh, they might strut around and act like they be and think they be, but believe me, they ain't. It ain't their world, son, and it ain't yours or mine." Her big soft hands cupped my face. "Look at me, baby. I ain't mad. I love you more than anything, Billy, and I don't want to see you treated bad, but I ain't mad with nobody. Don't feel bad or angry, baby, 'cause sooner or later it's gonna be all right. Jesus is gonna see to it. This is His world, and in His own time, He's gonna make it right. And, listen, Billy, He's gonna make them treat us right, too. You understand me, baby?"

Well, the truth was, I didn't understand her, and I really didn't want to! I wanted to know why those things had happened to me. I wanted those bad kids to get a whipping. Perhaps most of all, I wanted my dime's worth of Happy Jack Cookies back. And she looked into my eyes and she knew that.

"Listen, Billy," she said, "Grandma's gonna get you some more of your cookies. But you need to let this whole thing be a lesson to you. You've gotta find peace in this world 'cause you gotta live in it with all kinds of people. Some people are just gonna hate you and be mean to you because you's colored. I know it don't make no sense, but that's just how they are. Some of them are confused people, son, and some of them are sick with hate in their minds and bodies. Now, what we don't do is act like them. We don't give back hate for hate. We give love for hate, that way love is gonna win out. That's the way it is, Billy. That's how God planned it. I can't tell you

I understand God. All I can tell you is that I know Him. And I know He wants us to forgive them children that was mean to you. So, you know what we're gonna do, Billy?"

"No, ma'am," I said, finally stopping my sniffling long enough to listen to her. Promising me my cookies back may have had something to do with my renewed attention to what Grandma was saying.

"Did you do anything wrong out there with them children?" Grandma asked, shaking her head side to side. "I know you didn't, son. So we don't need to do nothing for you or ask God nothing for you. But, we do need to do something for them children that did you wrong today. And that's what we're gonna do, Billy. That's what we're gonna do. We are going to pray for them. You and me, right now, we're gonna get on our knees, and we're gonna pray for them."

Grandma Matt took my hand and led me back into her living room. She knelt down in front of her sofa and made me get down on my knees, too. As we knelt, I looked up against her wall, and there staring down at us was a picture of Jesus Christ hanging over her sofa. I was staring up at it when she said, "Put your hands together, Billy, and let's close our eyes." And then Grandma began to pray out loud. "O, Lord," she started out, "as we bow, don't let us bow for form or fashion or as an outside show to this cruel world, but with a pure heart. Lord, forgive us for our many sins and wrongdoings, and we come acknowledging our unrighteousness. Have mercy on us. I ask you, dear Jesus, to let us surrender everything to You and let us come as humbly as we know how before Your precious throne. I don't have to tell You what done happened down here today, 'cause You already know all about it, and we are just mentioning it to hand it over to You. Lord, we are puttin' it in Your hands. Jesus, help us to forgive our enemies and them who spite us and who use and abuse us. Please, Jesus, we pray You, forgive them young white children who attacked and wronged my sweet grandboy, Lord. Help them to understand that hate is wrong, God, and that love is Your way. Let them see Your way, Jesus, and forgive them. Touch their hearts with Your love, Lord. Open their eyes to Your truth that we're all Your children, all the same. Now, Lord, look down on all Your children and have mercy on us. Fix our hearts, Jesus, and give us clean hearts and a right spirit to serve You. Strengthen us on our Christian journey and teach us to wait on You. So, Lord, we are giving it all back to You—all the troubles of this world. And, we ask You, Jesus, to remember us down here, and bless us any way You see we stand in need of. And, when it is all over down here in this mean old world, we ask You to please receive us into Your kingdom where all troubling and worry will cease, and we can live out eternity with You in Your kingdom in heaven. Thank You, Jesus. Thank You, Lord. All of these things we ask in Jesus's name. Amen."

I opened my eyes and looked up at my Grandma. She was already beaming in perfect peace and glowing and bubbling with joy. Staring into her eyes, for some reason, made me press my hands real tightly together, and I said, "Amen, too."

Grandma smiled at me, and then she laughed out loud with her catchy laugh, and it made me laugh too. "That's Grandma's little man," she said. And she gave me her squeezy, squeezy, Grandma hug, and another snuff-filled, juicy-lipped Grandma kiss hard against my face. She picked me up, carried me into her bedroom, and laid me down on her big, goose-feather-stuffed bed and covered me with her colorful, patchy bed spread, and I fell asleep.

When I awoke, right next to me was a brown bag. I looked inside, and it was filled with Happy Jack Wagon Wheel Cookies, twenty of them. I opened my bag of cookies and took a big, long-awaited bite of one of them and savored its creamy, sweet, vanilla flavor. Then I leapt up toward heaven and shouted out loud so Grandma could hear me, "Thank You, Jesus!" I just wanted her to know.

A wise son maketh a proud father; but, a foolish son is the heaviness of his mother.

PROVERBS 10:1

A Fish Story

MAMA WAS RIGHT TO warn me to be careful when I went fishing that morning. But I wasn't listening.

Mama had just finished serving me a good breakfast of flapjacks and maple syrup and cold sweet milk, when I decided to go outside to find something better to do than just sit around with her. My older brother and sisters were out working, and I didn't feel like playing with the baby ones. I didn't see that I had anything or anyone to play with. So, I took out my pocket knife, cut a part of a low-hanging sycamore tree branch, and started making circles on the ground with the stick, some big and some small, some close to my front porch steps, and some farther away. I was gonna use these circles to practice throwing my pocketknife.

I had finished drawing my circles, and I was just about to throw my knife to the circle that was the farthest away, when a big, brown rubber knee boot stomped down right in the middle of that circle. It was the "Big Boy." He was big and fat. From his floppy jowls to his jellyroll gut to his elephant-leg calves and ankles, he was big—B-I-G—big. That's why we called him the Big Boy, and that's the only name I knew for him. I thought to myself, *He must not have a thing to do himself either this morning, else he wouldn't be standing in my front yard in the middle of my circle, messing up my game.*

I said to him, "Man, you almost got stuck in your big ole foot jumping in front of me like you did when I was about to throw my knife. I didn't hardly see you."

The Big Boy just stared at me with his arms behind his back. "Your eyes must be pretty bad then," the Big Boy answered laughing, his belly jumping hard. *Right about that*, I said to myself. "Anyhow, I got something more fun for you to do," the Big Boy grinned. "Wanna come and go across the levee with me to fish?" The Big Boy moved his arms from behind his broad back and showed me his fishing pole that he was dragging behind him.

My heart leapt in excitement. I quickly forgave the Big Boy's intrusion on my meager game. "Yes," I said, before I even thought about it. I dropped my stick and folded up my pocketknife.

It was late in May now, and the high waters of the Mississippi River, which just a few months earlier were at the top of the levee, had gone way down, leaving patches of ponds, some that were like small puddles and some that were pretty wide and deep. The really deep ones we called "bar pits." Some of these bar pits were covered with green algae and moss-like stuff and looked really dark. These were the ones that were most likely to have big fish in them—big fish that were swimming deep in the river when it was high, only to be trapped in these deep dark pools and left behind as the river flowed out to the Gulf of Mexico. I hadn't ever had a chance to go and see if I could catch one of them. Daddy wouldn't take me, and Mama was afraid of the earthworms that were used for bait, so she never went with me either. And she wouldn't let me go by myself. All the fishing I had ever done was for crawfish in the ditches close around, and sometimes I would catch some little perch there. But I'd sure heard a lot about some big catches made over the levee this time of year. I'd also heard enough descriptions to know what a good fishing spot looked like.

I didn't know the Big Boy that well, and had only played with him once before. So, before I let myself get too excited and let my emotions really cut loose, I had to be sure of what the Big Boy meant. "You mean you want us to go to fish for them big fish in the bar pits over the levee?" The Big Boy nodded yes. Now, I was so, so excited. Right then I saw myself landing some of them big catfish or buffalo fish hidden in the blackness of them bar pits. I was excited, so excited that I started to jump around like when I was going to pee on myself.

"Let's go," the Big Boy demanded. I really wanted to get my fishing pole, dig up some worms and get across the levee to fish with the Big Boy right there. But I knew I couldn't just go off like that. I knew I had to go inside and ask Mama if it was okay. The Big Boy was twelve and I was nine. He said he didn't have to ask his mama nothing. But, I knew I did. When I asked Mama if I could go, she came out of the house to take a look at the Big Boy.

"You Lutie Mae's boy, ain't you, son?" she asked.

"Yessum," the Big Boy said, drawing his chin down to his chest, making himself look as small and innocent as possible. The fact is the Big Boy was so big and fat that he looked a lot older than he actually was. Even though Mama knew his mama, she still gave the Big Boy a good looking over. The Big Boy smiled at Mama, and then he came and stood next to me and put one of his heavy arms around my shoulder. It was a strange reaction by the Big Boy, and I couldn't figure out whether it was helping or hurting our cause. I didn't know anything different to do than to flow with the Big Boy, though. So we both stood there smiling at Mama. Mama looked at us both real hard for a good while. She must have liked what she saw 'cause finally she said, "Y'all can go, but you better be real careful. Them bar pits is so black and so deep now, that if y'all fall in one of them, ain't nobody gonna find you till late summer." My heart started beating a mile a minute. I felt sooo excited. I started to fidget again. "You listenin' to me, boy?" Mama asked. "You hear me and you hear me good. Them bar pits is dangerous. If you fall in one of 'em, ain't nobody gonna ever find you, and you'll be dead and gone. You understand me?"

I stopped squirming and I crossed my legs to hold myself still. "Yes, ma'am," I said. "Yes, ma'am. I'll be careful. I promise."

She started to walk away, and then she turned back to me. "Pee before you go 'cross that levee." "Yes, ma'am, Mama," I said meekly. "Yes, ma'am."

As soon as the door slammed behind Mama, I burst off the porch to the side of our house to get a rake. I rushed to an area under the trees in our backyard that was always moist in the springtime, and full of earthworms, just a rake-scratch below the surface of the ground. I had gathered only a handful of worms when the Big Boy said, "Come on. Let's go."

"I ain't hardly got no worms at all," I complained to the Big Boy, and I started raking a lot faster. I wanted to catch a pile of fish that day, and I didn't want to miss none 'cause I was out of bait. A few minutes later, the Big Boy barked again. "That's enough, let's get our little Black butts over that levee!" His big butt jiggled, and bounced around from side to side, as he struck a trot toward the levee.

"There ain't nothing little about his butt," I laughed to myself.

I was thinking about whether he'd hurt any of the stuff he was carrying when he yelled back at me, "What you standing there for? What you staring at?"

"Nothing," I shouted back to him, picking up my fishing pole and running to catch up to him. "Nothing." Pound for pound that was probably the biggest lie I have ever told.

"I think I know a good place to go, and it ain't too far, either," I told the Big Boy when we got to the top of the levee. My cousin had told me a few days earlier that he'd caught a monster buffalo in this bar pit just across the levee from our house. But the Big Boy didn't answer me. He just swiped the air with his big right arm and motioned me to follow him. I just stood there and looked at him, 'cause I was real worried that I might lose my chance to land the cousin of that big fish my cousin had brought home.

Finally, the Big Boy said softly, "I know a better place to fish. Ain't even no little fish there no mo'. The big fish done ate them all. Now they's feedin' on each other, and the ones left are just gittin' bigger and bigger."

I couldn't believe it. "Really?" I asked. The Big Boy just looked at me. "Honestly?"

"Hell yeah. You ask too many questions," the Big Boy said firmly. "Now, you goin' with me or not?" I nodded that I would go with him, and I followed him.

We trudged along for better than a mile before the Big Boy said we'd come to the right spot. "Here is where we gonna do our business," he said with a sly look. I didn't understand the weird look on his face. *Maybe he's just trying to make some confusing joke,* I said to myself. Truth be told, though, the fishing hole the Big Boy pointed me to looked pretty good. There were clumps of trees around it, a lot of moss on the water's surface, and it looked a mile deep. I hurriedly baited my hook, set my stopper real high on my line so I could fish down deep, and threw my line in. Any minute now, I thought, some unsuspecting, monster buffalo fish or catfish is gonna make the fatal mistake of grabbing a hold of my hook and bending my pole to near its breaking point. And then he's gonna be mine—I'm gonna land him, I'm gonna land him good. I clinched my pole real hard in my hands and steeled myself for the big bite.

Then I heard a *plop, plop, plop* from the bar pit. Something was striking the water right where my sinker was bobbing. I turned around, and it was the Big Boy. He had fists full of clods of dirt, throwing them hard into the bar pit. "Hey man, what you doing? How we gonna catch fish with you scaring them and running them away? We can't catch no fish that way at all," I yelled at the top of my voice.

The Big Boy just laughed, but it wasn't a funny, joking laugh. It was a mean, evil laugh, and it scared me. "I don't care. I don't wanna catch no stupid fish no how," the Big Boy shouted back at me, even more loudly than I had at him.

"Look, I wanna do something a whole lot more fun than fishing right now," the Big Boy said in a lower, more composed voice, and now with a friendlier look on his face. "Come on with me, and we can fish later. Just leave your pole in the grass under the tree there and we'll pick it up on the way back. Come on." He gave another swipe of his massive right arm, and just like that I laid my pole down on the bank of the river and followed him like he was some kind of messiah.

So the Big Boy and I started to make our way to the top of the levee, with me not knowing where or why we were going. I was beginning to build up my courage to ask him what was going on when suddenly, as we neared the top of the levee, the Big Boy whispered urgently, "Stop, get down on your belly." I dropped down on my belly, and the Big Boy got down on his belly too, right beside me. The Big Boy was breathing fast and hard like he was in a panic. His breath was hot and stinky, and his whole body gave off this sour, sweaty smell. I was getting sick to my stomach, when he spoke up again. "Now, let's crawl on our bellies to the top of the levee and look over, and keep your head down." We slithered like water moccasins the rest of the way up the banks of the levee, through the Johnson grass, the mud, and the sand and gravel until we could look down below us to the other side. "Be quiet," the Big Boy whispered. At his command, I lay there as still as a mouse—scared, sweaty, muddy, and confused. By now, I had forgotten to ask what I was doing these things for. I had a bad feeling, but I just stopped thinking. Fear took me over. I was too scared to speak or to think or to fight back. I really don't know why.

Gaining enough consciousness to look out from the levee's top, I saw the broad, expansive fields of cotton that this levee was there to protect. And, right below us, at the foot of the levee, across a narrow, dirt road, were two small, shotgun houses, about forty or fifty cotton rows apart. These houses looked a lot like ours, and like a lot of the other houses that we poor Black folks lived in. There were a few dogs and a few horses and cows around them like at every such house. There was nothing interesting or unusual about them—nothing I could see. Yet the Big Boy couldn't take his eyes off of them. He kept looking at one and then the other of them, from one to the other. I was starting to wonder what he saw down there that I didn't see. He might have again felt one of my questions coming on, for at this point he looked to me and said, "Jus' wait." And, so we did, we jus' waited, and the Big Boy kept on watching the houses. After ten minutes or so, the front door to the house that was most directly below us pushed open, and an old lady came out. She stretched a little, gave out a wide yawn, and then started to walk slowly off her porch toward the other small house. "Now!" the Big Boy said urgently, "let's go."

He jumped up and I jumped up and we ran down the levee in the direction of the old lady's house. We were running so fast, that I was sure that the Big Boy was going to trip and tumble and hurt his fat self real bad. *If he falls that hard,* I was thinking, *he's gonna leave a big ole grease spot on the side of this levee that ain't nobody gonna ever clean up or ever get no grass to grow there again.* Fact is, I was kind of hoping something like that might happen to get me out of what I was doing since I couldn't seem to get myself out of it. But the Big Boy pounded the levee side as he raced down it, and while his whole flabby body shook violently, he proved a surprisingly quick and nimble runner. At the base of the levee, the Big Boy again commanded me, "Git down." I fell on my belly again. The Big Boy crouched in the tall grass and weeds there on the side of the road and peeped out in the direction in which the old lady was walking. A truck passed while we were hiding in the grass. The Big Boy put his head down. I put my face down too. Then, with another swipe in the air of his big right arm, he motioned to me. He got up and dashed across the road, and I trailed after him.

The Big Boy and I ran up to the old lady's house, and along its side. The Big Boy pressed his back against the side of the house, acting like he was trying to flatten himself out, and walking crab-like, sideways along the length of the house till he came to its end. I followed, walking in a regular way behind him. At the end of the side of the house, the Big Boy stuck his neck out to peer around to the rear of the house. Without a word, he turned the corner and headed toward the back door. He slid stiffly along the rear of the house till he reached it. He pushed at the back door. It opened, and he went in. I was still standing at the end of the side of the house, when the Big Boy poked his head out of the back door and nodded for me to join him in the house. I stood still. Then, he swiped his arm hard. It was the hardest thing I'd ever done, but, halfheartedly, I marched in behind him. I'd never done anything bad, or crazy, or wrong that amounted to much. I'd always tried to do what Mama said I should do. I didn't know what I was doing now. I felt deep inside like it wasn't right. I hadn't asked Mama, and that right there was enough to make it wrong.

Now, inside the house, my mind and parts of my body were pounding. I started to wriggle again, but I really wasn't faking like I might pee on myself out of excitement. This time, I felt like it might happen for real.

"Hello," the Big Boy called out timidly. "Is anybody home?" He waited for a minute. "Anybody home?" No one answered. "Good! All right!" the Big Boy said. "Let's eat."

We were in the kitchen of the house. It wasn't much of one, not even as good as Mama's. For one thing, it was very small, and for another, it didn't have a nice sit-down table in it like we had. The cupboard was half the size of Mama's. I didn't see any icebox, but I figured there had to be one in another room because she had a milk cow outside. Surely her milk would spoil without an icebox. I guess I was thinking about this while remembering Mama's sweet milk, which to me was the best part of being in her kitchen around breakfast time. I was just trying to keep my mind occupied with good thoughts, because I sure didn't want to think about where I was and what we were doing. That's why I was keeping my mind as full as I could of thoughts of my sweet Mama and her sweet milk.

Then the Big Boy exclaimed, "Look at all these good vittles! Time to eat, so we can get going."

Boy, did I ever want to get going, so all of a sudden eating the old lady's food didn't seem like a bad idea. Looking around, she did have a good breakfast spread. On her small, black wood-burning stove was a pot of freshly cooked grits. A soft-looking dishtowel covered some newly baked biscuits. And, partially covered with another plate on top, were some hard fried strips of fatback. So I accepted the Big Boy's offer to me of a shiny porcelain plate that he had taken from the cupboard.

The Big Boy piled his plate with grits, a handful of fried fat meat, and three fluffy biscuits. I took just one biscuit, a spoonful or two of grits, and the littlest piece of meat from the old lady's meat plate. I was feeling guilty. While I nibbled at my food, the Big Boy ate like a pig. Then I asked a dumb question, because I just needed to try to justify what was going on. "Is it okay to be in this lady's house and to eat her food?"

Without looking up from his feasting, the Big Boy said, "Course it is, else I wouldn't be doing it." I didn't protest or ask another question. "Okay," I offered, under my breath. That was gonna be answer enough.

He ate and I ate. We drank some water to wash it all down. Then we left. We left the dirty plates and all the mess, and ran out of the back door and back across the levee.

When we made it back to my fishing spot, I found my pole, picked it up and baited it. I threw my line back out into the bar pit, trying to get back to normal—back to where we were before we went into the old lady's house. But I couldn't concentrate anymore. If a big fish had hit my line at that moment, I suspect it would have yanked my pole right out of my limp grip. *What had we jus' done?* I kept asking myself. I wanted to blame the Big Boy. I wanted to ask him why, if it was okay to be in the old lady's house and eat her food, had we crept around and come in through her back door? I wanted to cry, but I couldn't let the Big Boy see me in tears. He was standing behind me, and I could feel the burn of his eyes staring at the back of my head. *What was he thinking about?* I wondered. *Was he thinking about pushing me in the bar pit to get rid of me so I couldn't tell what we had done? Why wasn't he fishing?* The Big Boy didn't give me a hint. I just sat there with my line in the water, and the Big Boy stood leaning against a tree, never saying a word. After a while, the Big Boy threw another big fistful of clods in the water, right over my head and right at my line. I was too scared to yell at him this time. I was too scared to look around at him.

Then, the Big Boy said, "Fish ain't bitin'. Let's go." I never thought I would feel relieved hearing him say that, because starting out I had wanted to fish so bad. But I jumped to my feet, and dropped my pole in the water right then and there. I threw my worms in the water for the fish to eat, the only thing I felt good about doing all morning. I was so ready to go back to my house with Mama, so ready to go back to my stick and knife game. The Big Boy and I didn't say anything else to each other. The Big Boy went one way, and this time I didn't follow him. I went my own way, home.

As I was walking home, I was wondering what I would tell Mama about that morning. I didn't want to lie to her. I never did tell her anything that wasn't the whole truth. I looked up to the sky for answers, but none came. I guess I didn't deserve to hear from the Good Lord. I felt like I had let Him down. And I was thinking that He probably felt the same way too. So I made the long walk home alone.

When I got to my house, I decided to stay outside for a while. I looked for the stick I'd dropped when the Big Boy came by for me. I went back and started to redraw the lines of my circle, when Mama came to the front door. "What you doin' out here in the front yard? I didn't know you was back. Y'all catch any fish?"

At that moment, I forgot every thought I had about telling Mama about what had happened. I just blurted out, "No, ma'am, I didn't get no bite at all."

"The other boy catch anythin'?" she asked.

"No, ma'am. He didn't get a bite either," I sensed I wasn't looking Mama straight in the eyes, and that my answers were kind of short, so I looked at her and I said, "When the fish didn't bite for us, there wasn't anything to do but come home, 'cause it wouldn't have done no good to just stay there for nothing."

Mama just looked at me. "I'm gonna sit out here on the porch for a while. You want to sit out with me?"

"If it's all the same to you, I'd like to go inside," I replied, sounding like I was tired.

"You hungry? I still got some of our breakfast in the kitchen if you are."

"No, ma'am, Mama. I'll just wait for lunch time," I said in an even wearier voice. I went inside.

"Jesus," I said as I fell onto my bed. "Jesus Christ." I'd almost fainted outside when Mama had asked me if I wanted to eat. Now, I was lying on my bed trying to convince myself that I really hadn't lied to Mama. "After all," I argued with myself, "the fish didn't bite, and the other boy didn't get a bite either." I knew that we never really went fishing, and I knew I needed to tell Mama this. But I didn't. I couldn't. Instead, I lay there wrestling with the Devil until I drifted off to sleep.

The next thing I knew, Mama was beating on my door and screaming at me. "Git out here. You git your butt out of that bed and git out here right now." And then, as if changing her mind and not wanting to wait for me to show up outside, she busted into my room, grabbed me by the back of my collar, and pushed me toward the front porch.

"But, Mama," I started out.

"Shut up, and git yourself out front." I wanted to do more than wet myself now. I wanted to go to the outhouse and jump in. I didn't exactly know what was going on, but I instinctively felt that it had everything to do with what I'd done with the Big Boy. Mama pushed me in my back again, harder than before, and I staggered and fell out through the front door onto the floor of the porch. I was going to cry, "Mama, why are you pushing me around like this?" when I looked up and saw her.

I shook my head. I rubbed my eyes, and she was still there. It was the old lady.

The old lady whose house I had gone into and whose food I'd eaten, was sitting right over me, right on our front porch. I felt a soft tinkle inside my pant legs. "You know this lady?" Mama asked.

"No, ma'am … I …"

"Don't 'no, ma'am' me …don't act dumb with me …don't you

lie to me no more," Mama said, her voice cracking. Somehow I couldn't stop lying.

"But, I don't know her, Mama," I protested.

"Then why did you go into her house and eat her food, if you don't know her, for God's sake. Why did you go into her house?"

I couldn't say anything else. I couldn't answer her anymore. I couldn't lie anymore. I just crawled up and stood in front of Mama and the old lady with my head down. The old lady got up to leave. Mama thanked her for coming by. They shook hands and hugged each other.

Mama turned and looked at me. Then she sank to her knees. Mama shook her head, over and over again, and cried and cried and cried.

It was the last time she cried for me.

But as for you, ye thought evil against me; but, God meant it unto good, to bring to pass, as it is this day, to save much people alive.

GENESIS 50:20

Gotta Go Up North

THE SOFT BREEZE MOVING through the tear in our front screen door whipped my mother's large dress against my face. She was a big woman by any measure. At five feet eight inches and well over two hundred pounds, Mama more than filled up the front door of our small four-room wood-frame house. I was ten, skinny, and short for my age. I was well-hidden standing behind my mother, as I was clutching as much of the skirt of her dress as the wind would permit me and trying to peer around her. It was slightly before midnight on a muggy July Saturday in the Mississippi Delta. But, because of the large pecan tree that draped over the front of our house, this July night was somehow managing to deliver a cool breeze. Ordinarily, by now my mother would have shooed me out of the night air with a stern warning that if I didn't do so I would catch my "death of cold." But we all felt a very different kind of danger to our family this night, one a great deal more threatening than the common cold.

The way Mama dealt with the situation this night recalls a sermon our pastor gave some years later. The particular scriptures that he used escape me, but I remember the essential message. It happened, the preacher said, that a certain cat lived under a certain house. A bulldog lived under the house next door. Every day the cat would cower in the presence of the bulldog. Were the cat to emerge from the darkness and dankness of its home under the house and attempt to stretch itself in the sunlight or merely take a walk, the bulldog would harass it, not for any reason other than he was big enough and mean enough to do it. When the bulldog would reach out and smack the cat, the cat would go tumbling, and screaming, and scrambling for cover under its house. This scene would send the bulldog into a fit of laughter, and he would strut along the streets, and glory in his strength and his power to intimidate. But one day, the dog realized that he hadn't seen the cat for several days. The dog was again looking for some fun at the cat's expense. So he went to look under the house where the cat lived. He called out, "Hey, cat. Come out of there!" The cat didn't answer. "This is bulldog, cat. Come out now, or I'll come in and get you." Still, quiet. So, the bulldog advanced, mad as hell, looking to find that cat and beat some sense into it. As he approached where the cat was resting, he could see its eyes glowing in the darkness. The cat stood up. Then it arched its back. It raised its tail. Then it exposed its claws, ready to fight. The bulldog was dumbfounded. "Have you lost your mind?" the bulldog asked the cat. "What? Why, I'll"—and the bulldog pulled back its big paw and took a powerful swipe at the cat. But this time the cat didn't cower, didn't scream, and didn't run. The cat dodged his blow, and struck back with one of her own, clipping the bulldog on one of its shoulders and drawing blood. Now, the preacher continued, his voice having risen to its sermonic crescendo, "The bulldog fell back. As he sat there dazed, on his haunches, the bulldog's eyes started to adjust to the darkness. Then, he could see them. There around the feet of the cat were six squirming kittens, holding close to her." The bulldog exclaimed to himself, "She's a mama cat." Then the cat spoke: "All these years, I've been running, and hiding, and afraid of you. I'm still afraid. But, I can't run anymore, because it's not just me. You see," she gestured toward her kittens, "now I've got something to fight for. Although that sermon had not yet been preached, something like this was on Mama's mind.

I didn't know much about what people meant when they talked about "up North" back then. On this night in 1956, literally hiding behind my mother's skirt tails, I only knew that two of my sisters had already moved up North to Chicago to teach school. They had sent us Easter clothes the spring before—nice satiny, frilly dresses for my sisters, and green plaid sports coats and green trousers for my brothers and me. It was the closest thing to a new suit I had ever gotten. On their first trip back home after relocating to Chicago, I remember my sisters going on and on about having seen Moms Mabley and Pig Meat Markum at shows in Chicago. They cracked up retelling some of Moms's and Pig Meat's jokes, and their laughter engulfed my entire family because of my sisters' contagious expressions of happiness. I tried to stay up late and laugh right along with them, even though I did not understand what Pig Meat meant as he carried on as a heavy-drinking judge, proclaiming himself, "high as a Georgia pine." Nor did I then understand Moms's classic explanation of the two women out walking who smelled hair burning when one of them exclaimed, "Maybe we're walking too fast." But my sisters surely did, and that they indulged me in those times with them was all that mattered. To me, then, up North, symbolized by Chicago, appeared to be a place to go after growing up—a place that was new and exciting, and where you could get a good job and buy nice clothes. I looked forward to someday going there. Indeed, up to this night, everything that related to up North in my young mind was pretty positive. But this was all about to change, and it was all because of what happened to my oldest brother, Fred, that night and of how my mother dealt with it.

The evening had started out innocently with Fred at his usual Saturday night job of shining shoes at Morris's Barber Shop. Like everything and every place in Sweet Providence, the small town just north of the twenty-five-acre farm where we lived, Morris's Barber Shop was rigidly segregated. Black people could work there, cleaning, sweeping up, racking pool balls, shining shoes and the like. But not one of us dared to sit in a barber chair or attempt to shoot a game of pool for fear of losing whatever little life or liberty we might have. So my brother shined the shoes of the white men and white boys who frequented Morris'. No one cared what his real name was. They just called him "Shine." He endured the Saturday night requests of the white cops for an "ass-kicking shine," knowing without question whose asses they had in mind for kicking. Fred was seventeen years old and in his second summer working at the barbershop.

Mr. Morris was not an easy man. Short and stocky, he looked almost stuffed into his off-white barbering frock. His near fully bald head and patchy side burns were poor advertisements for quality hair care. Mr. Morris usually appeared indifferent to the things going on in his shop. But he really was slyly watching every move of his employees and patrons. He preferred to be spoken to only after he had clearly offered an invitation to his employees to talk to him. For more than thirty years, Mr. Morris had come to work promptly at six o'clock in the morning, opening his doors for business at six thirty , and closing down at seven o'clock at night, except on Saturdays, when he might open at seven thirty in the morning and close as late as nine o'clock at night. The few loyal customers that he had were there because he was dependable, got them in and out of the chair without wasting time chattering, and gave them a consistently cheap cut—cheap as in just fifty cents a head. He was a good barber, but an unpleasant, poor salesman of his craft. He didn't like people nearly enough to be in a people's business. And, naturally, for our town and the times, he liked Black people a whole lot less than everybody else.

Unfortunately, Mr. Morris's faults were not clear to him, and he drove his employees to mirror his habits, good and bad. He required them to be sticklers for detail, and to watch the customers like hawks. There had been two other barbers in his shop earlier in his career, but now he was down to just two helpers, my brother and an elderly white man named Cecil. Cecil had the job of asking the customers who came in for shaves whether their towels were hot enough. Cecil was an amiable man, though, who entertained the shop's customers with engaging stories, which itself was worth Mr. Morris's small paycheck to him. And he was nicer to Fred, often spending time talking to him, checking on Fred's progress, and urging him to stay in school. Cecil worked every day except Saturday, so, regrettably, he was not in the barbershop when Fred ran into his trouble. Had he been, things would not have gone as they did.

In spite of Mr. Morris's odd traits and habits, and despite his indifferent behavior toward Fred, my brother turned out to be well-suited for Mr. Morris's job. He always came to work after school on time, around four o'clock each day. He showed up promptly at seven thirty each Saturday morning. During the summer months, Fred worked all day, usually arriving at the shop well before his required starting time. His primary job was to shine shoes, but he pitched in on any job that needed to be done. He was just as happy not to speak to Mr. Morris, as Mr. Morris was not to be spoken to. Through his hard work and quiet manner, he had won Mr. Morris's confidence, as much as a young Black man could. It had not always been this way between his boss and him.

When Fred first started working for the barbershop, Mr. Morris would do a strange—and, for Fred, a very dangerous—thing. When Mr. Morris left Fred alone in the shop while he went next door for a cup of coffee or out for a brief walk to stretch, Mr. Morris would go to his cash register and count the money in it before leaving the shop. Upon returning to his shop, Mr. Morris would immediately go back to his cash register and recount his money to see if any of it were missing. Thus, every day, my brother's freedom hinged on whether Mr. Morris made the slightest mistake in the initial count or the recount of his money.

But, Fred persevered. He developed a sense of pride in his work, and even a sense of duty to Mr. Morris. On that night, then, after the cash register count had come out right every day for over a year, Mr. Morris made no count of his money before taking his coffee break. In fact, things were at the point with my brother and Mr. Morris where, when Mr. Morris went on break, he would leave my brother in charge of collecting and depositing into his cash register any money coming in during his absence. It would have been better for Fred that night if Mr. Morris had never come to trust him to handle his business.

About eight o'clock that evening, Mr. Morris went out for coffee, leaving Fred alone in his shop. My brother took advantage of the lull in activity to tidy the shop, sweeping up hair and wiping the sinks and mirrors. Disrupting this calm, three boisterous white boys, around my brother's age, swept into the shop. To Fred, these boys were just customers he had to accommodate until Mr. Morris returned. From his perspective, their entry was unremarkable. But, unbeknownst to him, through the eyes of these three white country boys, the place looked completely vacant. Fred's presence, and hence, he himself, was irrelevant to them. Their minds immediately turned to mischief. In what was to them an unmanned, empty, barbershop, the question was, "What can we do here quickly that's fun and free before anyone shows up?" Sizing up the joint, they glanced past the cash register, and almost as fast past the hanging bags of potato chips and neatly stacked candy bars. Then, the boys' eyes fell on the one thing in the barbershop that met their hankering for some innocent, free, quick, fun—Mr. Morris's pool table.

The pool table was in the back of the barbershop, away from the two barber chairs. The chairs themselves were in the middle of the narrow shop. The shoeshine stand and the small concession stand lined one wall up toward the front of the shop, while the waiting sofa and chair lined the opposite wall. The pool table was also in a rather dimly lit area, both because there was no illumination in the rear of the shop from the streetlights, and because it suited Mr. Morris and some of his customers to have it that way. You see, from time to time, some of Mr. Morris's billiard patrons, as well as others in the shop during a pool game, might make friendly bets on a game's outcome. Since the betting is "only good if the money is on the wood," these gamblers would clump their cash bets on the apron of the table. Should a sheriff's deputy stroll by and observe this illegal gambling, he could cause trouble were he of a mind to do so. Most cops didn't care. But the threat existed that some outraged Bible-belter might prod the sheriff into action. Thus, the dim lighting in the pool table area made it hard to see the cash on the wood from the street, and provided enough cover for the players to snatch the money from the table's apron and conceal it if the need ever arose. Tonight, the boys thought, the table's location and its lighting would provide perfect cover for a free game of nine-ball. If Mr. Morris came back in, he might not catch them. If he caught them, well, okay, they would pay up. If not, they would have just gotten one in for free, no witnesses and no one the wiser. They went for it.

Now, Fred knew that Mr. Morris had strict orders for pool customers—pay before you play. In fact, it was written on the wall on a big placard, just below the one listing the price of haircuts, shaves, and lines. There was no mistaking it. My brother thought his duty to Mr. Morris was clear. He had to collect the money. He spoke up. "Excuse me. Mr. Morris says the game is a dime. Mr. Morris says you have to pay before the game starts."

Were they to believe their ears? Fred couldn't be speaking to them. This Black boy had to be crazy trying to collect their money. What did he have to do with this? They didn't have time for crap, especially from him. "N——, you ain't talkin' to us, is you?" one of the white boys snarled.

This was Billy Ray. Fred knew him. He lived on the Brown plantation. He was dirt-poor and had dropped out of school in the eighth grade to work in the fields, just like a lot of the young Black boys who lived on Brown's place. Fred knew that Billy Ray was a big mouth and a hothead, and that he had even spent a night or two in jail for drinking and fighting with his girlfriend. Now, he also knew that Billy Ray and his boys didn't intend to pay.

"N——, you hear me talkin' to you? You deaf?"

Fred didn't answer. He knew it was better not to. He didn't want any trouble with this crowd. He just pointed to the sign on the wall.

But his blood was aboil. Being called "n——" by a white boy no older than he was just hard to take. He had promised Daddy that he would keep his cool, though, if anything like this ever came up. Besides, he had to keep his job, he said to himself. He had things to do with the money he was making—buy school clothes for his senior year, get his class ring, and help Mama with a few dollars. So he had to ignore the smear, no matter how outrageous the source.

"Cat got your lying tongue, Shine?" Billy Ray slurred, "Or you just too dumb, or just too scared to talk?" Billy Ray shook his body in a mock tremble.

Fred spoke up more boldly. "Mr. Morris says you can't shoot pool here without payin' first. So, you need to put your dime on the cash register ahead of shootin'. These are Mr. Morris's rules." Plaintively, he again pointed to the sign on the wall requiring advance payment.

Surely, now these boys understood they had to pay first. Surely, they saw that he was just trying to do his job. But the boys just looked at each other in utter disbelief. Fred, ever so carefully, walked toward them to rack the balls, extending his hand for payment. He didn't realize that Billy Ray and his cohorts were growing angrier and angrier by the second.

Walker and Billy Ray were of a pretty good size, each nearly six feet tall and around one hundred eighty pounds. They both looked pretty athletic. David, on the other hand, was built like a fire plug, thick and low to the ground. Up until now, neither Walker nor David had uttered a word, letting their leader, Billy Ray, do the intimidating. "Don't come nowhere near us," David threatened. "We don't want to hear another goddamned thing out of you. It's over. Now shut up. And, this over here where we is at is white folks' space, no n———s allowed. Come over here and keep runnin' your trap, and we're gonna horsewhip your uppity Black ass," David bellowed, his voice smoldering in anger.

By now, Fred had a pretty good idea that he had a big problem with these guys. Quickly, he ran through his options. He could reverse course, quietly withdraw to sit on the stack of Coke crates that were his seat in between shines, and indulge these intruders in the notion that he really wasn't there. On the other hand, he could take his chances, rack the balls, and once again extend his hand for payment, but this time more humbly. And finally, the last of the white boys had not yet spoken. Maybe he would bring the other two around. Fred looked Walker's way.

Fred knew Walker from when they were really young. They used to play together before they started fourth grade. His family lived about a quarter-mile from us. Walker was a good runner. He and Fred both had some good times as youngsters, racing barefoot over the hot, dusty road on which both our families lived. Each had won and lost some races. They had shot marbles, in a circle carved out of the Delta's sandy loam. They had played on even terms, lagging to see who would take the first shot of each game. And, they had spent time together at the various ditches cut through the cow pastures. These ditches swelled with crawfish in the spring. When one of them was short on fat meat to bait the lines to drag along the ditch bottoms to land these delicious mudbugs, the other would share with him. As very young boys, Fred had thought Walker and he would be friends forever. But, by the end of third grade, all of what they had done—the playing, the fishing, the time together—suddenly changed. Walker's parents wouldn't let them play together anymore, and declared their friendship over. Fred didn't understand it, and was upset that he couldn't be with his friend. But Walker seemed to be okay with the new arrangement, and started to act distant and aloof. The racial separation started then, and, as far as Walker's parents saw it, there would never be any time in the future when Fred and Walker would be permitted to treat each other as equals.

Yet, in this desperate moment, Fred hoped that his old relationship with Walker might serve as a counterweight against the scales now tipped against him. "You heard what they said, Fred, now git yourself back over there where you belong," Walker almost murmured. "Ain't no need to trouble yourself with what we're doing."

At least, Fred thought, Walker hadn't called him anything outside of his name, and he had spoken without apparent anger. But none of this changed the reality that Walker had sided with his friends.

Fred was not afraid of Billy Ray, or David, or Walker—or the three of them together. He was easily over six feet three inches, and he was a country-fed two hundred and fifteen pounds. He was a good boxer. None of the Black boys would ever have challenged him as these three were doing. They knew better. He was just that good. Boxing was well-accepted, even glorified in those days. Our school sponsored boxing matches, furnished the young pugilists with boxing gloves, and provided makeshift rings on the school's assembly room stage. This attitude toward boxing was influenced by the enormous popularity that boxing enjoyed with Black people because of the successes of Joe Louis, Sugar Ray Robinson, Ezard Charles, Archie Moore, and others. This gave every beaten-down Black person in America a vicarious, virtual win against some mean-hearted white person he secretly wanted to punch out. Fred had, over the years, established himself as the very best fighter on the school grounds, in the ring and out. But the three white boys who were now bent on horsewhipping Fred knew nothing of Fred's fighting mettle.

Yet, it didn't much matter. The racial climate of the day stripped Fred of the response he would ordinarily make to their challenge. He wanted to tell them to "just bring it on," but he knew he couldn't. He had to suppress his natural instinct to make the physical response for which he was trained and for which he was mentally predisposed. He gathered himself, and mentally withdrew. All he could say was, "Mr. Morris lets me work all over the shop. It's all the white side. There ain't no colored side here. I'm just tryin' not to lose my job; not tryin' to tell ya'll what to do. I wish ya'd pay Mr. Morris's charges the way he wants them paid. These ain't my charges. They're Mr. Morris'."

This mild summation was stunningly articulate, and for a moment these three boys seemed taken in. They hesitated, appearing to think about paying the dime they owed and doing the right thing. But Billy Ray couldn't bring himself to let it go. His throttled command shattered the silence, and tipped Fred's destiny on a downhill slide for the rest of the night. "N——, rack 'em," he said. "We're playing jess like we said."

Through all of the back and forth over paying for playing pool, Fred had kept moving closer and closer to the pool table. He was, in fact, close enough to "rack 'em" if he could have brought himself to do so. But he felt obligated to Mr. Morris's rule.

They had seen enough. Billy Ray picked up a pool ball. "Come any closer and I'll bust your skull," he screamed, turning red and looking as if he himself might burst. Fred was caught off guard by this sudden, violent escalation. He had not intended to push these three to a fight, not to inflame tensions. But it was now clear that things had spun out of control. So much raced through his mind. He was afraid. He hoped Mr. Morris would return. He wanted to fight back. Through it all, he knew he had to try to remember his place and to be careful not to fight the white boys. Yet he quickly decided, as well, that he was not going to become their victim either.

Suddenly, the pool ball that Billy Ray had picked up from the table whizzed past Fred's head and crashed into a big mirror in the barbershop. Somehow Billy Ray had missed Fred from only nine or ten feet away. Fred didn't remember ducking from the pool ball, but somehow he avoided it. Either that or Billy Ray was just poor at hitting a close target with an overhand fastball. Fred decided that whatever the reason, he was not going to give Billy Ray a second shot to improve his aim.

Fred reached for a pool stick. He cracked it across the pool table, snapping it above the tip, and creating for himself a sharp, jagged-edged weapon. Fred angrily lunged toward Billy Ray to back him away from the pool table and out of the reach of another pool ball. Billy Ray and his buddies beat a quick retreat to the farthest recesses of the barbershop, where they bunched up against the wall.

Then, as quickly as he had moved to immobilize these three,

Fred made his move to get out of harm's way. Backing out of the barbershop door, Fred menacingly used his broken pool stick to warn these boys against any advances. He needn't have worried. They were paralyzed with fright, and mesmerized by Fred's catlike quickness and his resourcefulness. Fred cleared the front door of the shop, then turned and ran, disappearing into the night.

After heaving sighs of relief, the three boys regained their composure and charged out of the shop into the street, hurling epithets in the direction they believed Fred might have run.

Mr. Morris, hearing the commotion, hastily made his way back to his barbershop. Later, the three white boys and Mr. Morris pressed charges of disturbing the peace and destroying property. One claim against Fred was that a mirror in Mr. Morris's shop had been broken, the break caused by the impact from a pool ball striking it. Another was for the breakage of Mr. Morris's pool stick. The third, of course, was for fighting and disturbing the peace.

No one knows how Fred got home that night. He didn't seem to remember. Oh, we knew he ran the mile and a half from town to our house, but we don't know what path he took. He ran in panic. He ran like a hunted man, like a runaway slave might have run. He ran wondering who knew what had happened, who knew what he had done, who was out to catch him, how he would explain to Mr. Morris, whether he would have a job, whether he would go to jail, what would happen to him. He ran blindly home. Fred knew that any white person who saw him and who wanted to exercise his "authority" could stop him, hold him, and, in effect, arrest him. I'm sure he also knew that he would look guilty of something if he had run through town, ducking between and around houses, so he wouldn't have raced that route. And, certainly he would have drawn attention sprinting along the highway at a furious pace. So he probably took a path that took him onto the levee, which he could have mounted about fifty yards from the door of the barbershop. He could have run along the top of it without being detected. There would have been no one there to notice him, except the livestock resting on the batture. So once Fred was on the levee, he could have streaked across it in secrecy for about a mile, before dropping off the levee onto some railroad tracks. From there, he would have continued along the tracks for about a quarter of a mile more, until the railroad tracks crossed the highway. At that point Fred could have hit that old familiar, dusty road leading to our house—ironically, the same road over which he and Walker had raced back when they were young friends. But Fred wasn't thinking much about that or anything else now, except getting home safely. He just ran. He just ran scared all the way home.

As he turned off the dirt road onto the narrow tree-lined path that led to our house, it struck him. Relieved as he was to get home, he abruptly realized that he was not home free. And once he got near our front door, the fear really gripped him. As afraid as he was of what the white folks might have in mind for him, he might have been even more scared of what Mama's reaction would be to the night's events. Fred wished there were some back door or some window by which he could enter the house and avoid our mother. At least, in this way, he could face her in the morning when his head was clearer and after he had had more time to figure out what to tell her. Perhaps she wasn't home, he quietly hoped. Maybe she was out at the grocery store with her sister, Aunt Sue. Fred knew that if Mama were home, she would be up. She was like a mother hen, waiting to account for all her chicks before tucking them under her protective wing and settling in to sleep. He would have to explain right there. As he reached for the front door, then, fear and worry re-gripped him. He had reason to worry.

Now, with all due respect, and with nothing but love in my heart for my dear mother, I must witness to the truth that my mother was not only a big lady; she was a big, tough lady. Oh, not in any moral sense. Mama was deeply religious—a mother's aid in our church. She enjoyed a good reputation in the community, and was president of the Colored Parent Teacher Association. But she had a bit of trouble turning the other cheek. Okay, slightly more than a bit. And, to tell it all, a mild cuss word or two would slip from her sweet lips every now and then.

Our mother was the disciplinarian in our house. When she said "sit down and shut up," we dropped into the nearest seat or onto the floor like puppets whose puppeteer had suddenly let go of the strings. Some say that once, when our mother was especially agitated and gave a "sit down and shut up" command, our father dropped like a rock too, just like we did. I never saw this myself, and I always remember her giving in to Daddy. But it's an example of how legendarily bad our mother was. She inspired such stories.

Her methods of discipline were fairly unrestrained, often creative, and always physical. It might vary from sending you to fetch a switch for your own upcoming whipping, to throwing her purse, her shoe or the closest thing at hand at you to make her point.

We loved her because she sacrificed so much for us, because she was always in our corner, always fighting for us, always talking about how we were going to succeed. But at the same time, and there is no other way to say this, we were very afraid of her. We had often heard her say, "I'll kill you myself before I see you go off to jail." It was a chilling thought. While she may have been saying this to scare us from getting into trouble, we children were sure she literally meant every last word.

This was not Fred's night. As he entered the house, he ever so gently closed the screen door behind him. As he tiptoed across the front room, he heard that voice that he so dreaded. "Fred, that you? What you doing home so early?" Mama screamed out.

Fred was dead. And he felt stupid besides. It was only about eight forty-five in the evening, and Fred usually didn't get home from the job on Saturdays till around ten o'clock. He'd come home much too early to avoid detection. He swore to himself a few of the choicest cuss words he knew.

Fred couldn't answer Mama. He just flopped onto the sofa, sinking deep down into it, as if trying to make himself disappear.

"Fred!" Mama screamed again. "Boy, don't you hear me calling you?"

Fred sat up. "Yes, ma'am, Mama, yes, ma'am. It's me," Fred

whimpered. "Need to talk to you. Gotta talk to Daddy too. It's a mess, Mama. It's a mess," he said.

Fred's tone unsettled her. He sounded like he was on the verge of breaking down. What was it? Now her tendency to scold him, to forcibly straighten him up, gave way to her mothering instincts. She rushed to him.

Fred looked terrible. But all she could think about when she reached him was, *Thank God he's in one piece.* She hugged him, then patted his back and sides to see if he was beaten or bleeding or injured in some way. Then she held his face to examine it, running her hand across it and looking into his eyes. "Oh my goodness," she cried, "Oh my goodness." His eyes showed shock and fear beyond any she'd ever had in all of her years. She hugged him tighter and cradled him like he was still her baby boy. Fred's body shook in her arms; he couldn't stop trembling. Even so, he was already feeling a world better with Mama consoling him, petting him up, ready to help get him through the mess he was in. They held onto each other for what seemed like much longer than the minute of their embrace.

Then Daddy came into the room, having been awakened by Mama's earlier commotion, and ended their special moment. "What's goin' on?" he stammered. Rubbing his eyes, he asked my brother, "What in the world happened to you, son?"

Now, it was back to reality, and time for Fred to deal with what was imperiling our family that night. He pulled himself together and painstakingly laid out to our parents every detail of what had happened at the barbershop. It was an all-too-familiar story to my father. He'd seen many an innocent Black boy unable to defend himself with mere truth. The response to a Black man's crime of forgetting his place, he knew, was usually certain, open punishment. But Mama spoke up.

"This is our son," she said, starting to sob softly. "This is our own baby, Mose. We've always taught our children to keep out of trouble. If they did, and if they always told the truth, we've told them that nothin' would happen to them. If this ain't so, then everybody around here might just as well be devils. This is our son, Mose, not some distant Black boy in trouble with white folks who we can shake our heads about and say what a shame it is his folks didn't teach him right from wrong and ignore the fact that the poor boy probably was just bein' treated wrong. This is our son." Our mother hardly ever cried about anything, but she cried a few more defiant tears. Her tears and her spirit compelled our father to boldness. He rested his big hands on Fred's shoulders to reassure Fred that he too was firmly on his side.

So they sat there, our Mama and Fred on the sofa, and Daddy on the floor. They had decided to stand, to stand together for Fred and for our family. Exactly how they were going to be able to do this was unclear to them. That would just be left in God's hands.

They told Fred to clean himself up and go to bed. Then Daddy went to the closet where he kept his guns and loaded his double-barreled shotgun and his forty-five pistol. He used these massive weapons of destruction for deer hunting, but tonight he just wanted them close at hand, he wasn't quite sure for what. Mama got up from the sofa and pulled her rocking chair near to Daddy. He had sat himself back down on the floor amidst his guns.

There, in the front room, they rocked and prayed. They prayed that the night would pass, and that the morning would come without trouble. They prayed that if racial retribution could not pass, and they had to face difficulty tonight over their son, that God would see them through. For over two hours, with just a few words between them every now and then, they held watch, with only a dim light separating them from the thick darkness. Having worked all day, they grew groggy, nodding off to sleep and then jolting awake.

Nodding at about the same time at one point, they heard what seemed to be the scream of sirens. They looked at each other in surprise, as if to question whether each had heard the same thing. Then they rushed to the front window and took a look outside. It was real. For accompanying these terrible, piercing siren sounds that were stabbing their eardrums, was the unmistakable flashing red, white, and blue lights of the Sweet Providence sheriff's office. At least it wasn't a mob, Mama thought gratefully, but those damned sheriffs had waited right up until they had turned off the dirt road onto the path leading to our house before turning on their sirens and lights, she cussed. They had meant to scare the hell out of everybody in our house, and they had damned well succeeded. Instantly, our little house became a swarm of us children trying to find our parents and to see what was going on. We saw them there in the front room, our father, grim-faced, now taking a seat in our mother's rocking chair. Mama strode toward our front door. Most of my brothers and sisters piled quietly onto our daddy's lap. He shushed us to be more quiet. Mama was going to do the talking. I ran to where my mother was, grabbing onto the back of her skirt. She took her position, blocking our front door.

Peering around my mother, I could see two sheriffs' cars parked in our front yard. Three sheriffs' officers slowly got out of them, adjusting their pistol belts as cops always do. As they walked toward our front door, I could see two big sheriffs and a little short one. The short one spoke up. "Don't mean to wake y'all up so late, Angeline, but we've got a situation here involving one of your boys that we have to deal with tonight. So, we've come to get Fred and take him to jail for what he's done. After that, y'all can git back to sleep. He's got to meet Judge Ragman in court Monday morning, and if y'all want to see him then, well y'all can just come on down to the courthouse," Sheriff Filbert offered coldly and matter-of-factly. Mama stood there for a moment, trying to measure this man and her response to him. Here he had come to take her son from her house in the middle of the night and this was all they had to say to her? They had come at midnight, as if this couldn't be handled later, and for what? At most, Fred had tried to prevent harm to himself and at the least he had run away from a fight. She steeled her resolve to see this thing through.

First, she would try diplomacy. "Sheriff, why don't you let me bring him to the courthouse first thing Monday morning? Whatever's happened ain't so bad 'til it can't be taken care of that way.

We're gonna obey the law. We always do. I'll bring him to you as early Monday as you say. You've got my word on it, and you know you can trust my word."

Indeed, Sheriff Filbert knew he could trust her to do exactly what she said. Why, he even knew that while she was dirt-poor, merchants would allow her to vouch for Black people traveling through town so that they could get their checks cashed. He knew she was telling the truth. But, he had come for Fred and, by God, he was gonna get him. With a haughty sneer, the sheriff responded, "You don't have nothin' to worry about, Lina. He'll be all right with us tonight. We'll take real good care of him. Now you can see him in the morning, rather than Monday, if you need to. Now, git him up and git him out here. Stop wastin' my time. Git him out here so we can all go to bed tonight."

To my mother the sheriff seemed to have vacillated. He'd gone from tough at the start of his statement, to nice in the middle, to kind of nice at the end. But he'd disregarded her promise and her proposal. Taking Fred with him tonight was still his bottom line. It couldn't be hers.

Mama was confronting the high sheriff of the parish, Sheriff Vaughn Filbert. He wasn't a man to take lightly. He didn't like taking no for an answer. In the case of Black people, he didn't even like taking "no, sir" for an answer. He didn't mind telling Black folk that he owed them nothing, because they didn't vote for him. Never mind that it wasn't legal for them to register to vote. It was a cruel joke, which he told often, and he liked to laugh when he told it. But he was not essentially a cruel man. Yes, his department had a reputation for always solving crimes and closing cases. That it didn't always do so with credible evidence or by convicting exactly the right person was another matter. Brutality, forced confessions—there was no line the sheriff's office wouldn't cross to get the man it wanted. Curiously, most Black folks confessed to whatever "crime" they were charged with, especially if it involved offenses against white people. These "crimes" always commanded the special, personal attention of the high sheriff himself. But Sheriff

Filbert didn't see these practices as wrong. It was just the norm for policing in his town, practices which always sported a healthy distinction between the Blacks and the whites, and the rich and the poor. "That is just the way things are," the sheriff would explain, and in those days that phrase covered a lot of territory and covered up a lot of sins. Most white people looked the other way, so long as they were able to feel safe themselves and so long as the sheriff's transgressions didn't involve anyone they cared about. Filbert knew what it took to get elected—over and over again.

But my mother's reputation for being a strong lady did not extend only to her household and to Black people. A white insurance man had said she was dangerous after she chased him across our field with a tire iron because he accused her of lying about not having money when he was attempting to collect an insurance premium. She was regularly in the faces of the all-white school board members arguing for more books and good teachers for our colored schools. And she was always taking the literacy test to register to vote, believing one day the registrar of voters would admit she'd passed. When the registrar once told her she would register to vote over his dead body, she stirred up things when she replied to him that she could live with that, provided it happened soon. And she had told a white store manager who wouldn't let her try on shoes in his store, as white woman were able to do, that she'd just go "barefoot, like Jesus," and tell her story in Glory of how she was mistreated.

So she was well acquainted with the sheriff's reputation, and he with hers. That's why he'd shown up with a third of his police force tonight. He didn't know what to expect from Mama. what to expect of herself. She was operating on the adrenalin of a mother's love.

"What y'all say he did?" Mama asked. She was hoping that by having them recite the facts of what had transpired in the barbershop, the ridiculousness of this whole matter would be exposed. She thought this might help to persuade the sheriff that the deal wasn't as big as he was making it out to be, and certainly not an emergency, needing attention this midnight.

"For fightin' and for destroyin' property in town. You already know it for yourself, Angeline. You know what he did. I ain't gonna stand out here all night. Now, what's it gonna be?" The sheriff's tone was more urgent, more insistent, than at any time tonight. He was trying to force her to comply with his demands, right then, at that moment.

But Mama decided she was going to take her time and tell her son's story from her own lips, and let them deal with it from there. Mama started out, speaking carefully, her emotions under control, retelling to the sheriff and his men what Fred had so meticulously told Daddy and her a few hours earlier. She was thoroughly convinced that Fred had told them the truth, so she could repeat it with passion and confidence. She told how he'd tried to protect Mr. Morris's place of business, how the white boys had started the fight, and how Fred had tried to keep things peaceful.

As she concluded, the sheriff and his men looked as if they knew there was no righteousness in their cause. To persist in his pursuit of Fred, then, the sheriff was left to fall back on the same Old South standard that was at the heart of his conduct of his duties as sheriff—to that of enforcing racial norms, even if it really didn't have anything to do with enforcing the law. "Well," the sheriff began, "whatever happened, your boy can't be fightin' white boys in this parish. If he wants to fight with white boys, then, by God, he's gotta go up North." This was what it was all about. This was the real bottom line. The facts, and right and wrong didn't matter. This was the reason Sheriff Filbert had shown up on her doorstep in the middle of the night. He wasn't there to arrest Fred because he was some dangerous criminal, but because he wanted to be able to answer to white folks that he was keeping Black folks in line.

The time for strategic moves was over. Mama was simply up against it, up against all the racial discrimination and hate she found so hard to accept—to abide, to endure. She boiled over.

"He's gotta go up North to keep somebody from whippin' his ass?" she screamed out. "He ain't goin' nowhere." Mama had a big voice to match her size. Tonight, with this declaration, her loud voice seemed to echo off our towering pecan trees, through the pitch black night, and right straight across Black history.

Sheriff Filbert was flabbergasted. He'd played his hand at intimidating Mama into handing over Fred, and it hadn't worked. He hadn't anticipated this standoff, not this way—not so decisive, so irrevocable. Daddy sat there in Mama's chair with his guns at the ready; he wasn't going to let anybody hurt Mama, no matter what it meant. We all just stood up, amazed at our mother's strength, and she simply stood immovable in our doorway. Her mind was fixed, as she glared down upon the sheriff and his men.

"Damn," the sheriff muttered under his breath. He wanted so badly to pull her out of the door and drag Fred out of the house, and beat the hell out of him and teach her a lesson. He reddened with anger. He took another long look at Mama, and she didn't look away. "God damn."

He nodded for his men to follow him. They all turned, the sheriff and his men, and slowly walked toward their cars. There, they huddled for a while. His men stood erect, and the sheriff was wildly animated as he talked to them, his arms flailing as if he were fighting a swarm of wasps. He was, indeed, still mad as a hornet. He railed on for what seemed like a good five minutes. We don't know what Sheriff Filbert was saying to his men. Perhaps he was cussing Mama out. Maybe he was merely letting off steam. Or, just maybe, he was telling them how stupid he felt letting Mr. Morris and those three crazy white boys make him come out to our house at midnight to arrest Fred for next to nothing. Now, the only way he was going to get him tonight was to kill this unshakeable Black woman in the door of her house in front of all of her children, with at least one of them holding on to her dress.

We thought it was likely the crazy-white-boy thing. In any case, without another word to Mama, the sheriff and his men got back into their cars, killed their flashing lights, and drove off.

I got crushed as Fred and the rest of my brothers and sisters rushed in and hugged and kissed Mama. But I was too numb for it to hurt. We didn't know what the rest of the night or tomorrow would bring. Would they come back? We stayed up all night, watching.

Eventually, we got to watch the sunrise together. We used to dread seeing the sunrise, because it meant that we children were up working early. But that morning was the most beautiful thing we'd ever seen. I was glad that Fred was right there with us.

He didn't have to go up North like the sheriff had said—at least not for now.

In the year that King Uzziah died, I saw also the Lord.

ISAIAH 6:1

Saving Grace

DADDY WAS A DEACON. In fact, he was the head deacon in our church. The church was across the field from our house. Every day when we left home, we saw it. And we passed it on the way home. It was impossible not to be aware of it. It went by a seemingly simple name—Sweet Canaan—but, that name was, in reality, a constant reminder of what lay ahead for the believer, in yonder life. Next to it was a graveyard, a reminder that life on this side was sure to end, and that there were consequences, one way or the other. A few graves bore headstones, a few twisted, time-worn, metal markers. But most were sunken over time, with hardly any reminder of the name of the dear departed whose earthly remains inhabited that piece of ground.

My grandfather Oliver Harris's grave, however, bore no such ignominy. It was covered by a full cement slab, with his name permanently etched. He had given the half acre that held the church and graveyard, which abutted the twenty-five acres he had given my mother upon which she and my father had built a home. Oliver Harris was a man of some means—holding about three hundred acres of good cotton-farming land, and running a cotton gin, in whose profits he shared with some white men. He looked white himself, his ancestry undoubtedly dominated by Europeans, which may explain why those white men partnered with him. He had come from Indiana, my mother had said, by way of Alabama, and, as I think about it now, he had something of a Midwestern accent. His "Now, now, Billy," which he would say to me if he thought I was getting a little unruly, would come out "Nyoo, nyoo" with a distinctive, non-Southern twang.

I never got to know him well. He was married to someone much younger than he, named Jessie, whom we called Mama Jessie. I don't think she much cared for us, his grandchildren, and we never spent time at Grandpa's house, or that sort of thing.

Mama Jessie, of course, was not the mother of my mother, who was near her age. My mother's mother's name was Matt, and my grandfather had never been married to our Mama Matt. When my mother was born, my grandfather was married to another woman, Francis. So my mother never stood in line to inherit anything from him, and upon his death at ninety years old, she got nothing. Jessie got all of his leavings, since my mother, an illegitimate child in the eyes of our laws, had no right to claim anything.

To my grandfather's credit, however, he always openly acknowledged my mother. In his Act of Donation of her twenty-five acres, he called her "my dear daughter." Mama Matt was jet-black and my mother nearly so. But he must have known for sure she was his, else he could have easily denied her and us. My mother and father called him Dad. He called my mother "Dear Angie." All of us called him Pa Pa. But I don't think he felt close to us children, because I remember him once asking me "Billy, do you like old people?" I did like him, but I never knew him, and I remember thinking it strange that he thought I should.

I do remember him talking to me often about joining church, which is where I mostly remember seeing and talking with him. He was Deacon Oliver Harris, who trained my father in the life of a deacon and laid the groundwork for Daddy to become head deacon when he died. He was the benefactor of our church; his name was first on the church's cornerstone; he was the preacher's right hand man. All of my brothers and sisters who were older than I had, mostly at his insistence, joined church by the time they were seven. I was ten and had not yet joined. I was becoming an embarrassment to Pa Pa and to my father because of it. This made me the object of their's and the church's special attention.

I was expected to be serious about this joining-church thing. Unknown to them, I really was. Maybe my problem was that I was too serious. I wanted to be able to testify about my conversion, as Mr. Stove had done.

"I prayed all night long," Mr. Stove had testified, when he, at seventy-three years old, had stopped drinking and gambling and decided to join church. "My face was wet with the morning dew. And, then, I seen a little baby, just crawling near 'round me. I said 'Baby, where you going?' And, that little baby spoke right up." At that point, somebody in the congregation asked, "What did the baby say?" And, Mr. Stove cried out in a loud voice, "That baby said, 'Don't be scared, come with me to meet my daddy.' And I knew just like that, it was God's child, who had come to save me. I said, 'Yes Jesus, yes Jesus, I'm gonna follow you all the days of the rest of my life.'"

It was this kind of stuff that had me messed up. I wasn't trying to defy my grandfather or my father. Indeed, every time I heard a conversion testimony, I actually thought about how proud my folks would be when my turn came to stand before the church and give mine. I just thought that if the Father and the Son were inviting Mr. Stove, a lifelong sinner, and others like him to join church that way, that, if I prayed all night under His heavens, why would not I, innocent by comparison, meet Jesus like that too? I truly wanted to be saved, but pretty much, personally, by God himself. But there was so much pressure to get on with joining church that I was starting to doubt that I would have time to keep praying for my conversion revelation. And, then, my Pa Pa died.

At Pa Pa's funeral, my eldest sisters cried, maybe because they knew him best. My father spoke about him adoringly, almost reverently—"not just a good man, but a great man, committed to God, the church, and family." My mother was openly weeping and wailing. "Oh God, what am I going to do? I'm going to miss you, Dad!" And she would rise from her seat every now and then and scream something like, "Oh, no! God, oh no! He's gone!" She was his only child, and she was making the most public of displays of her affection for him, and, perhaps, hoping, inferentially, of his for her. The ushers would rush to restrain her. She would quiet down for a minute, and then start up again. The other six children, including me, sat quietly. We didn't know how to react to Mama's outbursts, and we didn't know how to act ourselves. So we just sat there respectfully, like we thought people would think our Pa Pa would have expected.

I really can't speak to what my brothers and sisters were thinking, but I was occupied with my own odd thoughts, thoughts only slightly connected to the things going on around us at the funeral. I was thinking about how I probably should have joined church when Pa Pa had asked me to. I was nearly eleven and still outside of God's arc of safety. Was God going to punish me for not listening to my Pa Pa? Had I blown any chance that He would show up and save me? Had I missed the best opportunity I had to talk to someone old and connected to God to help me with my conversion? What would Pa Pa say to God about me when he got to heaven? This last question really worried me the most. I didn't know where to start to get answers to any of these questions. But I was thinking how desperately I needed to have a word with Pa Pa to get the right message to God. I wanted him to tell God how much I loved Him, that I wanted to join His church, but that I was just waiting for a sign. Just as I was meditating on that thought and trying to make contact with Pa Pa before they took him out of the church, Mama shrieked again, and I lost my concentration.

So they laid Pa Pa under his perfect-looking cement slab. And, as I walked away from it with the rest of my family, somehow I was struck with the overwhelming conviction that, although he was now placed beneath a thick layer of concrete, he would be easier to get through to than ever before. I knew it was just his dead body there in the ground, and that his spirit, his soul, was either in heaven with Jesus or on its way there. But since I had not yet been saved by Jesus, and He had not yet had a word with me, at least not in the way I had wanted Him to, it seemed to me more than ever that I could still talk to Pa Pa about my salvation, and that the best place to start that discussion was over his fresh grave—maybe even before he went on to heaven and had his first little talk with Jesus. On this slightly chilled October night, then, I crept across the cotton field to the graveyard to talk to my Pa Pa about his Jesus.

It was a strange freedom I was feeling. I would never have been bold enough to just walk up and say hello to Pa Pa while he was still alive. Maybe it was because I knew I would not be confronted by that fearful scowl he had on occasion given me, with his large menacing eyes peering from beneath dark bushy eyebrows, when I spoke to him without an invitation. I wouldn't be scolded for speaking out of turn, or for speaking while grown-up folk were having a conversation. I didn't have to worry about what his reaction would be to me. Pa Pa had a gold pocket watch, that it always seemed to me he was taking from his vest pocket and looking at, as if he might not have time to talk. And, if not that, then he was fingering his derby hat, turning it upside down, then right side up, as if he wanted to place it on his head and rush off to go to someplace more important. But while seeing him lying there in his casket—hatless, watchless, his eyes hidden—my fear of him passed away in an instant. It was weird and wonderful. Finally, I was ready to talk to him, and, surprisingly, intuitively, I felt he was ready to listen.

Pa Pa's new grave was just a few feet away from the cornerstone of the church, which was the keystone of the church's foundation, holding up its right-hand side. As I passed the cornerstone, the impulse came upon me to stop and kneel there before going to Pa Pa's grave site. I got down on my knees, and before I knew it, I was brushing his name with my hands, trying to distinguish each letter. My eyes welled up with tears and I started to pray out loud, like my Mama Matt had taught me to pray. I asked God to forgive me, for nothing in particular, but just for any and everything I might have ever done to misunderstand or disobey Him or Pa Pa or anyone I should have listened to. I asked Him to let Pa Pa and me have a good talk, and I asked to meet Him, right there tonight with Pa Pa and me. I told Him I wanted Him to come and save me. And, then, like a story from the Bible, I heard a voice say, "My son, you are already saved." I was so engrossed in my praying and crying that I wasn't even stunned by the voice. I didn't know what to say, or if I should say anything at all. I remembered from Sunday School, however, that Samuel, as a young boy in an Old Testament story, heard the voice of God, and after some coaching from a seasoned prophet, Eli, answered by simply saying, "Speak Lord; for thy servant heareth." I was thinking this through as a possible appropriate response, when I felt a cold, heavy hand on my shoulder—my right shoulder, the one closest to Pa Pa's grave. I didn't know what to do. The fear returned. Would I turn to face my grandfather, now, perhaps more powerful and difficult than ever, or would I simply faint away and join him in the grave tonight? I made up my mind to rise up and to face him, or them. I didn't know what to expect.

As I tried to get up from my knees, the cold, heavy hand pressed downward. So I stayed there. I was shaking, but I decided to wait for a suggestion from whoever was now in charge of me. "My son, you are already saved. Just accept Jesus right now. There is nothing to see. Simply believe on Jesus, as you already do, and speak it. You are saved by grace." Now I started to smile. I recognized the voice and that familiar heavy hand, made cold by the night's chill. It was the new head deacon, who had made his way across the cotton field to talk to Pa Pa too—about some other church business.

And they put it in the hand of the workmen that had the oversight of the house of the Lord, and they gave it to the workmen that wrought the house of the Lord, to repair and amend the house.

II CHRONICLES 34:10

F Is a Crooked Letter

MOST EVERYTHING IN LIFE is relative. When you live in the country as I did and depend on the yield of the land for sustenance, you develop a sharper understanding of this theory of relativity. "If and Then" become the common ways life is discussed, but not the ways in which one traverses mental exercises or works through math problems. If it rains by a certain time in a certain amount for a certain period, then we can expect a good chance of a good crop. If it isn't too hot for too long, and if the seed is good, and if the boll weevil spares the crop, then so on and so forth is likely or not to work out this or that way. That is and was the way it is. This sort of thing everyone, rich and poor alike, in farming country or not, had to deal with. But one of the most crucial determinants in working through the "If and Then" situation in our lives in my growing years had nothing necessarily to do with the weather or even with our crops. This was a different drill. It had to do with the relativity of travel time. This was especially true if you lived where and as I did, and you and your family rode around in a car or truck supported on may pops.

Please notice that the travel time equation is "if and then," not "if and when, then." That is because the "if" is sure to happen. The "if" will occur. In our equation, it is the "then," then, that is the cause for the uncertainty, the "then" that had to be figured out.

My first memory of our 1941 Ford was when my daddy was spreading hot black tar over the top of it to keep the rain out. I was a little over twelve years old. The black car had been given to us by our grandfather, Oliver Harris, about a year before he died. It was apparently a well-used car when we got it, because my daddy always had to work on it. It had gray cloth seats that bore lots of blotches and old spots on them, and there were places on the seats that were re-stitched where some of the stuffing was still poking out. Daddy sat on a cushion that he had placed on the front driver's seat, the most-used part of the bench row car seats, which covered protruding springs and the cotton insides. The running boards along the sides of our car were prominently rusty in places where some of their rubber surface had worn down. The headlights were so far apart that, to the inexperienced eye, at night, they did not appear to be on the same car, but rather as two people carrying separate lanterns, strangely, at equal heights. Ours had one light out so often, however, we seldom presented that trouble to an onlooker. The dented bumpers evinced encounters with other vehicles, and were so severe that it was plain that the other vehicles had prevailed. The still-shiny black exterior of the car recalled days of past glory, when the car was probably a striking black beauty. But we knew that the unmasked, ugly truth was that a lot of things that the car could not be proud of were going on, way out of order, under its shiny hood. However, we were not alone in dealing with car issues. Almost no one in our part of the country had a new car. Most of the cars were not only used, but pieced together contraptions. That they ran as well and as reliably as they did was a tribute to the legions of shade-tree mechanics that sprouted up under the sycamore and pecan trees to meet the demand. Almost every man and teenage boy around could "fix" a car, and the numerous jacked-up cars in front of houses and barns and alongside the roads awaiting a part or a fixing were unimpeachable evidence of that fact. My daddy, out of necessity, was one of those men who could fix anything wrong with a car. I wanted to become one of the boys who could too.

I spent a lot of time watching my daddy work on the various break downs and near break downs that happened with our car. When the cement blocks, which were always handy around our car's parking spot in our front yard, were not in use to hold our car up for one of its repairs, I was a fixture standing on one of them to peer over into the engine area as my daddy worked on the carburetor or water pump or the timing chain, or some other trouble spot. If he were under the car, I was excited to hand him a filthy rag to wipe oil from his hands or a greasy wrench to remove or tighten a nut. I hoped to be a real help to him, as his work on our car started to extend to repairing problems on an old John Deere tractor that he had bought. But, I soon learned that I added little to the efficiency of my dad's work, and that sometimes I was even in the way. "Daddy, let me help you put the gasket on," was often greeted with an impatient "Son, that's okay, I'm in a hurry to get this on so I can get going." Daddy preferred to rely on my older brother, Fred, to help him with these things, I guess because he was a lot bigger and stronger than was I. But, Fred didn't share my passion or even interest in this kind of work. Still, I soon got the message that if I was to be able to hang around Daddy as he worked on our car and tractor that I couldn't ask to do things that I thought would help, but just to help in the little ways that he determined that he wanted to use me. I decided I would just observe and maybe he would see that he could depend on me and let me work more with him down the road.

"Want to go with me to the hardware store?" Daddy asked me one day, as I was standing around handing him wrenches. Just by handing him things, I had had to learn what a one-sixteenth versus a one-quarter ratchet wrench socket looked like, and the other wrench sizes. I'd learned the difference between oil weights and greases, and the thickness of gaskets and a little about carburetor and alternator covers and components.

With Daddy's question, I felt like he was noticing my progress and starting to see some value in me as his helper. "Yes, sir," I shouted in answer. I'm sure it sounded pretty stupid, since I was just a few feet away from him. But it was just the repressed joy of his including me in buying a part or of recognizing my commitment to auto and tractor repair, or something like that, that burst forth in the form of my ridiculous response. No sooner was my shout out of my mouth than the thought occurred to me that I perhaps was risking ruining his invitation by again appearing too anxious to get involved with his car fixing. So I followed my ear-shattering shout of "Yes, sir" with, "Sorry, Daddy. When do you want to go?"

He hesitated. "Right now," he said, chuckling. "I'm in a hurry to get a few parts for the tractor, so we need to get going. The rains are gone now. I'll be able to plow in a day or so."

I had gone outside barefoot this morning, so I darted into the house to put my work shoes on. I wasn't sure whether Daddy was kidding about being in a hurry, but I wasn't taking any chances.

I sat up as tall as I could in the front seat of our car as Daddy tooled down the dirt road leading from our house to the highway into town. I was proud to be with my daddy, but I also wanted to have a good look out of the windshield so that I could read the ruts, and anticipate the kind of ride we were going to have. The dirt road was usually bumpy, and if we were to find ourselves behind another car, usually very uncomfortable too, because we were often forced to eat its dust. But today's dirt road ride was especially challenging. It had rained a day earlier. We didn't have to worry about the dust, but we had to navigate ruts that had been made by other vehicles when the road was real muddy.

The ruts always told a story. In places where they were remarkably deep, some poor devil had been stuck there; when there were tractor tire marks near that spot, the tractor had done the rescue job. Where there were double ruts, some driver had been unable to stay in the first rut that had been made, either because he was driving too fast or too inexpertly. It was left to the drivers coming after them to decide which rut to take. Old cars like ours left narrow ruts, since their tires were a lot less wide than the ones that were built later, so we could often tell when the one or two new cars, belonging to large plantation owners, had traveled our road to town after the rain. If a hay truck had gone down the road, the ruts would have been wider still, and keeping our car driving in a straight line in one of those would have been a piece of cake, compared to following a rut made by a car like ours. Tracks left by herds of cattle or horses across the road could mess up the best ruts, however, big trucks or not. Running into this kind of trouble, or just driving too fast and leaving the pattern established by the rut, could end you up with your car stuck in soft mud on either side of the road, particularly if your car were old and weak like ours and unable to forge its way as a first-tier rut maker as some more able vehicles might. That day, the ruts seemed fine starting out, but near a half mile up the road, right as we approached the highway, traffic was stopped, with three or so cars idling in front of us. We thought we knew what the trouble was right away. It wasn't the ruts. It was the one thing that most often got in the way of people in a hurry on a narrow dirt road after a rain—the inevitable flat tire.

A tire's inner tube was the most patched-up part of a car in our area. No one had much of a car to speak of, and the often severely used car had severely used tires on it. And every tire had an inflated rubber inner tube that seemed to explode and expel ts load of air at the slightest prick. Flats were inexorable, inescapable, preordained, unavoidable, bound-to-happen consequences of driving a car back then. We thought of them and accepted them in that way. Flats were a certain, predestined, fated, expected part of our traveling experience. The longer the trip, the more they happened. But even short trips involving daily or frequent travel wrought the same results. Getting a flat was so common, so usual, and so predictable that it became a part of our everyday usage in speaking of arrival time at a destination. "How long will it take you to get from your house in Sweet Providence to my place in Pecan Grove? When can I expect you?" The answer would come back unfailingly, matter of factly, and, indeed, truthfully: "If I don't have a flat, I'll get there in around forty minutes." We kidded around calling our undependable, well-worn tires "may pops," when, were the truth told, we should have called them "will pops" or "for sure to pops." As our three- or four-car traffic jam was proving today, and as experience showed, travel time had to be figured with flats in mind and accounted for with fuzzy flat figures. And, as I have said, the "if" in "if I don't have a flat, then" does not bear the usual meaning. Rather, it is a predictor of what will surely happen. But this certainty made the length of time of the journey, made on our bad tires, uncertain. It prevented us from giving a straight answer to the trip time question, the arrival time question. One could only give a response that was, well, crooked. In our country environment, where words were largely learned, not from books, but from the pronunciation of words by others, "if" came to be pronounced "ef," as the sound of the letter "f." Thus, this doubtful prognosis, regarding the notion of time of travel, over time evolved into the short hand, mangled expression or saying, "Ef is a crooked letter," meaning there is no way to be sure of the thing spoken of. And, like so many figures of speech born of an oral tradition, its origin got lost as time went on. Growing up, we young folks thought that when people said "ef is a crooked letter," they were talking about the way the letter "f" is formed, with a bend at the top, not knowing that it had anything at all to do with the word "if." This "un-straight" letter's configuration, then, was to us the cause of its meaning. So, whatever the subject, we found that one of us would finish the sentence of another. "Well, if I don't get things lined up as I would like ..." would be interrupted with "Ef is a crooked letter." "If I can find the time, then ..." led to, "Ef is a crooked letter." "If my mama lets me I'll stop to play ball ..." was met with this skeptical observation, "Ef is a crooked letter." And, indeed it was. The interruption told the story.

It was a flat world. The smelly hot patch ruled. Of the things I learned quietly watching my father, nothing proved more valuable than how to apply a hot patch to a leaky inner tube pulled from a punctured tire. Knowing how to take a starter out, or bleed brakes, or repair a radiator seepage, or scrub spark plugs carbon free, was not nearly as helpful as successfully floating an inner tube in a huge black kettle, otherwise used for submerging slaughtered hogs to remove their hair, locating its leak, drying that area off real good, roughing it up so the patch would adhere, gripping the patch tightly to the inner tube with a small vice, lighting the fire on the patch's underside, and keeping it tightly in place so that when the fire died out, after the right amount of time, there was presented a seamless, leak-proof tube at the end. Cranking the car was an everyday thing. Fixing its flats was next on the list of a car's things that had to get done to get its day started and to keep it going. Figuring all this stuff out was adding value to my relationship with my daddy.

Daddy got out of our car to see if he could help out, and I followed him. Cars were idling and spewing exhaust as we passed them on our way to the front of the stopped car line. The smoke and fumes were burning my eyes. Some cars were starting to run hot. All of them were old cars, like ours. So none of the drivers were brave enough to leave the path of a one-day-old rut, the day after a hard rain, and risk getting stuck in soft, rut-less mud. They were waiting out the time, waiting until the lead car's flat would be handled.

A lady about sixty-five was sitting in the driver's seat in one of the cars, the one just before ours—a sight to behold because not many women drove back then. She was a big woman with a slight growth of hair under her chin. She didn't laugh like a lady either—hers was very loud and from the belly. "Mose," she yelled out, "get that damn trap up yonder fixed so I can get the hell out of he-uh." Daddy nodded and smiled at Mrs. Mary Jones and went on. Mrs. Mary had no children to help her and Mr. Jack worked their farm, so Daddy and Mama hired us out to pick cotton and to pick up pecans on the half on Mrs. Jones place, when the work on our small farm was done. And, while I am sure Daddy didn't want to indulge her foul mouth this morning, he was not about to offend her.

Brother Eugene Matthews, a lead gospel singer and piano player in our area, was in the next car up. He was healthy-looking enough and young enough to have gotten out of his car to help out. But he was humming a soft gospel tune, appearing not to be in a big hurry to get back to moving down the road. He acted a lot more ladylike than Mrs. Jones most of the time anyway, and I just guessed he didn't want to risk jamming or bruising one of the fingers he made a living with fooling around with somebody else's car. He ignored us as we passed him up, looking away and down at his fingernails, and kind of slinking down in his seat, probably thinking that if he avoided eye contact, he could avoid getting asked to help check things out. Daddy disregarded him too.

Mr. Doc Rayford, in the next car about twenty yards ahead of the piano player, would have helped if he could have. He was old and had a bad leg. As a younger man, he was a powerful logging man, pulling trees out of the woods with his mules. One day, my daddy said, some logs got free from the heavy chains he used to bind them with for hauling, and as he was trying to re-stabilize his load, some logs slipped more, trapping his legs beneath them. Mr. Doc had a bad limp when he walked and had a weak left leg when he drove. Daddy said he had burned up a few clutches because of his leg getting stuck in position too long on his clutch as he applied his brakes. Anyhow, we understood when Mr. Doc greeted us with a big wave of his straw hat and an even bigger smile, but stayed in his car, a whole lot more than Brother Matthews sitting the trouble out. We stopped for a minute. Daddy warmly shook his hand and said hello.

It was more of a mystery why the person stopped in the lead car, the one causing all the trouble and delay, was still sitting in the car. The car was clearly out of the rut we and the others were following, as it was kind of angled across the road. Maybe a blowout had caused it to move out of place? Even so, it seemed that the driver should have been outside, at least looking around, interested in seeking help, if not working on the car's problem. But the driver was just sitting there.

As we came up close to the back of the car, Daddy started laughing and talking to himself. "No she didn't. I know she didn't," he muttered through laughter. There was a big Bible on the rest in the back window, and delicate-looking white napkins lying around it. Daddy wiped the smile off of his face, straightened himself up, and stood a respectable distance from the driver's-side window. "Morning, Ma'am. What in the world..." Before he could finish his sentence, the young woman behind the wheel burst out crying, a little loudly. Then she composed herself somewhat and started making whimpering sounds into her white gloved hands, holding a handkerchief with pretty flowers around its edges.

I knew her from church. She was the preacher's wife. She looked up, cleared her throat and began to speak. "Deacon, I know I shouldn't be out here. I know how the reverend feels. But, I just don't want to be one of those women so dependent on my husband that I can't do little things for myself, my children, my family and my church. You understand, don't you, deacon?" Daddy didn't say anything. "Deacon, I'm sure you will have to tell Rev and I don't blame you for that. I know you will have to. But, just help me get out of the road now before other people see me out here like this."

Daddy nodded to her. "Yes, ma'am."

Trouble was, as it turned out, Reverend Gant had preached quite a sermon on the place of a woman. He had made it quite plain that a woman's place was pretty much where her husband wanted it to be, but mostly at home waiting for his instruction and direction. He had spoken of new evils, new temptations that drew women out of their traditional roles and about how this was making family life unstable and children wild, sassy, and disrespectable. He was against women in the pulpit, against women working, and against women speaking out on certain subjects. The new evil, television, for those who had one or who had heard of one, was to be watched—not literally—but for what it might do to bring outside influences into home life that would make it harder for a woman to keep order and pay her whole attention to her family. And he said it might keep family members from having to talk with and listen to one another, especially mothers to their children, and make them forget about praying, and reading the Bible together, and forget about God. But the thing the good Rev railed against most, with respect to new evils attracting women away from their responsibilities at home, was this recent devil of mobility that had rolled into our lives, the automobile. His solution—keep women from behind steering wheels and they would steer clear of neglecting their homes and families, and they would not go out into the cold world seeking to see and do things that might make them less than virtuous.

Reverend Gant's wife, Mrs. Sarah, had had a front row seat for this sermon. While the others cried out round her, "Amen, pastor," she had kept quiet. She was a student of the Bible, too, she was thinking, and she hadn't read anything, ever, about women not working, or not witnessing for God, or not taking advantage of the modes of transportation of their day. To the contrary, not to contradict her husband, but it had seemed that the women of the Bible had done most of the work, had seen at least half of the heavenly visions, had witnessed first on Easter Sunday, the day most important to the faith, and had run their households just fine. With the preacher out of town on this Monday morning, Mrs. Sarah decided to teach herself how to drive—not so much to disobey her husband, she told herself, but just in case she needed to know how to do it for the sake of her house and her family. She didn't want to drive to sightsee or take away family time. Rather, she told herself, she might one day even be of help and support to her husband, even in his ministry, in case visits to sick congregants had to be made, while he himself might be busy or ailing, or to help him to get to places with him and the children, if he felt like relaxing while she drove. She thought of a thousand good usages for her learning to drive, and none of them were inconsistent with her Christian faith. But, directly disobeying her husband, who had refused to teach her to drive, worried her mightily, since, as much as she tried to think of herself as a modern woman, she still believed that she should follow him as he followed Christ. It was the "him following Christ" part, with regard to her not driving a car, where she felt the disconnect. She had resolved this dilemma in favor of secretly teaching herself to drive, and leaving it there—leaving this new learning on the shelf, not to be utilized except in case of an emergency so dire that even her husband would be glad that she possessed it. In this thinking, there were a few problems, but we need mention only two: She was clueless about driving at all, and chose to debut in rut driving, which is not at all like and a lot harder than rutless driving; and, most importantly, she knew not one thing about the propensity of her tires to pop on her. Both of these demons had conspired on this fine day after the referenced Sunday's sermon to bring this fine lady to this moment of desperate tears and shameless pleadings with my daddy.

Daddy nodded to me and I sprang into action. After racing back to our car to get a jack and a hot patch, I went to work like a pit-crew ace. We saved the preacher's wife's secret, if not her honor. Even she, as sweet and innocent a creature as God had amongst us, had fallen to the curse of the "Ef." "If only I had known," she moaned. Now, she knew what every true driver in my early years knew. "If I hadn't had a flat, I could have gotten back home undetected," she wept.

"Ef is a crooked letter," I said to myself. Indeed, it is.

Remember ye not the former things,
neither consider the things of old.
Behold, I will do a new thing;
now it shall spring forth; shall ye not know it?

ISAIAH 43:18,19

A Majority Perspective

FLASH BACK...

IT IS A BEAUTIFUL, crisp fall morning in our hometown, Sweet Providence, Louisiana. The date is October 3, 1966. The sky is clear and sunny, and the temperature is hovering around forty-five degrees. An almanac of October 3, 1863, exactly one hundred and three years earlier, recorded nearly identical weather. On that date, General Grant's Union troops bested the Rebel armies up around Vicksburg, forty miles north of home. In fact, just after their Vicksburg victories, a few Union troops made it down to Sweet Providence, to look for provisions and to take advantage of the abundant fishing in its lakes and streams. All these years later, shreds of evidence of the Union troops still linger through the presence of a few weather-worn stone markers showing the soldiers' points of ingress and egress. These markers stand uneasily against the persistent backdrop of Jim Crow laws and practices here, perhaps as uneasily as those young Union troops stood back in 1863 in the then-enemy territory that was Sweet Providence. But these two dates have more in common than just the weather. These were days with events that sounded virtual trumpet blasts for freedom for Black folks. More than that, they were milestones along the pilgrimage toward universal human freedom. You would think that days embodying such high-sounding American ideals would be broadly celebrated, especially in a flag-waving town like ours. Well, you'd be wrong, but you'd be right, too. You might find a big flag-waving celebration going on in Sweet Providence on either or both of those days, or you might not. Whether you did would depend entirely upon the side of our little town to which you went to look for the party.

Sweet Providence is deceptive like that. Take its lovely little Courthouse Square, for instance. It houses a sheriff's office and a jailhouse. It is the administrative office for the parish where road construction and public works are looked after. Of course, the courthouse itself is there for the conduct of the parish's legal proceedings. And, importantly, it is home to the office of voter registration. The courthouse is a gleaming white building with tall columns seeming to reach for the sky. It is surrounded by historic gray and white stone buildings, which accommodate the other offices I just mentioned. Lush, emerald green elm trees secure the square's perimeter. These rich features, together with the smallness of the square, give it a quaint, yet majestic look. The inviting appearance of the place and the square's picture-perfect setting, however, belie the ugly truth that the parish seat and the courthouse unjustly administer the laws of the parish and the state to easily half of Sweet Providence's citizens. To them, its Black citizens, the square is too often a place of the worst kind of mistreatment, done in the name of the law. On the issues of racial justice, the square's stand has not changed since 1863. The square saw Grant's troops arrive and leave, and then waited out the federal presence during the Reconstruction era that followed the end of the Civil War. It also protected the early Jim Crow regimes that came to town when the feds of Reconstruction left the South. Now, the square, this morning in 1966, true to its history, is standing firmly against the changes that appear to be afoot. At the same time, it is still cleverly managing to show the same false face of neutrality that it has worn for more than a few hundred years.

The movement toward freedom for Sweet Providence's Black citizens that the federal presence promised in 1863 was thwarted by a hundred years of racial intimidation and official segregation. Today, the federals are back in our town, carrying a promise of newer and greater freedoms. Thus, their presence in Sweet Providence, on this day, is almost as important as that of Grant's troops in the region in 1863. But I know the square. I know it believes this morning that it can wait these new feds out, too. We, Sweet Providence's Black folks, well know of the square's stout capacity to resist change. The stories about the square's enduring resistant powers have been passed down from generation to generation. And we are also well aware of our spotty history of success on civil rights in our town. So you would be right in allowing that today, like the square, a lot of us Black folks in Sweet Providence are a bit skeptical of our chances of winning with the feds this time around.

In fact, it was in the square that my parents suffered the most degrading experience of their lives. It was when a certain well-known governor of Louisiana came to town to campaign for re-election. Black folks came out in large numbers to hear him. They identified with his populist message of lifting the downtrodden and sharing the wealth of the nation's rich companies with regular, working people. They thought it included new hope for them. So they got to the square early, and some of them got places at the head of the crowd. They waited eagerly for more than two hours for the governor's appearance. Then came the reward for their waiting, an announcement over the loudspeaker that the governor had arrived: "Folks, I give you our next governor!" the announcement came. The crowd erupted in a sustained, excited celebration. But what happened next my mother still can tell only with great sadness. The governor was still exulting in his thunderous welcome as he approached the microphone that was set up for him on the porch of the courthouse. He looked out over the crowd, which ex-

tended the length and breadth of the Square and then spilled over
into the side streets, clear back three blocks toward the highway.
Then he looked down front and right into the faces of a good number of Black folks, all wildly clapping and hooting, just as excited
as all the white people who were there. The governor's face turned
pensive, as he struggled to stay with the celebration. His broad
smile suddenly looked frozen. He looked disturbed in his spirit.
This was his dilemma. There were all these Black folks up front,
and loads of whites that had less good places to stand. He made
up in his mind to fix this problem before he got into his speech.
So, ahead of getting wound up, he said something that was like a
sword passing through the hearts of all the Black folks there. That
he said it in a way that made light of their feelings drove the pain
deeper still. "I'm glad to see you colored folks out to see me," he
started out, "but I need y'all to do something for me so I can get
on with my talk. I need y'all to move from where y'all are at back
yonder behind this crowd of white folks so they can move up here
up front, right up front here where y'all are standing. Now, I want
y'all to see me and hear me like everybody else. I ain't trying to
be hard on you. But, y'all know as well as I do that y'all can't vote
like the white people here can. So, I'd appreciate it if y'all would
move out of the way up here as quick as y'all can." Mama, Daddy,
and the other Black folks stood stunned and embarrassed. They
couldn't move for a moment. Then he pushed them on. "Y'all go
on now, git just as fast as you can." So my parents and their friends
stumbled away from the stage. Adding to their shame were the
laughter and the exhortations to "hurry up and get back where y'all
belong" raining down on them by some of the whites in the crowd
as they made their ignominious exit from the stage area. Most of
the Blacks didn't stay to hear his speech. Mama and Daddy surely
didn't. They drove straight home. Now, Mama, Daddy, and a number of the Black townspeople who were there back when that governor drove them away from the front steps of the courthouse were
back in the square again, today. This time, they didn't expect to be
told to step back.

FLASH FORWARD...

So on this fresh morning, Mama and Daddy got to the square at around seven o'clock, waiting for things to get under way. Around eight, the federal people showed up. Mama went inside with them, and Daddy got right up front in line near the porch of the courthouse in the square. A lot of people had shown up early, Black and white. But how the Blacks and whites felt about the things that were happening there that morning was as different as ebony and ivory.

Among those who were out early looking over happenings in the square was our town marshal, Henry Vane. Vane was a tall, gangly man who had a grim look pasted on his face most of the time. His shadowy, dark beard gave him the look of a young Abe Lincoln. And, though history shows that calling Lincoln "The Great Emancipator" is an overstatement of Lincoln's commitment to freeing the slaves, you can be sure he had nothing in common with Vane. Vane was a hater. Today, he was standing on the side of the square nearest the courthouse, observing one after another "po' n———," as he saw it, pull up in some old dilapidated car or truck to take his or her place in line on the square's grounds. He shook his head in disgust. "What a ridiculous sight," he was heard to say. "It turns my stomach just to look at it." Others in the town looked on in agreement with Vane.

It had been a long time coming, but it was finally here. For the people in line, it was a day of unimaginable exhilaration. For those looking on from a distance, it was another day of occupation, like when Grant's men were there. It was a day when Vane's kindred souls felt control of things slipping away, a day when they were forced to accept what seemed to them a gross absurdity. For there they were, all lined up, these wretched Negroes, seeking to participate with them, and every other white person in town, in the exercise of the most priceless treasure available in a democracy. To them, it was an extraordinary waste of time and an unwarranted federal intervention.

Around eight thirty that morning, a slight Black preacher, Reverend John Huey, emerged from the courthouse. At the sight of him, those in line seemed to straighten up their shoulders. They adjusted their clothes and brightened up. They, too, had been somewhat nervously watching Marshall Vane and the others eyeing them from a distance. Reverend Huey's appearance calmed their fears and emboldened them.

Just to look at him, you would never think the reverend would have anything like that kind of command presence. He was a willowy wisp of a man, just five feet four, and no more than a hundred twenty pounds. Like most of the preachers in our small town, he worked only part-time at his church. His church was too small to support his rather large family of eight. He spent the greater part of his days setting traps for muskrats, raccoons, beavers, minks, foxes, and other fur-bearing animals in the area. Reverend Huey worked alone, never hiding his comings and goings, and always in a position of vulnerability. He would trap across the levee near the Mississippi River, and walk or drive back the several miles to his home. Were he walking, he would carry his traps and furs flung across one of his shoulders, with his Bible slipped inside of the waist of his pants.

A few years earlier, one of his enemies took advantage of his predictable behavior. On his way home from checking his traps, an attempt was made to assassinate him. Luckily, he was riding in his old Chevy that day, and luckily his shotgun-wielding would-be-killer was a bad shot. The shotgun blast left a gaping hole on the driver's side of Reverend Huey's car. But the assassin's aim was low. Even so, Reverend Huey was seriously injured, left with a broken arm, and a number of broken, bloodshot ribs. He vowed never to fix that hole in his car as a kind of statement about what hate can do and how it had to be defied. He had the body of a whippet, but the heart and courage of a lion. That's why people in line stood up straight for him that day.

Inside the courthouse, a sign hung in the window of the local registrar's office: "Closed for Business." Registrar Riley Mills had decided that if federal voting rights laws were going to force him to register "Nigras," then he would just close down shop and register no one from then on. He was determined that his act of defiance would match that of the federal government and of Reverend Huey and "his people." The federals who had come to town this day were the federal registrars. They had been sent to town to break the impasse between Mills and the town's Blacks and to enforce the new 1965 Voting Rights Act. They had come to register every unregistered adult Black person in the parish. And the Black people had come into town in droves, and were lined up for blocks, to sign their names or make their marks and register. This was the spectacle that so revolted most of the white townspeople. That Reverend Huey was being accorded meetings with and apparent respect by these white federal registrars, and treated like a conquering hero by his people right in front of their eyes, added immeasurably to the appalling, sickening feeling that possessed them. Reverend Huey was our local civil rights leader, head of the parish chapter of the NAACP. But, today, he was being treated, his detractors felt, like he was head of the whole damn town.

I was nineteen years old at the time, and accompanying my mother, who, like Reverend Huey, was already a registered voter. Both of them, after many tries, had "passed" the literacy test for voting a couple of years back. And, she, like Reverend Huey, was working the line, making sure that the folks standing there were as comfortable as possible and knew just how to answer the federal registrars. Today, they would only have to provide proof of eligible age, proof of residence in the parish, and swear that they were who they said they were. This was a far cry from the rigorous and ever-changing "literacy" test that Blacks previously had been forced to take as a precondition to voting, a test not required of whites. Among other things, Mr. Mills's literacy test usually required a Black applicant to recite the preamble to the Constitution, name the presidents of the United States in order, and compute his or her age to the year, the month, and the day. For an illiterate Black person, the test posed an impossibility to voting. But Black schoolteachers and other well-educated Blacks also routinely "failed to pass" the test. Everything depended upon who graded the exam papers. That was always Mr. Mills, and he kept the voting rolls darn near clean of Black folks, or "Nigras," as he called them. Of course, the voting rolls in the parish were filled with illiterate whites, but no matter. Somehow their voting while illiterate posed no threat to the proper workings of democracy and was not scandalous to the body politic. Mills had hoped that by letting my mother, Reverend Huey, and three other Blacks pass the test, they would stop their insistence on the right to vote. But instead, they intensified their efforts, their voter drives. Mills found out, much to his dismay, that their demands for voting rights were more than personal. He found out that their insistence on the right to vote extended to every blessed, disgruntled, prospective Black voter. Now, the results of their labors were standing right there in front of them, lined around the courthouse for all the world to see.

As I stood there with my mother contemplating these things, I saw Marshall Vane emerge from his car and make a beeline to Reverend Huey, who was standing no more than ten feet from us. Reverend Huey, alerted by someone in the line that Vane was approaching him, turned to face Vane, who was by now storming toward him. Vane could not contain his consternation any longer. His long legs quickly ate up the ground between Reverend Huey and him. Now, he was right in Rev. Huey's face, towering over him. "Huey," he said, "why in the hell are your people lined up here like this? Look at 'em. There ain't one of them fit to hold office. Who y'all gonna put in?"

Reverend Huey took his time, as if he were in deep thought over this question. Then he responded with an answer as smooth, yet as powerful, as a hot knife cutting through butter. "Well," he said, "we may not have anyone we want to put in. But, we sure do have some folks we want to put out." Indeed, a while later, there were successful efforts made to put some people out of office. Included among those put out was none other than Marshall Vane himself. Vane lost in a landslide in his next election to a more moderate white merchant, Howard James. This victory for James was courtesy of the folks who were lined up around the courthouse that day seeking the right to vote.

FLASH FORWARD MORE

"Go back to Kentwood, Bug Eyes," Mr. Broussard, an elderly African American, shouted at me. "You ain't gonna win nothin' around here. Nothin'." Just thirteen short years from my standing in the courthouse square with my mother in Sweet Providence, I was actually standing for election to the Louisiana State Senate. I was, in fact, trying to put someone out. I was the beneficiary of that same Voting Rights Act that empowered people to vote in 1966. This time it was being used not just to register African Americans to vote, but also to require our state legislature to carve out a majority-minority senatorial district. Running in one such district, I found strange things happening in this newest of democratic processes. Black voters were torn between two paradoxical views, two perspectives: that of a constrained minority, which they lived, and that of a free majority, which they had come to know about, but had not yet experienced in an election or anywhere else. This has been a large part of the duality in perspective that was being tactlessly expressed by Mr. Broussard. He had seen other Black candidates run against this white senate incumbent, with whom I was competing, only to lose badly. These previous competitors of the incumbent were more established in the community than I was at the time of my contests with him, and were born and raised in the district. Mr. Broussard wrongly accused me of being from Kentwood, Mississippi, but his point was that I was from somewhere in the country, and if the local fellas had lost against this white senator in a Black majority district, I surely had no shot at winning. His was still a minority perspective. Were it otherwise, he would have thought of himself as a part of a new majority, fully able to organize and rally around a candidate of his choice and win.

So just thirteen years later, and the long lines are gone from the Courthouse Square. We now call ourselves by the empowered and proud appellation, "African American." Back in 1966, referring to ourselves by the now mostly discontinued "colored," or "Negro" labels, even the threat of physical danger couldn't keep us out of the lines for registering and voting. Now, with no hint of the kind of dangers that Reverend Huey and "his people" faced, we are found struggling to provide strategies for how to turn out the African American vote. Many of the descendants of those in Reverend Huey's voter registration lines now unfathomably wonder whether their votes count or whether voting makes a difference. Many have come to see themselves as weak, the political system as unyielding for them, their candidates as unproductive and unresponsive, and winning on their issues unrealistic. Yet the familiar adage, "majority rule, minority rights," captures the essence of American polity. But it also seemed to rob the minority of my would-be constituency of the awareness to think in terms of ruling. "What if a minority group member strives, not only to enjoy the rights it has in common with the majority, but also the influence, power, authority, and prestige of a member of the majority racial group?" It is this question that Mr. Broussard was finding it impossible to comprehend. For him, the exalted and precious privilege of ruling would always be the exclusive province of the majority—not the new majority that the voting laws had created, but the old majority that had dominated and cemented his political thinking all of his life. But during my maturation, the feeling of the power that the vote generated in the square that day never left me. I still identified with the feeling that sprung from Reverend Huey's gentle retort back then with Marshall Vane in the square—that feeling of a majority perspective.

"It's all about how one looks at things," I have repeatedly explained to my friends and colleagues. Take political parties. Whichever party is in the minority at a given time is continually trying to shake that position. If minority status is tolerated at all, it is only so tolerated as temporary. Once a party accepts its minority station as its way of life, then that is exactly what it becomes. For a party to deal with its minority status in this way would mean that it would accept a more or less permanent incapacity to rule or to be a part of a ruling group. The difference, of course, is that while it is possible to change the status of a political party from a minority to a majority party by adjusting the numbers of the minority party upward in sufficient numbers, in the cases of race, gender and religion, such a literal change is either impossible or unthinkable. In the cases of race, gender and religion, with numbers lacking, majority status can be achieved only through the way the minority thinks and acts. It is determined by the way it deals with and views its supposed minority limitations. It is defined by the minority's perspective on them. In these instances, such achievement will depend upon the extent to which the minority is able to see the world through the eyes and from the vaunted place of the majority, or to adopt the perspective of the majority as it makes decisions and pursues choices. It throws off its perspective as a limited minority and takes on that of the majority, with all its rights and privileges, including the privilege of ruling.

FLASH FORWARD?

It is another beautiful, crisp fall morning in my hometown, Sweet Providence. The date is October 27, 1979. The sky is clear and sunny, for tonight I will win my race for the Louisiana State Senate handily. African American voters will respond to my candidacy magnificently. But some will hold back, especially some leaders. And, for a few days that follow, I am troubled by Mr. Broussard's remarks to me, for I know that too many others feel the same way. So I sat Mr. Broussard down and explained to him my thinking on these matters, hoping that he would revise his and bring some others to a clearer understanding. "I've got it," Mr. Broussard exclaimed after two hours of discussion. "All that you have said to me may be summed up in a few words," he said. "You want every person who is of a so-called racial minority group to live and perceive life in such a way that when he or she dies, that he or she may deservedly have etched on his or her tombstone, 'Here lies a minority who had a majority perspective.'"

I knew he didn't get it. But since I didn't want to dampen his newfound enthusiasm, I feigned agreement. Still, I had to let him know that I was not encouraging this limited view of the subject at hand that he was prepared to embrace. "That's good, Mr. Broussard," I interjected. "What we need are minorities with majority perspectives. But, I hope we can get this done and acknowledged a little before we minority group members all die."

He agreed it was important to work with me on this. But, since our meeting had already gone on for some time, he implored, "Could we get after this timing issue just a bit later?"

Verily, verily, I say unto you, except a corn of wheat fall into the ground and die, it abideth alone; but if it die, it bringeth forth much fruit.

JOHN 12:24

Dying Is the Easy Part

I NEVER LIKED VISITING an old person who was very sick and near death. I know that sounds a little selfish, since a time near death is probably when the dying person most wants to see those with whom he or she has shared life. But I had thought it was even more selfish on the part of the dying person to insist on seeing those close to them. Dying is the most personal and individual thing that we humans do. At the time of birth, there has got to be participation of some sort by one's mother. At least two people have to be involved. But dying is different. One does it entirely by oneself. You can't really be assisted in dying, because in the end, whether you're handed a poison pill or reach for it yourself, the act of dying can't be shared with anyone or by anyone. At least, that's how I saw it. I surely didn't see what my Cousin Honey's final illness had to do with me. We called her "Cuttin Honey," and today I was being forced by my folks to pay a visit to her. They said she was asking for me. Cuttin Honey had been on her deathbed for more than a month. Now, she had taken a turn for the worse. I was going to see her because I had to, but I truly didn't want to go.

Cuttin Honey was ninety years old, born in 1875. She had steadily lost more and more of her eyesight until she'd come to depend for the little sight she had left on thick and foggy-looking glasses. From a robust one hundred sixty pounds she had dropped to around ninety-five. As she explained it, she had arthritis "reel regula" in her joints, especially in her "knee bon's and her fangers"; a "rat smart" measure of high blood "press'na"; and a "tech" of sugar "di'beties." Her toothless mouth was drawn into a small, wrinkly opening. Her full head of hair was braided into soft, snowy white, ribbony plaits. But she wasn't soft and frilly. She got her name because of her honey-brown color, not because she was all sweetness and light. She had a sharp tongue and a fiery spirit, and could signify with the best of them. If some of our really dark-skinned cousins would get upset with her about what they would say was her "white folks mean streak," they'd tease her with their little biting, signifying ditty, "The blacker the berry, the sweeter the juice, an ole red Negro ain't no use…" Before they could finish it, though, she'd shut them up with her comeback—"Yea, say what you wants to, but ain't nuthin' sweeter dan honey, but money baby, an' y'all ain't got none of dat, jus' lak me." She didn't really mean it, though. Deep down it hurt, because she wanted to look as black as they did. But to say something back to them, to out "jaw jeck 'em," as she put it, was just her nature.

She came to derive a certain pleasure from winning these verbal sparrings. Were anyone in our family to even come close to making an utterance that seemed to challenge her in the slightest way, she would cut her eyes at them in one of her well-mastered, menacing glares, or say to them, "Okay, you can start up wif me ef you wants tuh, but don't start what you can't finis'." Either her well-placed words or a well-directed eye cut had the unfailing effect of rattling my unkind kin, sending hands up in surrender, accompanied by subdued, submissive whimpers of "All right, you got me, Cuttin, I give." Mostly, this would happen before she would have even spoken a word! To this surrender, nodding her head up and down and extending her neck in a rooster crowing-like gesture, Cuttin Honey would strut her exultant response, "Well all rat den, well all rat." These were usually the last words spoken in such a tête-à-tête. Yes, all of our folks knew better than to pass words with Cuttin Honey or to get into a haughty, pretentious exchange with her, to mess with her. On this particular day, however, I would prove myself a slow learner in this regard.

When I got to the house where she stayed, the front door was open like always. I went in and called out to her. She answered softly, inviting me into her bedroom. Her room was large and stuffy with a glass-paned door shut tight that led to a veranda where she used to sit for hours on end watching over her beloved chicken yard. The door served as a view of that yard. Cuttin Honey's chicken yard was the one thing she had insisted upon holding on to when her children moved her to town from the country. She had well over eighty chickens in her yard when she first left her farm. Her favorites were her Rhode Island Reds and her Dominica hens. She often talked to them by name as she scattered their corn feed across the yard each morning. Now, after six years in town, she was down to just five or six chickens; all the rest had died off or been stolen by hungry or just plain larcenous neighbors. But she still was reminded of the country life she had loved just by getting a glimpse of her few chickens every now and then.

She had moved from the country into her daughter's four-bedroom house. All of the children had moved on. With her daughter still working every day, she indulged the feeling that she was living alone. But she wasn't lonely. These times restored the feeling of independence she longed for after she had come to live at her daughter's place, filled then with the sounds of her daughter's noisy teenage boys.

Were she still on her farm, this would have been a time of relative quiet. By now, in late August, she would have laid by her cotton fields from chopping by early July. She would have already beaten back the boll weevil too, and would have been enjoying something of a respite from the fields before the cotton-picking started up in late September. During these dog days of August, she would don her wide-brimmed straw hat, draping a towel from it like an Arab headdress, and stroll around her place, just checking things. Finally, she would rest in the highest heat of the afternoon in the shade of one of the four huge pecan trees out front of her house and look up, squinting, through their branches at the wild geese sailing in great V's high above or at the squirrels, closer in, darting among their limbs. Around this time, too, her truck crop of purple hull Crowder peas would be ready for the gathering, and in the relative cool of the late afternoon, her neighbors would come by and help themselves to as much as they wanted. In the Delta, everything would still be green, green, since there was no abrupt separation of summer and fall. Things would usually turn brown gradually, after the first frost, which routinely came in the second week of October, and, with the cotton leaves then dying and withering away, this browning would signal the best time for picking cotton in earnest. Till then, she would have been more or less free to cook and clean, take care of her animals, check her fences, and, when her children were growing up, get them cleaned out with castor oil so they'd be ready for school. These thoughts allowed her, depending on the season of the year, to feel the same independence she enjoyed and missed from the country.

But, now, Cuttin Honey was bedridden and spent the greatest part of her time doing the few things she could do from this much-diminished vantage point—looking over the pictures in her Bible, looking out of her windows at her chicken yard or her neighbors' comings and goings, staring at the walls of her room, and remembering. The room's wallpaper had been freshly painted with her favorite bright pink color when she moved in, but time had repainted it faded and dull. The walls were covered with old family pictures, though, that captured timeless, undiminished love and good times. Family pictures also adorned her dresser, which stood next to a small, flowery cloth-covered divan. She was the mother of thirteen, seven boys and six girls. They had filled her life, and now their pictures filled up her bedroom. The bedposts were solid oak, with the sturdy look of carefully crafted furniture. Her mattress was hand-made and lumpy, however, stuffed with cotton and corn shucks from her own fields. But she was used to the feel of it, and refused to change it for something modern. The bed was covered with a bright quilt of many colors that she and her last living sister, Jessie, had made just before Jessie's death more than ten years earlier. She was lying in her bed, curled into a fetal position. Her head rested comfortably on a fluffy down pillow, which was yielding a few grayish feathers around the edges. She looked real frail. But she seemed alert, at ease, and at peace. The traces of a smile creased her face when she saw me.

"Come on in, Billy," she said weakly. "Look ober dere on de dresser. I's done put somethin' ober dere fuh you. Dat's hit, rat dere in dat raid bandana. Mus' be five dollars in dere. Take hit wif you. Yo mama tol' me you was gonna go to college, an' you can n'use dat lil bit tuh git you sometin' tuh take wif you. Git you some soap, Billy, some of de kinds dat mens use, dat smells so good. Yo grandma, my Antee Stella, tol' me you was gonna come tuh mo dan de res' of us in de way of learnin'. An' yo teacher at Sundi school, Miss Mae Shorter, she said how you tuck ober de class, hepin' her teach an' ever'thang. Y'all chilin sho is blessed, Billy, sho is blessed. I known you was rat cleber when I seent you readin' dem books all de time, jus' sittin' dere an' readin' an' readin' till you couldn't hold yo heid up". She paused and laughed under her breath, then, to herself, like she was remembering something real pleasant. "Yea, Billy," she went on, "I ain't had no book learnin' myself, but I sho do 'spects dem dat does, 'specily us' cullud ones. You gonna be all rat when you done finis' yo schoolin'. I wants you to git yosef a fine suit of clothes, an' maybe eh pipe, lak dat cullud senator from Mis'sippi had in dem picture books you shoed me. What was his name is Billy? De one was settin' in dat chair puffed up lak a frog, wif a pocket watch an' all dat, what he name?" She asked with the happiest look of remembrance on her face.

I took in a long look of her. I couldn't believe she was going on like this, as sickly and as weak as she was. I wanted her to stop talking. I worried that she might keel over and croak with me there, and I didn't want that to happen. "Cuttin Honey," I said, "His name was Hiram Nevels. I showed you that picture a long time ago. How did you remember him?"

"Cause I got good sense, boy," she snapped. "Why you thank I 'members him!"

Now I thought she was getting a little testy, so I figured it would be a good time to ease out of our conversation. "Cuttin Honey," I said, "I want you to listen to me. Thank you for this present. I'm going to do just what you said to do with it. But I'm not going to use the soap. I'm going to put it on a shelf in my room down at the college and it's going to make me feel like you are right there with me. And when the others ask me where I got it from, I'm going to say from the smartest women I know—in college or not. Now please get some rest, and I'll go on home and finish packing and get ready to leave for school tomorrow. And I'm going to write you soon, and you can get one of your grandchildren to read my letter to you. I am going to come and visit you when I come back home for Thanksgiving."

Whew! I was secretly exclaiming. *I've done my duty, made my ritualistic, ceremonial, useless visit to the near-dead like everybody insisted and I am now outta here—out of this room smelling of liniment, rubbing alcohol, witch hazel, used bed pans and death.* I wasn't much thinking about what I had said to her, or how it had come across. I was just saying something—anything—that would get me moving in a direction that amounted to leaving and ending this visit I was obliged to make.

Suddenly, from behind her thick glasses, the sparkle that was in her eyes was taken over by the glint of a fire, foreshadowing an eruption. "What did I say wrong?" I asked, trying to stem this hint of an angry storm I saw coming.

"Don't y'all thank I already knows what's happnin' tuh me? I's dying, Billy, I knows hit. Why y'all keep talkin 'roun' hit? I ain't gonna be heh when you gits back from school fuh no Thanksgivin', an' you 'no's hit. So, why's you lyin' tuh me? Don't talk tuh me lak I's some chile or 'nother!" She was straining to scream at me. "Look at me. I's all curled up, lak jus' 'fo' I fust got ready tuh come intuh dis worl'. Don't hit look lak tuh you I's jus' gittin' ready tuh go out agin? Sho looks lak hit to me."

What she said shocked and saddened me so much. I didn't mean to hurt or offend her. I really loved her. I knew she was dying, and I knew she probably wouldn't last very long. That was precisely why I had let my folks talk me into coming by to see her before I headed out of town. But I didn't know how to handle talking about that. I didn't know what to say to somebody who was dying. I didn't want to be there to see her like she was, looking so small under her bed covers, like she was hardly there, and sipping in short breaths, like she was trying to drink something in a hurry that was still a little too hot.

"I'm sorry, Cuttin Honey," I said in a low voice. "You're right. I just didn't know what to say. But, I really do thank you for the soap," I stammered.

"Den, you ain't near as smart as I bin thankin' you was," she mumbled, shaking her head from side to side. "No, I'd say you is pretty stupid." Well, I didn't like being called stupid, but I figured she was old and she was dying so she could say whatever she wanted. "You's one dumb boy, Billy, purdee stupid," she continued, this time with a little glee in her weak voice.

Now, I thought, she is having a little too much fun at my expense. Anybody can be wrong, but stupid and dumb—well, there hardly seemed any call for that. But she was old and she was dying, so I decided that I wouldn't say anything back to her. "Okay, Cuttin Honey," I chuckled, "okay. I'll be leaving now."

"You's reel stupid ef you's skeerd tuh talk 'bout deff an' dyin'. I faces hit ever' day, an' I talks 'bout it ever' day. I even talks tuh him too, but ole deff he don't talk back tuh me. De onliest thang he ever did say was when he seent me fuh de fust time, an' all he done den was jus' tuh tell me who he was. An' when he do come by tuh visit wif me, well, hits de mos' comfitibal thang. We bin gittin 'long fine, 'jus' fine. Funny thang is ole man deff neber do visit me alone no mo'. He brangs a crowd 'long too nah. Sometime dey fills up dis heh whole rum. Yestidy he brung by Ike, yo cuttin Ike, my dead husman; an' he had wif him de onliest one of our chilin we ever los', Ray Lee. An' all my sistahs an' brudders dat's bin long gone, dey all come back by tuh see me, dey comes 'long too. Dey didn' say nothin', dey neber does. Dey jus' stan''round, an' Ray Lee, he some-time leans on my bed pos', close tuh me lak he n'used tuh do at de house. Dey all looks reel quiet lak. But, mos'ly dey looks reel happy an' be smilin' down at me. An' hit make me feel happy tuh see dem." Then, with a look of child-like wonderment, Cuttin Honey sighed a sigh of deep satisfaction. "Hit don't look hard fuh dem, Billy. Hit don't look hard whatsonever."

Now it was time for me to shake my head. I was thinking, *Talking about me. This takes the cake.* Anyhow, she was old and she was dying and I owed it to her to respect that, so I didn't comment on what she had said. But it did seem to me that she was talking out of her head, making not a bit of sense. Just then, though, she started up again. "I done jus' got reel ti'ed, Billy, like my win' is short from walkin' up a hill or somethin' lak dat. But, I's bin ti'ed one way or 'nother fuh mos' of all of my blessed days. Mos'ly, I's bin ti'ed of watchin' ober de thangs dat belongst to me—my farm, my peoples, my roosters an' hens, not tuh manshun my heff an' stranf. I done watched dem, an' watched ober dem, an' tuck kere of dem, tryin' tuh keep up wif 'em an' 'count fuh dem. But, no mattuh how much I watches out an' worries ober dem, I bin stidy losin' dem, losin' mos' ever'thang, one at de tim'. Dat's what's wrong wif dis worl'. You can't keep nothin'. You can't hol' on tuh nothin'. Dat's de hard part, Billy."

What she said really, finally, got through to me. It made me start to think about a lot of the things she had told me about how hard her life had been. I remember once, when I was about eight years old, how fascinated she was to find out that I could read already, and how after that, she would ask me to read something to her from one or the other of my books. She liked to have me read to her from books about things that happened after the Civil War ended. When I finished, she would say, "Now, let Cuttin Honey tell you somethin' 'bout reel hist'ry."

Cuttin Honey had lived long enough to be more than half as old as the United States government itself. She'd seen and lived through the most contradictory times for freed Blacks in American history, when the laws of the land didn't mean any protection for them. She'd witnessed firsthand the frightening reign of the KKK, the fearful cross burnings, the murders, the beatings, the intimidation, how they didn't have to answer "tuh Gawd or nobody else." "Rat up dere, Billy, rat up dere, at our own lil church, Sweet Cannan Misshunari Baptis', jus' spittin' distance from ware we's stan'in', dey burnt one, mo dan once, till dey runned ole Reben Dunn clare up tuh New Yuk fuh preachin' 'bout Pres'dent Lancon an' us' freedoms." Tearfully and angrily she told me of a Black physician who'd come to town, and who was taking care of the poor Black people in our Parish, "when de Kluxers, fuh no re'sin udder dan jealousy of his clothes and his drivin' eh new Model T Fawd, tol' Dr. Green he'd bettah git outta town fo' he was kilt." Then she would raise her voice almost to a wail and say, "An' de po' man, dis fine man, will, he was leabin' town undah dere t'r'et, an' he was at de train depot waitin' fuh de train fuh tuh take him somewares else, dem Kluxers shot him down an' kilt him rat at de depot, shot him down an' kilt him in broad daylight lak he was'n no mo' dan a rabbit." She'd heard of a few lynchings in her area too, "but I neber did wants tuh go an' see where one had done tuck place, 'cause hit was jus' too hurtin'." But she admitted, "I did knowed of one boy named Gates who was growin' up wif me an' who was no mo' dan sebentin yares old was hung fuh 'sposed tuh be sassin' a white uman ober a raid apple de boy wouldn' pay fuh 'cause de boy say hit was rotten." And, she "membered" to me on another of my visits that "Mr. Joe May, yo bus driber, fuh de school bus, his brudder, R. T., was shot and kilt by a white man instid of Joe May 'cause he looked lak Joe May, and Joe May was 'sposed tuh be tryin' to keep time wif some white uman down at de drug sto'. All dey said Joe May ever done was jus' tuh tip his hat at her." Shaking her head, she'd say, "We los' so many of us' good mens ober jus' white mens jealousy an' hate, ober nothin'. So watch yosef, Billy, watch yosef."

Even as horrible as she'd seen things for Black men, with them being killed, beaten, and run out of town, "Dat wasn't de wust of hit. Hit was de Black uman was vi'lated by de white mens dat was de wust." It was plain that this was a quarter of her life's experiences that was deeply troubling for her. Maybe it was just because of the circumstances of her own fathering or maybe it was something else. She never said. But it was known in our family that her daddy was a white man, that she knew who he was, that he was the owner of the plantation where she grew up, and that he lived nearby with his white wife and white children; and that throughout all her growing-up years he never spoke to her, let alone acknowledge her as his own. Folks said she looked more like his child than his white children, except, of course, she was a lot browner. This deep hurt and neglect stayed with her all of her life, and that her mother was a victim of an unwanted white man was surely a main reason why she dwelt on her heartfelt conclusion "dat de vi'lation of de colored uman was de wust of hit." She'd lived through it all—the KKK, lynchings, senseless killings, rapes, racial segregation, and hate—and my books about the Civil War, Reconstruction, and all that followed competed poorly alongside Cuttin Honey's vivid, personalized accounts.

Cuttin Honey had never gone to school. There was no colored school in her parish for her to attend, so she never had a chance to learn to read or write. But she'd point to her head and rub her hands together and say, "Nobody neber gived me nothin'. Ever'thang I has I got wif dis heh heid, an' dese heh hands." Indeed, her hands— rough, calloused, scaly, and gnarled—were more like that of an old man than an old lady, testifying to her claim that she'd "Don' don' mens work, pickin' an' choppin' cotton, puttin' up fence rows, cuttin' wood, takin' keer of a fahm, fuh near sixty-fi' years." At fourteen, she was a married woman. By the time her child-bearing years were over, she'd given birth to thirteen live babies, and had suffered through a stillbirth and three miscarriages. "One thang I alus said 'bout my chilin, Billy," she'd said to me with a voice full of pride, "dey all had de same daddy. Dat's a promise I made tuh myself as a young girl, 'cause my mama's chilin had four or five different ones. I said to myself dat my chilin would all have one an' only one daddy, an' he'd be rat dere in de same house wif 'em all." After that affirmation one day, she looked at me, wagged her finger, and admonished me, asserting, "An' you be sho, boy, dat when yo time comes for chilin, dat yern, yo chilin, has one an' de same mama too."

"'Course I will," I quickly reassured her, "Of course I will." She looked at me then with her face wrinkled in skepticism.

Cuttin Honey had lost her husband, Ike, and one of her sons, Ray Lee, more than twenty years earlier, in a farm accident involving a mule. It happened, they say, when one of their strong-headed, high-strung mules was spooked while pulling a wagon of hay with Ike driving and Ray Lee riding and working with him. The mule stampeded down into a ravine, turning the wagon over, and her son's neck broke under the wagon's load of hay. "Dat mule jus' keeped on runnin' wif my husman tryin' tuh heid him an' tuh hol' on, but de wagon turnt ober anyhow, killin' my sweet chile, Ray Lee, and tanglin' Ike up in de lines an' leids. De mule broke free aftuh de wagon turned ober, an' he runned an' drug Ike tuh his deff too, wif eh busted heid." She never understood or accepted how it happened. "How could one mule kill two grown mens at one time wifout some hep from somebody?" she'd ask. This uncertainty about why they died in that way made the pain of her loss of her husband and her son all the harder to take. Like so many other things, she had to finally take comfort in the assurance that she would have her chance to ask her savior "in de judgmint when I will sho'ly see him face tuh face."

Somehow, over her ninety years, she had dealt with all of what life had cast her way through her faith, her guile, and her wits. It was her mother wit, her uncommon, common sense, her intuitive understanding of what I needed to get from her that had caused her to call me to her room. I hadn't given her a chance to share with me what was on her mind.

I wanted to listen now and to tell her that I understood why she had called for me, so I drew closer to her bed and looked down on her. She was smiling back at me now, like she was as happy to see me as when I had first come in and stood by her bed to say good-bye to her. I leaned over and touched her cheek, then lightly brushed it with the backside of my hand. Then I took a closer look at her face, and it looked like she was smiling at nothing in particular, but kind of like a two- or three-month-old baby smiles at its surroundings for no particular reason. I looked around the room, but it looked empty to me. All of a sudden, her little body moved slightly, squeezing into a tighter fetal position, and she looked up at me and smiled at me once more. Then, she softly clapped her hands three times—clap, clap, clap—real fast, rapid-fire-like. "I'm gone, chilin. I'm gone," she whispered out urgently. And, just like that, Cuttin Honey was gone, drawing in a last earthly glance of me, all those pictures of her children on the wall and of what was left of her chickens.

It didn't look that hard.

He sits in the lurking places of the villages.
In the hiding places, he kills the innocent.
His eyes stealthily watch for the unfortunate.
Arise, O Lord, O God, lift up your hand!

Psalms 10:9, 12

A Mistake

SHE WAS PREGNANT AGAIN. And she was ashamed. My brother, John, knelt down next to where she was lying on the sofa and touched her small, bulging belly. She turned away from him, letting out a slight groan, feigning sleepiness. "Jadie, Jadie," he whispered. "It's me, Brother." She turned away further, pressing her face against the back of the sofa, burying it in its pillows, groaning and frowning more. "Come on, Jadie. Wake up. We need to talk," he said urgently. No response. He took a long look at her. She was still our little sister, in spite of everything. *Still so shy,* he thought. *Still acting like a child. Still a child.* It had always been her way to avoid facing him when something had gone wrong. He'd just come in from quite a hunting experience and he hadn't seen her pregnant this time. She probably thought he wanted to talk to her about that. He had never figured out how to get through his sister's wall. He'd always felt like he'd failed her. When he found out that she was pregnant this time, he swore to himself, "never again." So the problem was dealt with.

Jadie was the latest of his victims, in fact twice smitten by him. There were many others. All like her: young, gullible, impressionable, vulnerable school girls. All the girls were abuzz about him from the first day he'd come to our school. Hawk, the PE teacher, six foot four, good-looking, fast-talking, hard body, hard-playing, sweet smile, but ruthless—bad habits learned from big city life as a football star. He was from our place and he knew the traditions of our way of life and how people handled teenage pregnancies. When a young girl had had her "leg broken" or gotten in a "family way," she was sent somewhere, almost all the time. If a girl had a place to go—and there was usually someplace—to another town with an aunt, grandma or big sister, they'd send her away to avoid the shame. It wasn't much talked about after that; people just acted liked it wasn't happening. When people did talk about it, with the evidence removed, the talk sounded more like rumor. But the rumors came as whispers, so that even those who felt the need to talk about these poor children who had been sent away still showed respect for the tradition.

Hawk knew all about the tradition, and he took advantage of it. He knew nothing would happen to him. There was too much shame. No, not on his part, to be sure, but on the part of the unfortunate girl and her crestfallen family. Oh, he would go on about his business—teaching PE and watching the girls, dressed out in their PE shorts and thin blouses, looking over them like a stalking leopard, planning his next catch of the weakest and the finest of them. He would go on with his good life, while his confused young victims would have to make do. Sure, some people might early on wonder aloud whether he was the daddy, but that would be about it. That charge would soon be forgotten, and he would go—indeed had gone—blameless for all practical purposes. He would have to acknowledge nothing, and he would never open his wallet to her or the baby. He would go on with his proper wife and his proper children in their proper home. Only those children would carry their father's name, not his of the young girls. He would attend church services, speak at funerals and wear the veneer of respectability. He would sponsor athletic events and prowl the sidelines during football games, always introduced to warm if not thunderous applause. He would be hailed as a molder of young men, and celebrated as a builder of character for them. He would be accorded the honors of his profession, hoist trophies to toast victories, and hold his seat in the state football hall of fame.

The life of his young girl prey would be changed forever. She would be separated from the company of her schoolmates. She would lose growing-up time and sometimes take up the strange pursuits of prenatal care. She would not be called "a nice girl" ever again. She would move away from the familiarity of her family and be forcibly placed with new people, who pitied her or thought her bad or foolish. She would have her baby in this environment and she would almost always immediately leave it somewhere—where she had had it, or somewhere else. When she returned, there would be no outward evidence that she'd ever given birth. There would be no baby in her arms, and she would have a flat, young girl's tummy like before. At first, she'd have to tighten her bra so that her breasts wouldn't show the new sag from her passing experience with motherhood, but that wouldn't be obvious. Some people might wonder or whisper about her and a baby, but that would be short-lived, too. But the girl would be changed. And those close to her, family and dear friends, would know.

We saw it in Jadie. Her bright spirit grayed. She looked all of fourteen, but she had lost her playfulness. At times she seemed occupied in deep thought and content with idleness, much too much for a previously outgoing teenager. She had in some superficial way been made to become a woman—a sad, lonely woman—in just nine months. She had been crushed by the barbarism of rape—in this case sexual assault imposed upon her without consent. Too young to give independent consent for a driver's license, surely she was too young to have given grown-up consent to sex in the backseat of a grown man's car. Then, the tragedy of losing her baby—her baby, born of rape and then snatched from her bosom. Before the pain of childbirth subsides, her baby is taken. Before the first breast-feeding, the baby is gone. It is taken before it is held or hummed to, snatched from its mother's hands. Even before she has a chance to bathe it, or powder it or smell its baby freshness or hear it coo, she is separated from it. She is sent away from her baby with breasts swollen full of milk that will not be for feeding, and with the small first cries of her newborn ringing in her ears. There must be no bonding—a quick look, a word that it is a boy or a girl, and the baby is gone. History. Forever gone. It is the most unnatural thing for a mother to forget her baby, but she must. She must think of it, indeed accept it, as a mistake. "Go on, child," the old ones would tell her, "Go on. We got the baby now. Go on back to your mama and dem. Be good now. And try not to make no mo' mistakes."

John's shotgun clicked three times as he loaded it with three twelve-gauge shells. He cupped his free hand over his shotgun's action so that the clicks could barely be heard. Up close, a shotgun is the deadliest of weapons. Hawk would soon be only three feet away from him. They were readying to get into a pirogue, and John would be sitting at his back. Later, if they made it to the duck blind to their hunting spot, John would be even closer to him. At either range, a blast from his shotgun would cut Hawk in two. For today's hunt, John would take his shots on the left side of the blind. With twelve o'clock being directly in front of them, then, John was to shoot at twelve, eleven, ten, nine, eight, seven, and six o'clock. Hawk would hunt the right side, at twelve, one, two, three, four, five, and six o'clock. No turning into each other to shoot, no shooting over each other's head: those were the rules for the sake of safety. They would keep their safeties on until the last minute, when one of them would whisper to the other, when ducks were in range, "now take them," and the one so instructed would fire off a booming barrage of gunfire that would echo resoundingly across the marsh. It could be a deafening, ear-splitting sound, especially against the soft cackle of marsh hens, the distant muffled quacking of ducks, the periodic soft trumpeting of high-flying geese, and, when it was warm enough, the deep groans or hisses of alligators. Nothing resembled the blasting explosions of these powerful weapons in the marsh; nature had made no allowance for them. When the shooting had passed, and the shotguns had grown quiet and their hearts had stopped racing from the excitement of the moment, there was usually a fallen duck or two at death's door, fluttering in the muddy marsh waters. Then, all would go mostly quiet again, and the other birds would resume flights overhead as if all were forgotten, and the men would resume the game of watching the skies for ducks coming within shooting range, of looking them off with their eyes low, of calling the ducks down if need be, and of waiting for the whisper, "now take them."

But these were not John's thoughts as he tiptoed down a thirty foot long narrow patch of earth, nearly covered with water on one side, that was serving as a makeshift levee leading to the pirogue landing from which they would launch into the marsh. John was not thinking about dead ducks. His mind was on Hawk. He hated him. Many were the times he wished he could walk up to him and tell him so, but he didn't have the guts. He wished he could fight him over our sister and for the other little girls too, but John was sure Hawk would kick his ass. John couldn't call the DA or the sheriff to arrest him and charge him with rape, because they just didn't consider it much of a crime, and besides, they would think it just wasn't—hadn't ever been—done in our community. And John hated himself for smiling with Hawk and acting like they were friendly, asking him about everything under the sun except our sister—why he'd messed her up, why he'd continually lied to her about caring about her. When they saw each other on John's trips home, they'd talk about football, his football team. He'd ask after John's wife and children, and John would ask after his. They'd talk about his job at the school as a PE teacher, and John would talk about his as a minister in a growing church. It was as if John's little sister didn't exist, even as if God had forgotten about her too. As if John had. But his heart was torn for her. He hated Hawk. As a minister, he hated that he hated him; but he couldn't lie to himself. He so did hate him. Prayed about it, sought forgiveness for it, but he still hated him. Loathed him, despised him to the core. It was against everything John had ever been taught, against everything he knew to be right, completely against God's way. But he was unable to forgive him. He was so overcome with grief for our sister's lost chances in life, chances Hawk had robbed her of, that John just couldn't help but hate him for it. It was not the kind of hate that Cain had for Abel, for John certainly wasn't jealous of him. Abel was a good man. Hawk was not. John was a good man. But he wanted Hawk dead.

Now, John would have his perfect opportunity. Hawk and he shared one, and only one, passion: duck hunting. They didn't care about the conditions—hot, cold, rainy, windy—they hunted no matter what. On this day, it was cold, unusually so. John had even noticed ice on the little levee they crossed on the way to the pirogue. But John had made a plan to come home and to hunt with him, so they decided to go out despite the cold weather, alone, Hawk and John. It would be so easy to get the job done, so easy to have an accident— John would leave his gun loaded, forget about putting his gun's safety on as they got into the pirogue, hit a bump while they made their way to the blind or cause an unsteadiness in the delicately balanced pirogue, making the gun go off—an accident. No one would doubt John's word on that. He is a minister. A good man. That is John's reputation. No one would ever doubt his story.

Or, he could violate their shooting area in the blind. John could forget about his twelve, eleven descending order to six o'clock, and shoot twelve, one, two, to three right over his head, and right through the top of it—a tragic accident. Here, though, some might claim fault on John's part, and he would be blamed more if he died that way. Some people might even say he had been too careless, and he might have to resign his ministry. Still, everyone would take his word for how it happened. But our baby sister would be devastated. She believed Hawk loved her and thought she loved him. She would be quiet, real quiet. Every time John would look at her, he would see extended sadness in her eyes. But she would believe him, too. She might not talk to him for a while. She never did when things went wrong, but she would doubtless believe him. At least this time, when she gave him her treatment, he thought, he would not feel that he had failed her.

Although it was real cold, most of the signs of the morning

pointed to favorable conditions for a successful duck hunt when they started out. The sky was overcast, making for a somewhat low ceiling. The winds were blowing, not too much to make conditions unbearable, but enough to create small waves so that the decoys would appear to paddle about and dip like live ducks. The tide was high, usually good for hunting, because ducks don't like to go where there isn't much water. On the other hand, too much water means that the food they are looking for is harder to find. Ducks know this. Against the other good conditions, it worried John that today's tide might be too high, as the water lapped their boat. Still, on a normal hunt, all they needed were three or four good fly-bys of ducks and they would get their limit of five each. But, as I have said, other things were running through John's head that morning, deadly things to be sure, but not dead ducks. They talked about the ducks nonetheless. "Shouldn't take us long today," Hawk observed. "Either things will be real slow or we'll get our chances in early. I think we'll get what we came for," he continued, observing the high waters. "We'll know soon."

The sun was coming up over the marsh now and John had already missed his first chance to eliminate Hawk from their lives, our sister's and his. When they were paddling from the boat launch to the duck blind, John had done the one thing one never does in duck hunting, any hunting: he'd loaded his gun before he'd gotten to the hunting spot. He'd never done this in twenty years of hunting. But he'd deliberately violated this most fundamental safety rule. And he'd consciously breached the second-most important rule that closely follows the first: If you are going to have your gun loaded, make darn sure you keep your safety on so the gun won't fire until it's time to shoot. John had taken his safety off. He'd also done another very unsafe thing—pointed his loaded gun, off safety, straight at the back of Hawk. He'd left the sheath for his gun slightly open so he could slip his hand to the trigger when he got ready to discharge his weapon into Hawk's back.

They didn't hit a bump on their ride in, and John didn't create any commotion to cause the pirogue to rock or to ply an unsteady course. John started to wonder why he was waiting for these conditions to occur by themselves. In the end he was fully prepared to lie about what had happened anyway. But, I guess, he thought he would feel a little less criminal if he could set the scene where what happened might have been something like a real accident. So he thought hard about it, and waited for his self-imposed plot to unfold.

As time went by, it didn't happen, and he hadn't been able to free himself to take matters in a different direction. John had never sweated so much in the cold; he started to doubt that he would ever get this thing done. And as John was engrossed in this deep analysis over whether his plot would work, the pirogue docked at the duck blind, so that opportunity was shot. But there was a hole in his plot that he should have filled in a different way anyhow. He'd wanted to get access to Hawk's gun before they boarded the boat and slip a twelve-gauge shell into its chamber, and load Hawk's gun in the boat with the safety off. But Hawk had brought his twenty-gauge gun today, not his twelve-gauge, and John had no twenty-gauge shells in his pocket to perfect and carry out his plan. Shooting him in the back with Hawk's own gun, with his appearing to have violated the fundamental safety rules, was a far better outcome than John shooting him in the back with his. Maybe, John said to himself, he just didn't have the guts to carry out any plan like this, holes or not. He tried to refocus. It was time to get this thing done. He could still have a chance to get his gun in play if he would just do it and not think so damned much. Why couldn't he slip one of Hawk's twenty-gauge shells in his pocket while they hunted, then load Hawk's gun, safety off, as John handled it on the way back in, unless John got a chance sooner? John knew he had to be determined in this, and he wasn't ready to get right with God just yet.

As the sun spread its soft morning orange glow against the brown grasses of the marsh, John noticed in the distance three ducks, grayish brown balls, wings whipping constantly like those of hummingbirds, speeding their way. He touched Hawk. "There," he said, "at twelve o'clock. Three of them." They peered from beneath the bills of their camouflage caps, their eyes downcast, hidden from view of the birds' sharp eyes. The ducks looked like they were coming in. "Damn teal," Hawk murmured dejectedly, and he let his duck call drop from his lips. He wasn't about to waste his time calling in these little bitty ducks. In his mind, duck calling was for big ducks—mallards and grays. John was worried again now. He'd hoped Hawk would be preoccupied with his duck calling. If he were, he would be turned away from John, utilizing his corner of the duck blind as a kind of echo chamber to muffle his duck calls to make them sound more authentic. It would be easier to strike Hawk from behind without looking at his face from the front or the side. Watching these birds come in, then, John tried to get his nerve together. John wanted desperately for those ducks to hold Hawk's attention and fly his way, twelve, one, two, three, then Boom! Boom! An accident. An accident tearing off the top of his no-good head. Now these three ducks were just about on top of them, moving like cannonballs with wings, low and fast, never braking to land, making for a hard-to-hit target. Suddenly, they veered, all three of them, to eleven, ten o'clock. "Take them," Hawk whispered. Instinctively John complied. Boom! Blam! Blam! Two of the three ducks fell. "Yes!" Hawk screamed. "Great shot! Great shooting, my friend!" Hawk exclaimed, and he flashed his broad, beautiful smile that had bewitched Jadie and the others, and he slapped John on the back. John felt stupid. He didn't like having a good time with Hawk. He didn't like him cheering him on. He didn't like losing his head in a duck hunt and losing sight of the real target. *It's okay*, he said to himself. *Others will come soon. Surely they will fly Hawk's way.*

They waited. Some big ducks flew over. Too high, too far even to call in. Some more teal came in on John's side, one or two waves of them, and he purposely missed them. "Hard shots," he said to Hawk.

The sun hid behind the clouds and an hour and a half passed, and no real action. They both knew it was time to go. "Tide's too high," Hawk moaned. "Nothing worth our time is flying. Too much water." He looked John straight in the eyes. John wanted more time to put his plan into action, but he knew he had to act quickly. John peeked down into Hawk's open ammo bucket at his loose twenty-gauge shells. Hawk bent over with his back to John to empty his gun—ordinarily a good safety practice. But not this time, because John took that opportunity to reach into the bucket and retrieve a twenty-gauge shell. John emptied his gun loudly. Ka-chang! Ka-chang! Ka-chang! All three of his shells fell heavily to the floor of the blind. He looked at Hawk, his body language suggesting that he follow in this supposed safety ritual. John stuck his finger inside of the chamber, using it to search inside the barrel to make certain no shell was left by some oversight. It was empty. John left the action open, and to be absolutely sure that the gun could not fire, he put the safety on. Hawk unloaded, cleared and checked his gun in the same way.

Hawk got onto the pirogue first and stuck the long oar in the mud to hold it still. John handed him his gun, then John's gun, just before he boarded, with both gun barrels raised straight up in the air—as safety dictates. On board, John took his seat behind Hawk. He took the sheaths for both their guns and appeared to cover them, but John left Hawk's unzipped. As he pushed off from the blind, John sneaked the twenty-gauge shell from his pocket, slipped it into the open action of Hawk's gun, and quietly closed the chamber. John released his safety. He repositioned Hawk's gun in the pirogue from pointing cross-wise to pointing straight at Hawk's back. As Hawk paddled away, John placed his hand on the man's own gun near the trigger, waiting.

The place for their boat to dock was little more than a thousand feet away from the duck blind, so John had precious little time. They were already close to halfway back. Hawk was busily rowing the pirogue, on one side and then on the other. He enjoyed handling the pirogue and he was good at it. The little boat plied smoothly, mercurially at his expert efforts. He was absorbed with his brilliant performance, never noticing John's preparations. John had to act now. He found himself praying to God for the strength to do it—the strength to murder Hawk and to lie about it. It was out of place, but it was John's nature to pray. As he placed his hand on the trigger of his gun, the pirogue suddenly hit a big branch that was partially submerged just below the surface of the water. It startled John, and he jerked his hand away from the gun and gasped loudly. Hawk turned with a wide grin. "I got it, preacher. You're in the best hands the good Lord's made. Safe as in your mother's arms," Hawk laughed.

John sat up real straight, took in some deep breaths, and sighed loudly. *God! How could I do this? How could I screw this up?* he questioned himself. Hawk was looking back at John now, laughing and paddling without looking forward. He was showing off so much that he didn't notice his gun aimed at him. "You gotta believe, man," he said.

A horrible feeling came over John. He had failed our sister again. He had had the answer to her problem right on the tip of his finger and had let it slip away. The conditions of his plot played out beautifully and he literally could not pull the trigger. He was starting to hate who he felt like he was—a worthless, spineless worm.

At the boat launch, John disembarked, visibly shaken. Hawk shook his head and laughed some more. "Ain't that bad, preacher. It really wasn't that big a deal." Hawk took their ammo buckets from the pirogue, carrying one in each hand, and John followed him with their guns. "Come on," he urged John forward, "time to get out of here," he said, moving out at a brisk pace. John was starting to think again and starting to sweat a whole lot more. How was he going to get the shell out of Hawk's gun without him noticing? Hawk had double-checked his gun, as John had his, to make certain that it was empty. How then could it have a shell in it? How was the action that he was sure he left open now closed? They were traversing this long knoll back to the bank of the marsh, John's head lowered in deep thought, when he heard Hawk laugh out loud. John looked up and Hawk spun around to mock John again. "Preacher, you still ain't together. You still—"

Suddenly his feet slipped out from under him, and he fell into the deepest side of the icy water. He fell backwards and sideways at the same time, contorting his body as if he were trying to balance himself in mid-air. The gun buckets proved obstacles to his athletic, good balance and he held on to them as if they could break his fall. Instead they weighed him down as he landed hard and awkwardly, sinking under the water on his back. As he fought his way to the surface, he yelled at John through the breathy pant of a swimmer who'd taken in too much water. "Preacher, get me outta here. Help! I can't swim!" He was in a panic, grabbing at the water as if there were some chance he could clutch it. John's good nature took hold. He forgot about trying to kill him. He couldn't just stand by and watch him drown. John reached his hand out to rescue him, but he was too far.

Then John reached one of the guns out to him. "Catch on to the barrel. Hold on," John shouted. Hawk yanked at the gun barrel, pulling it down sharply into his body, somewhere near between his legs. Then, Blam! The gun went off. Hawk stiffened up and fell back, his eyes wide, his mouth open, disappearing almost instantly beneath the reddish-brown muddy water. John yelled desperately for him. He didn't come back to the surface. John threw both guns into the water away from where Hawk sank and ran for help.

That afternoon, the Hawk's dead body was dragged from the high swamp waters. John wasn't there. John didn't know what the authorities would find. After leading them to the spot where Hawk had gone down, he'd made his way to see Jadie to tell her what happened. But she wouldn't talk to him, so he left and went to his motel room. John needed to be alone anyway to gather his thoughts and get his story straight so that he'd be ready to deal with the authorities when they came to question him.

They didn't come. In fact, John got word that Hawk's body had been found from his old neighbor, who had come by to check on him and who had heard it from somebody else. John wanted to ask for details about how his body looked, but he didn't know what was going on or whether it would arouse suspicion. His friend didn't volunteer any details about Hawk's death. He seemed to be more concerned about John's state of mind. A few hours into his friend's visit, someone called the room for John, and his friend told the caller he thought it would be better if he called back later. "By the way," John heard his friend say to the caller, "Can you tell me what happened to him?" John's ears perked up. "Drowning." His friend repeated this word from the caller. John was startled. Drowning? It didn't make sense. Now John had to know. He had his friend call the police and find out the cause of death. Same report. "Drowning." Nervously, John took the phone. The official explained to John that as far as they could figure, when Hawk hit the cold water, it must have been a terrible, frigid shock to his body; his eyes were wide open; his mouth was agape. He appeared to have died, they said, of drowning associated with a highly traumatic accident.

John knew it wasn't the shock of the icy water that had so traumatized Hawk. It was the thought he was losing his precious jewels near where the gun went off.

It was his mistake.

*And ye shall...proclaim liberty throughout all the land
unto all the inhabitants thereof...and ye shall return
every man unto his possession, and ye shall return every
man unto his family.*

Leviticus 25:10

Into Africa

I ate a piece of the dirt of the African continent. It's true. I literally did. I don't mean I took in gossip about Africa's alleged bad habits or bad practices, or that I participated in any that might be real instead of rumor. I mean this in no figurative sense whatsoever. My mother used to send my sister for some freshly turned dirt to munch, as land was turned for the first time in the spring for planting season. Women expecting children held that earth gotten from the right place added iron and other minerals to their prenatal nutritional regimes. As kids in the Mississippi Delta, we routinely ate dirt. Yes, we would take a piece of God's good earth and chew and swallow it. It wasn't an everyday thing, and it wasn't a planned thing. No one ever said, "Know what let's do tomorrow? Let's go out to the field or to the river bank or near some tree roots and get some dirt to chomp on." No, it wasn't like that. It would occur as a casual happening. You would just be outside somewhere, and as you were talking, or playing, or just sitting around, for no particular reason and at no particular time or season of the year, you would just pick up a clod in the field, or a clump of soft mud, usually with a root or two attached to it or running through it, and bite into it or place a bit of it between your cheek and gums and let it dissolve there. I don't mean a large portion. No one I know ever made a meal of it. It was just a taste, almost without noticing you were doing it—like the earth was a part of you and you of it. It tasted good. It was always cool, gotten from a cool spot, a shaded place, just below the hot surface of a cotton field or near a stream or body of water. It was always refreshing. We didn't talk about it; it was just something we did as it came to us. I believe that if one of us had asked the other, "Hey, why are you eating dirt?" I suppose the other one would have dropped it from his hand or from his lips if it had already made entry to the mouth, because there was not a good explanation or perhaps no conscious explanation that could be given for it. But it never was handled that way. It was not accidental either, as when you drop your favorite cookie or piece of candy onto the floor or on the ground, and, because you can't part with this favorite treat, declare, for the sake of your own craving and your inability to walk away from it, "God made dirt and dirt don't hurt." No, not that. It was as if an animal that does not usually eat grass as its main dietary staple, like a dog, which you will sometimes see eating blades of grass, instinctively knows that there is a certain nourishment, a certain healing, a therapeutic value if you will, in taking this odd medicine that rounds out its sustenance and connects it to its place in the world.

I was not a little kid when I made my first trip to Africa. I was twenty-nine years old. And it was not accidental or casual that I ate of its earth. I planned it. I decided to taste a piece of the land of my ancestors, of my great-great-great-great grandfather and mother. It was somewhere in Cote D'Ivoire, beneath the greenery of a lush tree. There, I knelt down, and, from the roots of sweet-smelling vegetation, I took and ate African dirt. It was sweet.

We were all there, we Black folk from America in Africa for the first time, seeking a connection to our motherland. None of us knew quite how to make it. Some of us cried, some sang songs, some took in the open-air marketplaces, some marveled at how some African they saw on the street, or someplace else, looked remarkably like uncle or auntie or cousin somebody back home in the

United States. I ate dirt and went to church that second night after our arrival to get connected. I don't think anyone ate dirt with me, but a few others did accompany me to a church service that night. And, even though we could not understand the language, mostly French, we understood the worship. After a while, we joined in the call and response, and a kind of improvisation and innovation rose up on both sides, the African and the African American, which characterizes Black church music. Whoever said "you can't miss what you never had" knows nothing of Africa and African Americans. There at the church, and later the following day, words ran through our heads, capturing more than the moment, but rather centuries of missing things and missing places we never knew:

We sat at great-great-great-great grandfather's funeral place
last night
West Africa
And, thought of him
Apart from us, alone
In an ancient church
Cheeks sunken, eyes too closed
Till familiar music lifted us

Aroused, we whirled like angels in the sky
Like Angels meeting partners in the stars
And, long grass nightgowns flowed around our legs
Till the spirit came and tucked us into bed

Then, we lay stiff under dark cold sheets
Ruing that fate had not chanced us him to meet
But, matching baggage spoke our history
Then we broke our rigid poses
To think of sleep no more

So, flinging icy covers to the side
We jumped up all warm, rosy and renewed

And stomped jazz circles in the room
Calling, crying out to him
Africans all, but too strange to speak
Yet, connecting blood wrought our fluency
And tickled grandpa's fancy
Till Grandpa woke and rose to dance with us

We all knew that hundreds years of separation could not be made up in a virtual moment. We just decided to rejoice in our reunion—now. The three-month, death- and degradation-ridden middle passage from Africa, suffered unwillingly by our violated ancestors, mixing the bones and tears of Africans with the waters of the Atlantic, still reminded us of the distance the world fell, however. And, at the airports of the rich European capitals, where we caught the sights of these developed worlds, we were reminded still more that the divide in wealth between them and the countries in Africa was in direct proportion to the slave labor and exploited resources stolen from Africa by the Europeans. The same could be said, in great part, about the relationship between America's wealth and the African slave trade. In spite of it all, though, we determined that through our common effort, we could span, indeed could fly above that inky, watery Atlantic graveyard. In doing so, we thought, we could uplift each other and, through our example of reconciliation and striving together, give ourselves a chance to do our part to try to uplift others. We started to realize that we, from America, were like Joseph, reaching out from a new and strange reality, a new geographical place, to break the famine and help to end the suffering of our people. We could identify with their place of peculiar suffering and them with ours. And, we communicated. We lost awareness of our language barrier. We looked into each other's eyes, we held hands, we sang in tune and in time. We picked up a few of each other's words, too, but even when they are forgotten, as they surely will be, we will still remember what they meant, what it all meant. On this trip, we danced with our African ancestors and African brothers and sisters, and they, in turn, with us. That is what caught our flight of imagination and the fancy of our grandpas. It pleased them. Doing what would please them, we decided, must be what we do.

I do not know how the ancestors or my current family would feel about ingesting dirt, as a show of love or commitment or making up for lost time or as a way of connecting with one another or as a dietary supplement or for any one of a hundred good reasons. I am not recommending it for everyone. After all, there is, for some, something inherently unsavory in the thought of consuming a thing that has been trampled under the feet and shoe soles of the peoples and animals of the world. I can hear my wife, and I am sure you can hear your wife or mother as well, saying, "How do you know where their feet have been?" I understand this. I can only say that it worked for me, at least in this one very important instance. So, for those who can, I urge—try it—in moderation. Thus, when you see the slogan, "Let them eat dirt," remember it has nothing to do with an expression of the competitive hubris of a cross-country motorcycle racer. It has everything to do with promoting a proud, proven and sacrificial tradition, spread from the country folk of the Mississippi Delta to the good folk of West Africa. Respecting and eating each other's dirt, I, for one, believe can nourish, if not heal, what ails the world.

AFRICAN ANCESTRY

November 9, 2007

Mr. William J. Jefferson
1922 Marengo Street
New Orleans, LA 70115

Dear Mr. Jefferson,

It is with pleasure that I report our MatriClan™ analysis successfully identified your maternal genetic ancestry and our PatriClan™ analysis successfully identified your paternal genetic ancestry. The mitochondrial DNA (mtDNA) sequence that we determined from your sample shares ancestry with the **Masa** people in **Cameroon** today.

Mitochondria are subcellular organelles that serve as sites for the production of energy. Mitochondria contain their own independent genome called mtDNA composed of 16,569 nucleotide pairs that do not recombine, is maternally inherited, and is in high copy number. Due to their high mutation rate, mtDNA sequences hold a wealth of valuable information on evolutionary changes that occur in populations. We examined your mtDNA sequence differences using standard Polymerase Chain Reaction (PCR) methodology and DNA sequencing. Differences in mtDNA sequences correlate highly with the ethnic and geographic origin of the individual. The result is that you have inherited through your <u>mother</u> a segment of DNA that was passed on consistently from mother to daughter to you. It is presently found in Africa in Cameroon.

The Y chromosome DNA markers that we determined from your sample share ancestry with the **Yoruba** people in **Nigeria** today.

We studied polymorphisms (different forms of DNA) on the non-recombining portion of your Y chromosome (NRY). This segment of DNA is transmitted identically from father to son. A panel of nine genetic markers (also called polymorphisms) on the NRY was analyzed using standard Polymerase Chain Reaction (PCR) methodology. The polymorphisms we examined consisted of the slowly evolving ALU insertion/deletion polymorphism; and 8 highly mutable microsatellites or short tandem repeats (STRs). Differences in Y chromosome markers correlate highly with the ethnic and geographic origin of the individual. When compared to Y chromosome markers in large databases such as our African Lineage Database (ALD), Y chromosomes collected from individuals like you could be interpreted as genealogies reflecting the paternal lineage history of the human species. Although the informative stretches of genetic information along the Y chromosome represents less than one percent of your entire genetic make-up, it has proven to be a powerful tool for identifying and defining paternal lineages.

AFRICAN ANCESTRY

Paternally, you have inherited through your <u>father</u> a different segment of DNA that was passed on consistently from father to son to you and is presently found in Africa in Nigeria.

We have included several materials that reflect the results of your analysis. There is a copy of the mtDNA sequence and Y chromosome markers used in the analysis. The Certificates of Ancestry authenticate that your mtDNA sequence matches with the Masa and your Y chromosome markers match with the Yoruba. You can display them with pride among other family documents. In addition, we have included full color maps that geographically depict the ancestral regions of your maternal and paternal lineages. Finally, we have included the *African Ancestry Guide to West and Central Africa* to help you learn more about the peoples and cultures with whom you share ancestry.

Thank you for your support and interest in African Ancestry.

Sincerely,

Gina Paige
Gina Paige
President

Re: Kit ID# 1004637
    Kit ID# 1006148

Man that is born of a woman is of few days, and full of trouble.

JOB 14:1

These Colored People, They Just Beg So Much

THE MARKER ON HIS unkempt grave was hard to read. A slightly bent beige-colored metal card, however, saved the barest summary details of his life. After I spent some time clearing away a little rust and a little encrusted earth and straw, it revealed them. There, in perfect cursive etched into the soft metal card, was a simple statement. "Hiram Farley," it read, "Sunrise, April 1, 1910, Sunset, July 7, 1984." Hiram was his given name, but I had known him as "Mr. Boot Farley" all of my life. *A good long life,* I thought to myself, *but he should have lived longer.* Mr. Boot didn't die of natural causes. Those of us who knew him well always expected that he would not. We always thought that he would give Mother Nature a healthy assist toward his demise. He had.

Mr. Boot had at least three very bad habits of which I am aware. And he had them very badly. I'll mention two of them now, and get to the third a bit later. One of them was that he chewed too much tobacco and he chewed it all of the time. Another was that he drank much too much hard liquor. As a young boy, I didn't notice his drinking. I guess I didn't know the signs. But there was something about the way his face looked that struck me every time I saw him. Mr. Boot was nearly always chewing on the right side of his face, and there he had this huge, ever-present protrusion. There, where his cheek poked out, the skin that covered this ball was stretched so tightly that it made his jet-black skin really shiny in that spot. I remember wondering about it for the longest time, so one day I just up and asked him. "Mr. Boot," I said, putting my finger on the right side of my face, "what's that?" He looked at me with that kind of wild-eyed look of his and said, pointing to his right jaw, "Dis here? Hit's Red Man 'bacco. Hit's my chaw of Red Man." Then he reached into his pocket, got a square of his Red Man, clipped a plug of it with his pocketknife, and jammed it into his mouth to replenish his chaw.

Sometimes, Mr. Boot's chaw was so big that it gave him a real unnatural look, like he had a gross facial deformity. Sometimes, he didn't chew at all, and the lump just sat there, as he went about his business. Whether he was chewing his tobacco, or just holding it in his mouth, however, came the inevitable spitting. Were he indoors, Mr. Boot carried a tin can that he spat into from time to time. He didn't toss out this liquid, which he called "'bacco juice," nearly often enough, so it would frequently fill up and become ugly and smelly. Whenever he would miss his mark, the tobacco juice would dribble down the side of his can. To save a neighbor's floor from having to accept his dripping tobacco juice, Mr. Boot would catch this juice with his free hand, wipe it from the side of his can, and then wipe his hand onto his work clothes—his pants, his sleeves, his shirt, and in the winter, his coat. It didn't seem to matter. "Mr. Boot is some nasty," we kids would say out of earshot of our parents. "Ooo ooo wee," we'd say, "nasty, na-asty." We don't know if he ever heard us. If he did, neither what we said nor his own dripping, drooling, and wiping of his 'bacco juice ever seemed to bother him. Mr. Boot kept on carrying on. Were he chewing his tobacco out of doors, he would spit his 'bacco juice right straight onto the ground. The thick, dark-brown tobacco juice would seem to rest atop the dust momentarily, then sink slowly out of sight, burying itself into the soil. As Mr. Boot would get up to leave from a visit, he would make a final spit onto the ground or toss the contents of his tobacco juice-filled can there. Then he would always stand up and give a military style salute good-bye as he was leaving. We used to say he was giving honor and respect to another fallen Indian warrior, his tobacco kemosabe, Mr. Redman.

The chewing marked his already darkly yellowed teeth with streaky stains of brown. It looked awful when he smiled. And sometimes it looked worse than awful if his tobacco juice would ooze from behind his teeth during a smile. And Mr. Boot loved to laugh. He had a peculiar, long-lasting high-cackling kind of laughter. While engaged in one of his relished guffaws, Mr. Boot would sometimes lose a bit of his tobacco juice in one direction or the other. Not only might this tobacco juice drip out when he smiled or spoke, or squirt out when he laughed, but there was tobacco residue between his teeth as well—a little, brown, ugly, straw-looking residue. Yet Mr. Boot kept right on showing his frightful smile and laughing in apparently perpetual good spirits.

On school days at around six in the morning, my brothers and sisters and I would walk to the highway to catch our bus, a distance of about half a mile. If it were springtime, Mr. Boot was a fixture in the cotton fields around us. When we saw him out there, we knew we were in for a treat. He would be mounted on his noisy John Deere tractor, leaning forward in his seat, with the bill of his cap turned up, like a jockey on his steed. His big tractor popped and popped along as it pulled a large two-row middle buster through the soil that had been packed down hard by the winter's weather. This busting-up the ground was the first step in preparing it for new cotton planting, uprooting and plowing under what remained of the cotton stalks from last year's crop, and making a furrow, or middle, between the new rows that would spring up on either side of the middle buster as it plowed and dug its way through the field. For most tractor drivers, this part of the work was relatively simple. Almost anyone who could steer straight down an already existing straight row could produce a fairly straight middle, and hence a new straight row. It was easy to follow the previous row pattern. But once this first middle busting was done, the field was dragged or raked over by another set of implements to soften the soil and level the field. Now, this is where the real tractor-driving skill came in. It is at this point in the cotton-field preparation process that Mr. Boot separated himself from all others. And he did it with flair and style. Here, on these plain, unmarked fields, Mr. Boot would draw the straightest and most even-sized rows that can be imagined. His rows were so straight and so uniform that you would have thought that he was following a design that had been laid out on the ground for him by some master planner. And he did this at top speed, driving his tractor, whiz-bang, back and forth, up and down the field. For us children, this high speed middle busting was itself a great thing to watch. But it was not the best part. The high point of Mr. Boot's performance came when he got to the end of a newly formed row and made his turns, in an area at either end of the field, aptly called the turn row. Reaching it, Mr. Boot would slam his foot onto the tractor's brake, barely touching the clutch, while at the same time violently turning his steering wheel left or right, whichever way he desired the tractor to go. This combination of actions performed at high speed caused the tractor to quickly pivot on one or the other wheel. Then, in a flash, his foot was quickly off the brake, and in a seamless transaction, his right hand rammed the accelerator throttle forward with great authority. And, just like that, he was off up or down the field again, making another sweet-looking row. As we made our way to our bus stop on the highway, we stopped in our tracks from time to time to watch Mr. Boot make his patented tractor pivots and his maniacal middle busting. It was a thing of beauty, art on tractor wheels. So spellbinding was it that the timeliness of our arrival at the school bus pick-up point was often compromised. We dared not miss our bus altogether, and we had to race like hell many a spring morning to catch it. But we soaked up as many of Mr. Boot's free-whirling dervish tractor shows as we could. It was worth the wait and the rush.

What made Mr. Boot's tractor-driving displays even more spectacular was that he did them largely while under some influence of alcohol. Were he close enough to us as we passed him working in the fields, he might nod in our direction or wave at us. But for sure he would always acknowledge us, his fans, by giving his tractor throttle an extra nudge to make it pop for us, and he would flash that happy, foolish, terrible smile. Sometimes, when we would come home from school, he would still be out there plowing and churning the earth. Mr. Boot worked hard and he drank harder, a risky combination for one interested in a long life. But it is clear that Mr. Boot spent little time troubling himself with this morbid detail. He just got up early every day and went about his life, which for him was mostly filled with hard work and hard spirits.

As I grew older and knew the signs of intoxication, I can say with confidence that I never remember seeing Mr. Boot when he was not at least half drunk or drinking heavily enough to be on his way there. His breath smelled of alcohol; his eyes were blood shot; his face glistened with perspiration, even in winter. He always seemed anxious, and he chattered continuously and rapidly to anyone close enough to hear him, or just to himself. He used to brag, though, when people would admonish him against drinking, that he could hold his liquor. And, to be sure, it always appeared that he could and that he did. His gait was mostly steady, his hand was steady, and he never ever missed a day's work.

I don't think Mr. Boot had a favorite drink, except that he admitted favoring hard liquor over beer. But, he would take beer, or bourbon, or scotch, or gin, or still whiskey, or just about whatever there was available. He made lots of friends during his life, but it is fair to say that he held his liquor a lot better than he held his friends. He loved his wife, Alberta, and their seven children, but he wouldn't give up his drinking for them. He lost some of his children over it, but Miss Alberta stayed with him. "I works hard, and I mos'ly brangs home my pai and that's bedder dan mos' upright, everyday sober men do," he would say to his exasperated wife, close friends and relatives. Putting it that way, it was hard to find fault with Mr. Boot's argument. Folks joked that Mr. Boot would drink anything. In fact, this is how he earned his nickname. "You drink so much stuff, I bet you'd even drink shoe polish," a critic is said to have called out to him back when Mr. Boot was a young man. To this Mr. Boot reportedly replied with a twinkle in his eye, "Even boot polish, ifin you'd put the rat thangs in hit." Hence, he got the nickname, "Boot."

People used to say that Mr. Boot took up drinking early in his life, when he wasn't anymore than twelve or thirteen. They say it was because of his father's deeds. His father, Arthur Stewart, was a big man of considerable height and girth. He was a field worker, like Mr. Boot. Mr. Arthur wasn't a man to look for trouble, but he wasn't one to run away from a fight, either. He had a violent temper, which he kept under control at the house with his wife, Miss Helena, and the children, but he had had his share of run-ins outside of the house. Still, he was well liked and respected by those who knew him best, that is to say, by all the colored people in the community.

Even those who thought his temper was a little too hot admired the way he defended himself and stood up to white people. For instance, while he would say "yes, sir" and "no, sir" to white folks like the rest of the colored folks in town, he refused to address white people younger than he in that manner. He would say things like, "that's right," or "that's wrong" to avoid saying "yes, sir" and "no, sir" to them. By doing so, he would avoid directly challenging these young whites. But if Mr. Arthur were ever frontally challenged by a white person, with something like, "N———, do you hear me talking to you?" Mr. Arthur would back him off. He'd likely say something like, "Scuse me, boss, 'preciate it if you'd call me by mi raht name. My name's Arthur, and Arthur would be glad to do whatever you needs doin'." This was bold stuff in the South back in the forties, and Black folks thought of Mr. Arthur as something of a hero. But Mr. Arthur never saw himself in any leadership role. He was just acting on instinct, living out his personality.

To go with his explosive personality, and his demonstrated lack of fear of white people, Mr. Arthur always had his pistol with him. Now, you should know that this was not an unusual thing for Black men to do back then. Almost all of them had pistols at home, and in the car, and a good number of them had guns in their pockets. They weren't looking to use their weapons to rob or steal or hurt someone on a whim. They lived in perilous times, where they had no real rights and where they thought of their guns as true articles of self-defense. With all the guns they were toting, one might expect that there would be a lot of gunplay going on. There was hardly any at all. The only person who had been murdered in Mr. Arthur's parts was a fellow called "Man Green" who was shot by a jealous husband who caught and killed "Man" for breaking his wife's leg. I thought this was a rather extreme reaction to a mere bone fracture, until I found out that to "break a woman's leg" meant to impregnate her, and that this term was used as a euphemism so that parents speaking around children about illicit pregnancies could avoid saying that a woman was having a baby she shouldn't have been having. "Man" was caught when he was out bragging to some of his friends that he had not only broken a certain fellow's wife's leg, but that he had done so with a big stick. Most people could see how the humiliated husband was rightly let go by a judge on the basis of justifiable homicide. Other than that, the guns were never a problem for the Black men in Mr. Boot's daddy's town. That is to say, not until Mr. Boot's daddy used his gun one night in such a way that he had to leave Miss Helena, and his children, and, with their blessings, had to run out of town and out of their lives forever in order to save his own life and maybe theirs too.

It happened when Mr. Boot was about eleven years old. He, his mother and father, and his five siblings were piled into and on the back of their old, broken-down truck, headed home. They were coming from town after visiting kin folk. It was a little late, and some of the younger children had fallen asleep. Miss Helena asked him to stop at a little store next to a filling station to pick up some white bread and summer sausage . As he approached the store, it looked like trouble to him, because he saw eight or nine young white men gathered out front, some of them holding beer bottles. He expected he might have one of them yell out some racial insult, and this might start a problem. He almost didn't stop. But then he looked over at his wife and younguns, and he decided that he wanted them to enjoy their breakfast, and he wasn't going to deny them that, even if he had to run a gauntlet of insults. He pulled in. Before he got out of the truck, he reached across Helena's lap and got his pistol, a thirty-two snub nose, from his glove compartment and thrust it into the front, right-hand pocket of his overalls. Mr. Arthur strode past these young men, who didn't seem to notice him. He passed them without incident. In the store, he ordered a summer sausage, a slab of fatback, and got some white sliced bread and some yellow corn-meal grits. He paid for his groceries and walked out. That's when he found out that the young men outside had gamed him. They had just decided to delay their mischief until they caught him leaving. "That don't look like near-enough food for them hungry-looking, nappy-headed pick-a-ninnies you got in that truck, now do it, boy?" one of them yelled out to him.

Mr. Arthur never said a word; he just sped up his walk to his truck, opened his door, and slid onto his seat. Before he could crank up his truck, the white boys had fairly well encircled it, and were blocking his way, both in the front and in the back. Then one of them came to his door. "Git out and answer my question," he snarled.

Mr. Arthur knew he couldn't get out. Besides, he had his family with him, and he would leave them stranded at the mercy of these men if he got out from behind the wheel of his truck. He made up his mind to stay behind the wheel. "We ain't looking for no trouble," Mr. Arthur started. "Let us go home, and there won't be no trouble for nobody. My chilin and my wife is tied. So leave us go. Have your fun tonight somewheres else." Mr. Arthur locked his door and put his truck in first gear.

"N——, you gonna run over us? Turn that damn truck off, and give me the keys, or we're gonna turn this whole piece of junk over," the man at the truck door screamed.

Mr. Arthur had had it. He reached into his pocket and pulled out his thirty-two. He slammed it down on the car door where his truck's window was broken out. "Git out of our way! We're going home now! Git out of our way!" Mr. Arthur screamed back.

The man at the door fell back and ran. Most of the others scattered too. But the two men in the back didn't see the gun. "Why don't we just start with whippin' one of these little n—— back here, first, since the big one won't get out and take his ass kickin'?" He grinned.

With that, Mr. Arthur bolted from his truck. "He's got a gun," the other man in the back screamed.

"Who gives a damn, I've got a gun too," the first one said, sounding a lot like he had one beer too many. The young white man pulled out his pistol, and reached for Mr. Boot's sister, Maureen, and then for young Hiram himself, both of whom were in the back of the truck. Maureen shrieked. Hiram cried out, "Daddy!"

Mr. Arthur's gun exploded. The young white man grabbed his throat, spun around in a daze, and crumpled down onto the parking lot pavement. Mr. Arthur got his trembling daughter from the back of his truck, put her on his lap, and drove his family home. The young white man was left dead in the parking lot.

At home, Miss Helena urged Mr. Arthur to run away. She knew he was a dead man if he stayed. He knew it too. He gathered up what clothes he could. They cried and held each other and his family urged him to hurry up and go. Miss Helena said that he shouldn't contact them for a long, long time, and that they would be all right. She said she couldn't bear to see him hanging from a tree, even if it meant she would have to raise the children alone. "Please go now! Right now!" She said. "Please go. I love you." Mr. Arthur turned and ran from their home. Neither Miss Helena nor the children knew it then, but that was the last time they would ever see Mr. Arthur.

Part of the reason that Mr. Arthur and his family never reconnected may be that his family kept moving after he left. The morning after Mr. Arthur ran away, the townsfolk found the young white man's body, shot through the throat and with an unfired weapon in his hand. Mr. Arthur was immediately branded a cold-blooded killer.

Then, the rumors started. There was a theory, widely held by whites in the community, which was a part of the lore in many sections of the South, that held that if a Black man killed a white man, then his seed, specifically his male seed, would also kill a white man, a kind of poisonous fruit of the poisonous tree notion. Therefore, it logically followed, the proponents of this theory argued, that to prevent this inevitable future killing of a white by a Black, the young boy of the Black killer should be eliminated, preemptively struck. The talk started that some whites had decided to target young Hiram to be killed.

Within days, Miss Helena moved the family as far away and as secretly as she could, from North Carolina to Georgia. She changed the family name from Stewart to Farley, to make it harder for anyone to track them. A year later, she saw a prominent person from the town in which they had earlier made their home. Fearing they might be discovered, she ran with her children again, from Georgia to Alabama. Finally, before this second year was out, she felt forced to move a third time, which she believed was necessary for the safety of her family. This last move took them to Louisiana, to the Mississippi Delta.

Each time she moved, she made it harder and harder to be found by anyone, including her own husband, Mr. Arthur. By the time he may have felt it was safe enough for him to start looking to reconnect with his family, he probably couldn't have found a trace of them. For Miss Helena's part, after three or four years of not hearing from her husband, she feared the worst had befallen him—that he had been caught by the white men who were looking to avenge their comrade's killing and hanged. Besides, she couldn't go back to look for him. She just had to give up and focus on her children. Miss Helena spent the rest of her life in loneliness.

As bad as things turned out for Miss Helena, they were even worse for young Hiram. He was the only male child of Arthur and Helena. Therefore, he felt it was his fault that his family had to keep moving. He believed it was because of him that his father couldn't find them. He missed his daddy terribly. He was always in fear of his life. He was continually depressed and paranoid. He tried to cover it up by smiling and grinning his way through his sadness. He took up drinking to salve his pain. He was told that the way to stay out of trouble was to keep busy. So he forced himself to work hard, very hard. Over the years, he kept telling himself that the last thing he wanted to do was to get into trouble, like his father had.

You might think from what I've said so far that Mr. Boot died of taking in too much liquor, too much tobacco, or a combination of the two. Well, you'd be wrong. Yes, as Mr. Boot got older, these two bad habits slowed him down considerably, probably cut his work life short by a little, and even ruined his health in his old age. And, no, he didn't die from hard work, because, as everyone knows, hard work never killed anyone. None of these things, then, directly killed him. It was the third bad habit, of which I have not yet spoken, that really took Mr. Boot out, and actually directly killed him. The cause will likely surprise you. For, though it is obviously a sin, and maybe even a deadly one to the soul, it is not usually associated with the killing of the physical body—at least not as a direct cause. What killed Mr. Boot in the end was his selfishness, pure and simple. His habitual inability to share with others finally led to his bizarre and untimely expiration. Like most things that went wrong with Mr. Boot's life, this selfish streak probably developed from Mr. Boot's lifelong obsession of looking out for himself and being unreasonably afraid of others on account of his father's deeds.

I should have had an inkling of what might bring on Mr. Boot's end based on an encounter I had with him a few years earlier. My brother, L. C., and I were home for a Christmas visit after having been away from home for the better part of thirty years. After spending time with a few of our surviving relatives there, we had agreed to go out to a local store to get a few things for them. By this time, Mr. Boot was a little over seventy years old, and neither my brother nor I had seen him since we had left town. So when this bent-over, stick-figure of a man approached us, I had no earthly idea who he was. He was wearing a gritty, dirty old Army jacket that looked to have lots of grease all over it and lots of dark markings on its sleeves. He was working hard to control his walk, but he looked a little tipsy. The hood of the jacket was pulled over his head, virtually hiding it. This, together with the thinness of his body, gave him the appearance of the ghost of death, the grim reaper himself. But when he spoke to us, that rapid-fire speech pattern suggested someone we had once known well. As he cast back his hood to give us a better chance to identify him, a big rotten-toothed grin and a slight bulge in his right jaw left us wondering still more whether this might be who we were starting to suspect he was. But when he said, "Com' on nah, you boys 'no's me," and laughed that high, cackling, uncontrolled, unforgettable laugh of his, we knew it was Mr. Boot Farley. Yet we couldn't believe our eyes. This strong, muscular, hard-working man, we thought to ourselves, had come to this? "I needs you boys to let me have a dolla' and thirty-five cents so's I can git mysef a half point," Mr. Boot asked us. He laughed some more as he continued to speak, softly soliciting our support for his purchase of a half-pint of Old Crow bourbon. God, we felt so sorry for him. But we knew that the last thing we needed to do for him was to give him money so he could go on drinking. He read this message on our faces, and we saw a look of desperation come over his. He ratcheted up his pleading. "But, y'all knows Mr. Boot. Y'all can't do nothin' wif me. I can't do nothin' wif mysef. I is who I is. Don't y'all shame me. I jus' wants a little nip fo's I turn in. I knows y'all good boys and means well, but it ain't gonna hurt nothin'. I jus' takes it to bed wif me mos'ly. It don't mattuh no mo'. Sides, hit's Christmas time," he concluded, kind of half grinning and half sad. It was an Academy Award performance. We looked more closely into his now severely bloodshot eyes. They revealed pupils ringed by the familiar blue-gray tinge that often discloses how much a man has truly aged, and we knew that he was right. It really didn't matter anymore. There wasn't anything much left for us to protect Mr. Boot from, save our own self-righteousness. So we let him have the buck thirty-five. "Dis is a dolla' an' fo' bits," he said. "I'll give you yo change when I comes back out," he offered, letting us know that even though he had lost a lot over the years, he could still do a pretty good job of holding his liquor.

We stood there outside of the store as Mr. Boot went in to get his bottle. Maybe we stayed outside to avoid association with him and with what he was doing. Maybe we were just too steeped in sadness to move, as we watched this once fast-driving, fast-moving, crowd-pleasing, tractor stunt man turn into this plodding remnant of a man.

While we were gazing at him, he seemed to emerge quickly from the store, extending to us our fifteen cents in change. "Keep it, Mr. Boot," my brother and I said together. "God bless you and Merry Christmas to you."

Mr. Boot seemed in a rush, but he paused for a minute. "Thank you, an' same to ya," he said hurriedly. Then, Mr. Boot, apparently anxious to take a snort from his "half point," ambled a few feet toward the back of the store. We watched him as he stopped in the alley between the store and the filling station next to it. He made sure he turned his back to us, but we still saw the urgent action of his arms as he quickly opened his liquor bottle. We saw his head snap back to accommodate a fast slam of whiskey into his mouth, saw his bottle linger there between his lips as he savored a long swig of it. Then, he abruptly recapped his bottle, and, looking nervously from side to side, hastily thrust it out of sight into one of the big pockets of his Army jacket.

"Mr. Boot," my brother asked in a comforting tone, "Are you okay? Don't worry. You paid for your drink. No one is going to take it away from you."

Mr. Boot hesitated for a minute, surprised and confused by my brother's question. "Hell, I 'no's ain't nobody gonna take what's mines," he replied. Then Mr. Boot came closer to us and whispered, his eyes now wider. "But, you boys 'no' these colored peoples 'round here. You 'no's how dey is, don't y'all? Hit's hard to keep anythin' fuh yourself." Then the stunner. "Des colored folks," he said, his voice now even lower, the pace of his words considerably slower than usual, and his tone more serious, "Des colored folks, dey jus' begs so much."

Leaving us with our mouths open, the figurative black pot having unwittingly called the kettle black, Mr. Boot sauntered to the very end of the alley, unaware that he himself had become the beggar he detested. There, he continued stealing drinks from himself—drinking and looking around, drinking and looking around, like an antelope looking out for a lion at an African watering hole.

I stood there at his graveside thinking about his life, and that night at the store where I had last seen him. His had not been an easy death. Death by poisoning can be extremely painful. The symptoms of this brand of dying can also be very deceptive, especially when, as in Mr. Boot's case, he was accustomed to going to bed with pain, and getting up with it and never seeing a doctor. So when Mr. Boot complained to his wife on the night that he died that he "didn't feel too good," she asked him if he needed anything. He said, "No, I don't need nothin'. I's jus' sayin'." But Mr. Boot "jus' sayin'" anything about pain, which he had endured quietly for so many years, set Miss Alberta to worrying about him. She stayed awake that night, watching and listening to Mr. Boot. He couldn't stop tossing and he couldn't stop moaning. As the night wore on, his moaning grew louder and longer, until finally she couldn't take it anymore. "Boot," she at long last said, "Boot. Git up! Come on, git up. I'm taking you to the hospital." Mr. Boot resisted, saying he would be all right and that he'd put up with worse. But Miss Alberta had seen him through all of his worst times. This, she knew, intuitively, was unlike the others. He continued fighting with her over leaving the house, but she was desperate to get him to see a doctor.

Finally, she got him out of his bed. Somehow, she summoned the strength to hold on to him while she put a robe around him. She hated to take him to see the doctor without first cleaning him up a little, for Mr. Boot had felt so bad just after dinner that he had crawled, unwashed, straight into bed. But there was no time. She guided him to the gallery and sat him down in their rocking chair while she got the car. It was down the road a way. The tree next to the house dripped sap, bird droppings, and caterpillars on her car, so she never parked beneath it. Her husband had always complained that she loved that car more than she loved him and that's why she parked it so far away. As she raced to get it for him that night, she was thinking that he had never been more wrong. After pulling the car up close to the gallery, she dragged Mr. Boot's rocking chair backwards down the three steps to ground level. Once there, she unfolded him onto the backseat of their old car, and took off flying with him to the county hospital. Miss Alberta drove as fast as she could to get Mr. Boot there in time, like she knew Mr. Boot would have done for her, and like he had done all those years up and down the rows and turn rows of the cotton fields they passed that night on their way. She wouldn't let him die on the road. "Boot, hol' on now. We're gonna make it. Don't let yourself think about nothin' else. You hear me, Boot?" She repeated this over and over as much to encourage herself as him. Mr. Boot said nothing in response. By now, he was delirious. He just moaned and groaned, and tossed and turned the fifteen miles into town to the hospital. He didn't really hear her.

He was still alive when she got him there. Hospital workers lifted him from the car. He was wet all over from sweat, doubled over in pain, and gripped by overwhelming fear. Miss Alberta kept crying and praying and the hospital people did all they could. But Mr. Boot didn't last long. He grew quiet after a short while, and fell asleep for the last time. Later, the doctors said that Mr. Boot had ingested cotton poison, and that it had killed him.

This was very confusing. The cotton poison, I remembered, came in a powder form. "Did someone sprinkle it on his food?" I asked my first cousin, Catherine, when she called to tell me Mr. Boot had died. "Who would have killed Mr. Boot?"

She slowed me down. "Wait, wait," she begged me. "Nobody killed Mr. Boot. He did it to himself."

Dumbfounded at this response, I hesitantly asked, "You mean he ... committed suicide?"

Her answer didn't clear things up. "Not exactly," she explained. "He did drink some cotton poison, which no one made him do, and it did kill him, but he didn't commit suicide," she said impatiently. "It's confusing," she admitted. Indeed it was.

Now it was my turn to slow her down. "I don't understand any of this either," I said calmly. "To begin with, how is it possible for anyone to drink cotton poison? Let's start over. Take your time and tell me precisely what happened."

Finally, she explained in a way that made sense, that cleared everything up, and that, as I have said, took me back to that night at the store when L. C. and I had bought him that half-pint, or "half point" as Mr. Boot called it.

In his last years, she told me, Mr. Boot had grown more and more fearful of most things around him. Most of his fears centered on the worry that people wanted to beat him out of things. Mr. Boot had always had a reputation for being a little tight. He would make his neighbors pay him for a ride into town, something other farming people wouldn't think of doing. And while he didn't make it to church much, he never put more than fifty cents in any church offering. Besides, people knew that he would fuss at Miss Alberta if he ever heard that she'd put in even a few cents more. For a man who didn't have much in a material sense to lose, and who often had to depend upon the charity of others, you would think that he would render a good deed to the Good Lord from time to time in the hope of a return. But Mr. Boot was just naturally bone-cheap. When you combine the increasingly parsimonious bent Mr. Boot took as he got older with a mind that was going bad from years of heavy drinking, and that he was perhaps losing, well, it's a terrible thing. Nothing added up anymore for him and he started doing risky, insane things.

Of course, the thing he treasured most was his liquor. He hoarded it. He hid it so that no one could find it. Sometimes he even managed to hide it from himself. When this happened, it really got hard for Miss Alberta. Since she was the only person living in their house other than Mr. Boot himself, and since he knew she had grown to hate his drinking, he would demand that she find his missing liquor or accuse her of hiding it in the first place.

Eventually his selfishness and his weak mind collaborated on a fateful solution. The only way to keep his liquor all to himself, the way to be sure that nobody could find it and take it away from him, was to remove it from the bottles it came in with the obvious whiskey labels on them. That way, all those folks looking to steal his liquor, to hide his liquor, or to share his liquor wouldn't know where it was. And the additional beauty of this scheme was that he would no longer have to hide and look for his liquor; he could put it right out in the open, right under their noses, and they would not know the difference.

This plan worked well enough for a while. Mr. Boot would talk Miss Alberta into letting him keep a few dollars from his old-age pension check, from which he would buy his product. When that ran out, he would bum a sip or two from the corners of discarded liquor bottles, or beg a few dollars for his spirits. Whatever in the way of alcohol he got, through whatever means he employed, he took it home to his corncrib out behind his house. He would secretly pour the contents from his store-bought, bummed or begged liquor into containers out there—bottles, coffee cans, or tin cans. Thus, no one knew the vessels his drinks were in except him, and he always knew where they were, on the shelf in his corncrib.

But after a few months of this operation, Mr. Boot made a fatal mistake. By this time, he had used every dirty tin can and bottle in his shed and on his premises. Part of this problem arose because Mr. Boot rarely ever actually drank on the premises. He would take his liquor to go. He would go as far away from his corncrib as he felt would avoid detection of where he stored his stash as he consumed it. The more serious the drinking, the farther away from his house and his corncrib he would go. When he felt he was far enough away and in a safe enough place, he would start his routine, drinking and looking around, drinking a little more and looking around. Sometimes, he would get so loaded that he would forget to bring his container back to the shed for future use. Consequently, his supply of containers got lower and lower until, on the day of his deadly dose of cotton poison, he had flat run out of them. He wasn't about to stop his program of concealing his drinks, which, to him, was going so awfully well. There was a way to fix this problem, he thought. There were his neighbor's corncribs and barns filled with all sorts of containers all around. All he had to do was to go over to one of them and get what he needed. Mr. Boot knew that he couldn't walk up to a neighbor and ask for a used and discarded can or bottle like he might ask for a cup of sugar. He would have to just go and get a few without the neighbor knowing. He comforted himself with the thought that these containers were trash anyway, and his neighbor wouldn't mind.

The doomed plan was executed just around suppertime, at first dark. Mr. Boot sneaked across his field and onto the adjoining field belonging to Mr. Jack Puckett. Mr. Puckett lived alone, and didn't have any bad dogs that might alert him to Mr. Boot's presence on his property or otherwise present a problem for Mr. Boot. This proved a wise calculation, for Mr. Puckett had indeed gone to bed with the chickens already, and his place was quiet. His shed too was a treasure trove of cans and bottles, for Mr. Puckett's barn, right next to his corncrib, doubled as a repair shop where men working on their farm equipment often took their lunches. They left behind a rich refuse of tins and bottles. But here is where Mr. Boot's good timing failed him. On the very same day that he had decided to steal containers from Mr. Puckett's place, a cotton-poisoning machine had been brought in for repairs. To get down into that device to make the necessary repairs, some cotton poison had to be dipped out. A tin can was used for this purpose. Unfortunately for Mr. Boot, in the armful of empties that he carried back to his shed that night was that very can. You can figure the rest. Not wanting to share his cup, he drank and died of it. It was like he was hoisted on his own petard, or hanged on the gallows he had built for someone else, or something like that. Crazy, isn't it?

I turned to walk away from his graveside. As I did, I faced a newly planted field with straight green rows. *Looks as if someone had followed Mr. Boot's pattern*, I thought. Suddenly, something gripped me. Right then, I began to vividly recall my childhood memories of Mr. Boot when I was one of his biggest fans. It was unexplainable. But, with crystal clarity, I could see all of us children lined up alongside the cotton field applauding and cheering for him. I felt an overwhelming compulsion to honor him. So I spun around on one heel, as Mr. Boot had done years ago on one tractor wheel. Facing his grave, I saluted him as he had so often done in saying his good-byes to us. Then I spun back around in the same manner to face those straight rows again, and, on behalf of Mr. Boot, saluted them.

For what is your life? It is even
a vapour, that appeareth for a
little time, then vanisheth away.
Therefore to him that knoweth to do
Good, and doeth it not, to him it is sin.

JAMES 4:14, 17

Out of Order

"IT'S YOUR RESPONSIBILITY TO look out for your little sister," Mama scolded me. I sat speechless, with my face tear-streaked from a pretty good whipping. Those were her concluding words of a long tirade directed at me over my claimed inattention to her children that she had left to my care. I was the tender age of twelve. Maxie was five, and her face was bleeding, just a little, from an unfortunate encounter with the side of our house that my burly baby brother had pushed her into. The cause of the bleeding was a tiny puncture wound from a small splinter. But given the way Mama was carrying on and Maxie was bawling and boo-hooing, you would have thought I'd left her in the middle of the road and that she'd been run over by a big hay truck. I was angry at Archie and Maxie for putting me in this predicament, but I was plain mad at Mama for putting all the blame on me, and, if the whole truth is told, for giving me charge of her bad-behind children in the first place. As she had been flailing away at me with a green willow switch that she had made me fetch from a nearby tree, I thought, to the extent that I could muster a thought other than how to avoid the direct impact of her stinging blows as I danced about to elude her, that it really was her fault that she had made the bad choice of a babysitter and picked me instead of someone bigger and better for the job. I did not want to be my brothers' or sisters' keeper, not then, not ever, I was thinking back then.

As Maxie lay dead in her coffin at the funeral home, I was now thinking how I wished I had looked out more for her. The thoughts I had as a young boy of not wanting to take care of her had faded long ago. At a time like this, I felt strongly that I should take some of the blame for what had happened to her. She had grown to become a lovable, carefree, funny person. She made light of everything and every person she ran across, a genuine comedic genius who made all of us look forward to being with her, expecting some hilarious, ridiculous thing she would say or do. She was pretty, too, very pretty, a quality that is always a blessing and a curse for a woman. Maxie had the most attractive, big eyes imaginable— large and cheerful as a child, but compelling and seductive as a woman. Even her eyelashes were naturally gorgeous. Her skin was a smooth, chocolate brown, encasing a lovely, even-toothed smile. But the real story is that she was one beautiful person on the inside. There are wonderful people in our family, but I think we all would have voted Maxie as our parents' sweetest child. She was always upbeat, always helpful, always concerned and always intervening to settle disputes in her gentle way.

She loved, in fact craved, peace and quiet. She had moved herself and her two children from a dangerous neighborhood on the south side of Chicago to a suburban area that she expected to be safe. She hated guns and gunplay. She hated violence. Yet she had been killed by a handgun in the most violent way. A man who claimed he loved her too much to live without her had shot her in the head outside of her house in front of her children in her supposedly safe neighborhood. And, for someone so nice and special, this horrible death wasn't even quick, and in that sense merciful. Maxie had lingered for days after she had been airlifted to a hospital emergency room. Finally, on the evening of the fifth day, she was declared brain-dead and we, as a family, had to go through the wrenching decision of agreeing with this mortal diagnosis and cutting off life support. Only under the threat of civil action by the hospital were we prodded to let our precious baby sister go. With her big beautiful dark eyes, now glassy and bluish looking, with just a blank, fixated stare left in them, we knew she was gone. She was just thirty-nine. When we told our ailing mother that Maxie had died, all she could do was say out loud what we were all subconsciously saying: "Not Maxie. Not Maxie."

I should have taken more responsibility for my little sister, I was now saying to myself. *I should have known what was going on in her life, whom she was seeing, whether he was a good guy or not.* It was not that we hadn't talked recently. We had. We'd gone to a White Sox game on one of my rare, but recent trips to Chicago to see Bo Jackson. After the game, she came back to my hotel room and visited with me. I remember her sitting on the hotel room floor, searching through the various gift bags I had picked up during the day at my seminars to see what she might keep, knowing that she had the freedom of a little sister to take whatever she wanted. We joked around and she showed me pictures of her son in a basketball uniform, and her daughter at a birthday party, sporting wide smiles. The next time I saw her son he was sitting at his mother's bedside, holding her cool hands, sobbing softly, "Mama, I'll take you home and take care of you, but you just have to move, just a little, so the doctors can see. Come on, Mama, please." She didn't move, and her daughter hardly moved after that either, as she showed a stoic exterior that had to cover unspeakable shock and grief. The time I spent with her talking about her children seems more precious now than then. But it was too late to talk to her about the things that we all know now mattered most.

I did not know this young man, Brian, who killed my baby sister. I never got to meet him. After he shot her, he went to his car, took a seat, and shot himself in the neck. I slipped away from my family and went to his funeral, I was thinking, to make sure he was dead and to condemn him. I was sorry there had not been a trial where we could have testified to his face about the saint he'd killed and what he had taken away from us over foolishness, and to see him convicted. But his funeral was a tale of a wasted life, with his bewildered relatives literally fainting over his casket. A mix of grief and shame hung over the proceedings. Even the presiding pastor warned that suicide was a deadly sin, and that there was a need to pray for the deceased that his soul might somehow be redeemed. They didn't talk about the circumstances that led to Brian's killing of my sister and himself, but we knew. His rage against Maxie, and in the end, against himself, was set off ostensibly by her decision to marry another man. Mind you, the man she was about to marry, Jim, was not a man she had met in the middle of a relationship with her killer. No, this man, Jim, and Maxie had dated for years. When they broke up over Jim's reluctance to make the ultimate commitment to marry, somehow this new man came into her life for all of a few months. I later learned—too late as I have confessed—that he immediately became tragically possessive of her. He wanted to stay around her all the time. Over her objection, he showed up at her house unannounced. He followed her home without her knowledge, hanging in the shadows to observe her goings on. He stalked her. He pressed her to move in with her and her children. Maybe Maxie was just on the rebound from what she viewed as Jim's indifference after so long, and let her guard down and let this guy get into her life. Maybe he, who worked with her, watched her tears after the breakup and saw the chance to insinuate himself into her life as an apparent comfort to her. Maybe she was trying to show Jim that she could move on and live without him, taking up so soon with this misfit. Maybe she made light, too light, of his obsessions, and of his objections to her getting back together with Jim. Maybe. All we know for sure is that when Maxie and Jim announced that they were to be married, her young lover went off the deep end and vowed it would not happen. He told Maxie and his friends that he was thinking of killing himself. They didn't take him seriously; how could they, they said, when he had known her for what amounted to only weeks. In Maxie's lighthearted way, she probably laughed at him and told him to get a grip. She confided in her sisters and a few friends about his erratic behavior, but neither she nor they thought that she was in any danger. I left his funeral unfulfilled. Rather than wanting to spit in his face and possibly yell at his family for producing such a monster, I felt sorry for them. His death had cheated us of our day in court, but it had cheated them and him, too, and there was no triumph in it.

People say that the hardest thing in life is to experience the loss of a child. I'm sure that's so, for I saw it through my parents' eyes, and I know how much I love my own children. But I'd guess the next hardest must be to bury a younger sibling. Perhaps, as when a child dies, you cannot help but wonder if there was not something you could have done to make things turn out better. Whenever I hear an emergency vehicle or see a hospital aircraft hovering near a crime scene, I think of Maxie. Every newspaper story or television report of a shooting of a wife by an estranged husband brings renewed fear and worry, as I relive our tragedy with the affected families. I cannot watch a movie where a woman is stalked or abused. There is a part of me that is soft for every woman whom any man seeks to harm. I want to do something to protect them so I won't feel responsible for something bad happening to them. I suffer deep anxieties over each relationship with a man that my own daughters take part in, fearful that some nut will lose it with them and hurt them. I look into their acquaintances' eyes. I ask penetrating questions. Life is like that. It chastens. It teaches. It makes you regret saying stupid things as a little kid.

Daddy was philosophical when he heard of Maxie's death. I asked him, "Isn't it supposed to be that when a child honors her father and her mother, as Maxie did, that her days should be long on the Earth? Is not that God's promise? Is that not the divine order of things?"

Daddy replied as if he had answered the question before. "Maybe her life was long for her," he said. "Maybe she fulfilled her purpose a few years ago, and maybe God permitted her to stay around a little longer to keep his promise to her. Anyway..." His voice drifted. Then, he turned away, his countenance sanguine, ending the conversation.

"And, it came to pass, when the Lord would take Elijah into heaven by a whirlwind."

II KINGS. CHAPTER 2; VERSE 1

The Whirlwind

THE ONLY WAY HE knew where his grandchildren were was when the flashes of lightening illuminated them running across the muddy, cut over cotton field. He had the most severe headache, and there was blood mixing with rain water running from a laceration from his forehead. He didn't know how the children had gotten in the field; he didn't know where the laceration had come from; indeed, he didn't know how he came to be lying on his back, on the bare wood floor of his house, looking up at storm clouds and into pelting rain. Just a few minutes earlier he had been standing on the carpeted floor in his bedroom telling everyone to calm down. His wife, my mother, was sitting on the side of the bed, turned away from the side of the house where the storm was violently whipping mud against its old wooden boards and the bedroom window. Her eyes were closed in prayer. His three grandchildren, who were now running for their lives across the field, just moments ago, were sitting on the floor of the bedroom, with their teenage grand daughter, Anna, tightly holding the two toddlers on her lap. Then, the place exploded. It sounded like a bomb. Everything was gone. Where was his wife? "Angie!" He cried her name out as one facing an ultimate terror "Angie!" Silence. Dead silence. Now he cried out again. But, this time it was as one who was suddenly experiencing the grief and loneliness of a devastating loss and as one feeling the pain of what his life partner of 57 years must now be going through, had just gone through, all at the same time. "Oh, Angie", he cried softly. He had to find her. He tried to lift himself from the floor boards of what had been his family home for 50 years. Pain surged from his back and to his head. He felt like his head would burst wide open. He thrust his hands to the back of his head in a hopeless attempt to arrest the pain. A huge knot was there. And, there was blood there too.

Tornadoes had come through our area before. In fact one had come nearby before. Sometimes they were close enough to hear, like roaring freight trains. Some had been close enough to see; big black, scary funnels, eating trees and casting about cars and farm equipment. Once, one had even torn the roof off of a nearby church, just a quarter of a mile from our house. After that, the church had a meeting and put the preacher out. Many of them said, if they had done this before the tornado came, because they all knew of the pastors' sinning with a certain sister in the church, the roof would have gone untouched. But, no tornado had ever hit us directly. And we had never feared them. Unlike hurricanes, that spread their devastation across wide swaths condemning whole communities, touching the good and the bad mostly the same – perhaps because of the sins of a precious few—tornadoes cut discrete paths, taking out its targets with the kind of precision that brands one who gets hit by one, as a wrong doer, deserving something of what he got. Right or wrong, this is what a lot of people in our part of the world thought. So, as he started the panicked and confusing search for his wife, as the head deacon of his church, he was thinking "…for what might people say I am to blame?" "Why is God mad with me?" he was thinking. "What did I do to make him want to let me hurt so?" And, he let himself ask God a question he had always told his Sunday school class you should never ask Him. "Why, God. Why?" He was especially mystified about Mama. "She's a good woman, Lord!" "She prays and praises you more than me. She aint got no business being all broke up in no tornado and wallowed in the mud like no hog, Lord!" "Angie. Oh, Angie. Where are you? Where are you?" "God, where is my wife?"

Daddy knew he had to gather himself and look for help. He couldn't just sit there in the wind and rain, angry and bewildered. He would worry about what church folks might say and what God had to say later. The children were running in the direction of Miss Dump's house, the only neighbor within a half mile of our house. He would start his search for some answers there. Miss Dump had a brick house, a small Section 235 home, named for some rural homesteading plan sponsored by the federal government. But, it was sturdier than our old wood frame house, and it was built on a foundation that was set on piles in the ground. Ours was set off the ground on cement blocks, almost inviting a strong wind to knock it off of its tenuous perch. As Daddy made one gimpy step after the other to get from our floor boards, he realized that that was exactly what had happened. The floor of his house was now resting directly on the ground. The blocks on which it had sat were themselves gone. If the children had made it to Miss Dump's house, then he felt they might be safer there. It was black as a thousand midnights around his house, and as he stumbled over one thing or another that had been ripped from the house by the tornado, he hoped and prayed that he would not step over his wife in the cluttered remains of the storm. The pecan tree in his front yard, large and strong as any he had ever seen, was now a tangle of broken limbs, and protruding from its trunk was the rifle that he kept in his bedroom closet next to where Mama had been sitting, driven deep into the tree, bearing further witness to the power and violence of the tornado and to the dim hope that Mama had survived. He wanted to turn his thoughts from Mama so he tried to think of his other hunting guns and his rabbit hounds. What had happened to them? But, he trudged on, distracting himself by thoughts of all the things, large and small, that were probably lost forever. These thoughts and things crowded his mind and his pathway to Miss Dump's, but his strength to keep moving through the pain was driven by his overwhelming desire to locate and account for his wife and his grandchildren.

The howl of the wind and the rain seemed to die down as he

neared Miss Dump's front door. Miss Dump, as she was called, had a real name, Mamie Harris. She had earned the nickname, Dump, due to her short, rotund stature. She was a kind soul, a member of our church. Daddy hoped the children were there, as he was sure she would take good care of them. He could see the dim, flickering light of a kerosene lantern through her curtained, front room window. He knocked hard on the door, and as he listened with his head close to the door for a response, he could hear the sound of children crying. As Miss Dump opened the door, she almost fainted into his arms. "Mose," she wailed, "Mose. You are still alive! The children are here! Where's Angie?" Before he could answer, the children rushed to him, pushing for space from Miss Dump to get into his arms. "Grandpa! Grandpa!" they all screamed out together. "We've been so scared. We didn't know what had happened to you and Grandma. Thank God everything's okay!" Anna cried. And, the children squeezed him as tightly as they could. He kissed them and wiped away their tears. Anna had a homemade gauze bandage around one of her ankles that Miss Dump had wrapped. Daddy could see that the ankle had bled. He knelt down to get a closer look. She winced as he touched it. "I don't think it's too bad Grandpa," she whispered. "You will never believe what happened. When the house started to shake, I held on to the little kids as tight as I could. And, when the house burst open all around, the rug that we were sitting on was snatched from the floor and we somersaulted up into the air head over heels. We kept on spinning over and over, higher and higher, but I held on to the children. I wouldn't let go. Finally, we started to come down and I couldn't even see where we were going to land. And, then, I landed, SPLATT, hard on my ankle and my back at the same time, but into a pile of soft mud. I screamed, Thank you Jesus! Then, I grabbed the little ones and we ran over here to Miss Dump's. It's unbelievable, Grandpa. It's a miracle. And, now you and Grandmamma are alright, too. God is good, Grandpa. Just like you've been saying." He looked at her with pride. She had listened and believed everything he'd said to her over the years about God—that if you were good God would take care of you, and that He would be good to you. He felt in his heart that her precious grandmother was lost. Yet, he didn't want her to loose faith! And, he surely couldn't tell her that he was having his own second and third thoughts about God. He knew that the good sometimes suffer with the bad. He knew he should have thrown that in during her Sunday school lessons. Now, he blamed himself for giving her a one sided view of God and how he deals with His people – sometimes testing them; sometimes letting them suffer death to take them home to him to rest from earthly labors. He knew he had to tell her the truth. But, all he could say to her was, "Grandpa don't know where Grandma is right now; but, I know wherever she is tonight, she's with the Lord and He is with her." "No, Grandpa, No! Let's go and look for her. Let's go and find her and bring her in out of the rain!" Anna cried. He looked down at her ankle. "Forget about my ankle, Grandpa. I'm going with you to find my Grandmother!" Daddy could only smile to himself. "What courage, what strength. What a magnificent young woman. How she reminds me of Angie. Angie would be so proud," he thought to himself. "Come on baby. Let's go to the truck stop on the highway and see if Mr. Stanley is there with his big rig truck with the spot-lights and go home and look for Angie." The two of them took off limping, like wounded soldiers making their way from a war zone to find a friendly encampment to reinforce them in battle.

Half a mile later, they roused Mr. Stanley from napping on his couch. He had slept through the tornado, which had taken a diagonal path, south west to northeast. Stanley's house was north-west of ours. He couldn't believe what had happened. He had known Mama and Daddy for years and he was feeling the pain of Daddy and Anna. He dreaded the thought, though, of finding Mama amid the storm's wreckage. But, he couldn't tell them no. He pulled his overall straps over his shoulders and put on his rub-ber knee boots and his raincoat. "Take this shirt Mose, and put my overcoat on." It was November, a week before Thanksgiving, and there was a chill in the air. "Thank you," Daddy nodded. "But, let Anna have it. I don't feel much of nothing now no how." But Mr.

Stanley insisted. "You'll feel it in the morning, Mose. Come on now, take off that wet shirt of yours and take mine. I have more stuff for your granddaughter." Bundled up, they made their way to Mr. Stanley's big truck that he used to pull broken down mobile homes and disabled trucks from along the highway or into position at his truck stop. They pulled onto the black topped road leading to our house, once, years earlier, a dusty road that would have been near impassable under the present weather conditions. His huge spotlights searched along the road, across the field, along the tree line of the cow pasture, to the right, in the direction of the path of the tornado. For the first time Daddy and Anna saw how devastating and mighty was this tornado. Yes they saw trees flattened, uprooted and distorted. But, they saw more. The stove from our house was resting in our neighbor's field, shot putted a quarter of a mile. The refrigerator lay, wide open, smashed, just a few yards behind it. The carpet on which daddy was standing and Anna and the children were sitting was atop a tree, 40 feet high and 200 yards from the bare floor that was left of our once six room home. Daddy knew now how he had fallen on this back. The carpet was suddenly jerked from beneath him when the tornado hit, as he stood talking to mama and the children, causing his feet to be pulled forward out from under him, crashing him hard to the floor. But, as the truck moved closer and closer to the site of our house, he wasn't thinking of the pain in his head or his back. It was the pain in his heart that he was feeling now, deep inside. The truth is, it was pain mixed with crushing fear of how they might find Mama.

Turning off the black top, the big truck cut deep ruts into the muddy path leading to the site of our house. The searchlights were turned from the tree tops to the grounds in front of the truck and to the side yard, the side where mama's bedroom had been located. Daddy got out of the truck. "Wait for me here," he told Anna. She was having none of it. "I'm going with you grandpa," she said through tears. "I've got to go with you. Don't make me stay." Tears welled up in his eyes. He turned to her and signaled with his hands for her to join him. As the light stayed fixed on the same side of the yard, Daddy and Anna saw what was left of Mama's chest of drawers. Clothes from her drawers and her closet were strewn around the yard. Some picture frames were there, frames that had been on her wall. And in the most ominous sign of all, toward the back of her bedroom site, was the mattress from her bed, with the head posts and the foot rest and some slats from her bed broken into near splinters. Anna put her hands over her face and shook her head and sobbed quietly. Daddy hugged her, petted her. Then, he whispered, "Something tells me to keep looking. Come on." He asked Mr. Stanley to move his truck and his lights to the front yard. They picked up the search there. Stella, one of his best hunting dogs was there, dead, apparently struck by a large beam from the house that was resting on her back. Daddy sighed. "At least she was an old dog," he said to comfort himself. But, they saw no sign of Mama in the front yard. The electric pump and the butane tank had been torn out of their places. And, his old boat that he was fixing up for fishing was across the front field on its side, never to be good for anything anymore. Then, suddenly, as if out of nowhere, like a ghost appearing, he saw his black and tan hound, Bill. Bill licked his hand, and Daddy rubbed Bill's head and neck. "Good boy," he said quietly and reassuringly, "good boy." Then, Bill walked over and nuzzled the motionless remains of Stella. Daddy was relieved that one of his dogs was alive and well. Then, Bill came back to Daddy, and started to whine and to act excitedly, like when he was on the trail of a coon or a rabbit or a deer. There was nothing Bill couldn't track. Bill started toward the side of the house from which he had come. "Hurry up Stanley," Daddy shouted, "Bring your truck around to this side of the house." Stanley quickly thrust his big truck into gear, and brought it around as fast as he could, crunching everything in its path, what was left of a few tables and broken glass and appliances. He set his truck up, shining his lights along the side of the house opposite to where Mama had been sitting when the storm hit. Bill started down that side of the house, then turned and barked repeatedly, the light from the truck catching Bill's eyes, which shined right back at it. Daddy and Anna walked slowly, cautiously to where Bill was waiting and barking. "Hush dog," they heard a weak voice say. Then they quickened their pace to catch up to Bill. As they got to a bed that was alongside the bare floor on the right side of the house, they marveled at what they saw. "Mose, Anna," Mama said. "I knew you would come back for me." Mama somehow was on the bed from the room that had been next to hers. She was covered up, under wet bed clothes to be sure, but covered up nonetheless. Next to her resting place, was her wheelchair, one of the lightest things in the house, which had also been in her bedroom. Now, Daddy and Anna picked Mama up and wheeled her to Mr. Stanley's truck. Stanley was beside himself with happiness. "Come on in here Angie," he said. "Let's get you to the hospital." Daddy looked at Anna. "You need to go with your grandma and to get checked out yourself," he said to her. "What about the children. They will be scared if they don't see me come back. Maybe they all need to be checked out. Look at your head grandpa, maybe you do too." Daddy figured she was right, but he couldn't let Mama go alone. And, as attentive as Anna was, he felt that he had to check on the children. "It's okay, Mose," Mama said even more weakly. "Borrow Dump's car. Get the children, and meet me at the hospital right away. If you hurry, you will just be a few minutes behind us." She waved at Daddy. She smiled at Anna. She blew them a kiss. And, Mr. Stanley pulled off with her in his big truck.

Walking back to Miss Dump's house, Daddy felt ashamed. "Please forgive me for doubting you, Lord," he said. "Thank you for taking care of Angie." By the time they got to the hospital in town, Mama wasn't there. The nurses explained there were no doctors on duty to care for an elderly traumatized woman with a weak heart. They had asked Mr. Stanley to drive her to a nearby town, Grove Oak, just 14 miles away, where they had the personnel and facilities to treat her. Daddy and Anna were bandaged up by the nurses and given pain medicine. The children were attended to, and were fine. "God is good," Anna gleefully repeated. "All the time," Daddy chimed in.

The phone rang in the waiting room of the hospital where Daddy and the children were. It was my sister, Betsy, calling for Daddy. "Everything is all right Betsy. The house is gone. But, we all made it out ok." Daddy said. Betsy paused. "Not everyone," Betsy said quietly. "I'm in Grove Oak, with Mama."

At the church, Anna read the poem, she had composed for Mama. "God's voice, His arms were in the storm. He called her, cradled her and carried her home."

Answer a fool according to his folly, least he be wise in his own conceit.

PROVERBS 26:5

Going Along to Get Along

"HAROLD, I'M TELLING YOU for the last time, there is no one outside of our window, and no one watching us in the shower. Now, this is the last time I am going to tell you this," my sister Betsy barked.

"But, Betsy, I think we should call the police, or go outside and look or something," Harold pleaded.

"Then you call the police, Harold, you go outside and look."

Of course, that would not be the end of that conversation, if you can call it that. It would go on for a while, taking various twists and turns, until finally Betsy would stalk off angry, or Harold would fall asleep, or both of these things or something in between would happen to either or both of them.

My sister Betsy is an angel. She takes care of anyone without complaint. She would let anyone in our family live with her who needed help, for as long as they needed. So strong a Christian woman was she that we called her the church lady. And though her exchanges with Harold would often seem intemperate, the truth is she had the patience of Job. To put it another way, she had the patience of an elementary school classroom teacher in an overcrowded urban classroom—a test that even Job didn't have to face—on a daily basis for over thirty years. She had the gift of listening, waiting and taking her time, and talking and talking. She, in fact, was an elementary school teacher. Betsy had learned to listen to every individual need of every child, kindly and attentively. She responded to each of them individually and sweetly. She could talk them out of every disappointment; wipe out every tearful moment and wipe every sniffling, runny nose; and console them if they made a "mistake" on their way to the bathroom. She also knew how to mete out tough love too when and if it was necessary. A first-grade teacher, if she is good, and Betsy was, does the work of the Lord. It was these long years of practiced patience with these beautiful, but very needy, children that had prepared her for her sessions with Harold.

"They'll give you thirty-five dollars for turning in a crazy person," my daddy told Betsy. He was referring to an old practice from the days of his youth, when the state's asylums were part of the state's patronage system and offered decent paying jobs to those connected enough to get on the state's payroll. To keep this machine running, there had to be asylum patients. Good citizens were asked to help with asylum populating by turning in a crazy person for a fee—in Daddy's experience, thirty-five dollars a head. With enlightenment as to how to treat the mentally infirm and with the dismantling of the patronage system, the old practice of turning in crazy people for a price had been long ago abandoned. No one had bothered to tell Daddy, though, and he was still a creature of the old way of thinking. He was also wrong and outdated in referring to Harold as crazy, instead of more acceptably as "mentally infirm" or "mentally impaired" or "mentally disabled." But however it might be properly called, Daddy was right in his observation about the state of Harold's mind. It was in very, very bad shape. He was the brother of Betsy's husband, Jerome, living with them so her husband could look after him. But it was Betsy who ended up spending the most time with him. She was the one who continually indulged him in his delusions.

"Betsy, do you know why the president and the first lady are married?" Harold asked.

"No, Harold. Why?" would be her dry response to a question she'd heard a few times before.

"Because they are husband and wife," he announced.

"Do tell," she'd say, hardly looking up from her lesson planning.

He continued. "Betsy."

"Yes, Harold."

"Have you ever been to the White House?" he asked. "Did you get William to take you there?"

"Not yet, Harold."

"Can you ask him to take us?"

"No, Harold. I can't do that. I've told you that before. That is not going to happen," she said.

"Betsy, I hear that the White House is real pretty, and that there is a big helicopter and a big plane right there at the White House and that the president will give us a ride on it. Why don't you ask William to take us there the next time he goes?"

"Harold," she said, "William doesn't just go to the White House and ride with the president and show off the president's aircraft. Nobody can do that. How many times have we discussed this? Now, let me read."

He might be silent for a few minutes, and then he would begin again. By then, Betsy would seem to have forgotten that he had just gotten on her last nerve, and as he restarted talking she would engage him all over again. "Betsy," he'd begin.

"Yes, Harold." She'd drag out her response.

"I think I need to go and get a part for my car tomorrow. Can you take me?"

"No, Harold. I'll be at school. Remember, I work every day. Jerome is retired. So get your brother or someone to take you."

"But Jerome has already told me he can't go. He's too busy."

"Well, I'm busy too, Harold," she said, showing a little impatience.

"So, how am I gonna get a job, if I don't have my car working to go places?"

"Harold, you don't make any sense. You can't get a job, because you have a problem that we are dealing with. It would be too hard on you. Now, you've got to let me work now."

With a push like that, Harold might walk away to the back of the house and sit in his room and stare. Then he might get his flashlight and piddle around outside with his or somebody's car or motor or something. Betsy would look up from her work and out on him through her patio window from time to time to be sure that he was all right. "It's time to come in now, Harold," she'd call out, for she couldn't stay upset with him long.

"Betsy, I think I could do with some new tools. I can't find some of the ones I need the most."

"Harold, you don't need any new tools. You just got some new ones, don't you remember? And this was on top of that big boxful of tools you already have. Why don't you get to bed, now. You've got to be sleepy."

"I saw Osama bin Laden yesterday. He was driving a white van out on the expressway near the airport. We need to call and tell somebody so they can catch him."

"Let's get this straight, Harold. The whole world is looking for Mr. bin Laden: the Army, Marines, Air Force, the FBI, the CIA, the president and governments around the world. They have not, none of them, glimpsed this man, the most wanted man in the world, but you saw him driving out in the open down I-10?" Betsy inquired incredulously.

"Yep. And if you'll go with me I can show you," Harold said assuredly.

"So, what did he look like?" she asked.

"Like bin Laden," Harold said, "just like on TV." And she and he would go on and on from one degree of insanity to the next.

It was not always as easy as Daddy made it sound to diagnose Harold's condition, however. There were moments when he talked as if he were perfectly lucid, perfectly normal. Sometimes he would seem reflective, remembering a fond childhood experience. "Mama used to take us to see Christmas lights. The best ones were at Mrs. Mary Jones's house. They would cover her trees, her fence, every-thing. It was like a picture on a postcard, except there wasn't any snow," Harold might offer. In this, he would sound not just regular, but deep and poetic. But this limited evidence of his grasp of things would quickly fade, as he would soon drift into some other, poorly connected dribble.

Harold was a good mechanic. That is, he was able to fix almost anything that was wrong with a car. Somehow, for all that was taken from him in the way of mental capacity in his mother's womb, he was left with an excellent ability to take apart complex engines and put them back together. If a new kind of engine came out, in just a little while, he would learn it, too. But the problem was his attention span. He couldn't stay with a job long. He had trouble knowing where he had left off and what he needed for the job, unless he stood over the engine and took a hard look at it for some time. Of course, with these kinds of problems, he couldn't keep pace and couldn't keep a regular job in a regular mechanic shop or on his own. Since mechanic work was all that he could do, he couldn't keep a job at all, anywhere. But he would regularly forget about this limitation, what seemed like every other day, and he would talk about getting a job. Even when his words did not betray his lack of control of things, his look did. The regular tics, the impulsive giggle, the disconnected smile, his overly worried look and wrinkled brow, his ever-changing moods and almost constant nervousness, were clues to a disturbed mind. But no matter his appearances or how often Betsy heard one of his conversations, if you can call it a conversation, she listened and talked back to Harold. And whenever Daddy was around, like clockwork, he would tell Betsy to get the money for Harold.

On a certain Sunday, Betsy was primping in front of a mirror in the front room, fitting her dress in the best possible position before going to church, when Harold startled her. From nowhere he appeared in the mirror with her, forming a kind of picture of a kind of couple. "Betsy, you look good," Harold said matter-of-factly. Betsy, still a little surprised by the picture, didn't know what to say. "Betsy, you look good," he repeated.

"What are you talking about, Harold? Don't talk to me in that way. I don't think Jerome would like it at all," she stammered back, just saying something reflexively, as she was starting to feel a wee bit uncomfortable.

But Harold persisted with childlike exuberance at the picture in the mirror. "Look at us, Betsy. We look good," he said.

"Hush up, Harold, hush up," she whispered. "Don't you ever let me hear you say something like that again." Finally, Betsy was speechless. She glided away from the mirror and out of the door, a little sweatier than she was accustomed to being on her way to church.

Harold hadn't meant anything untoward, of course. He was just being Harold, with all of his immature imaginings. But it was the first time Betsy was worrying about him. After church, she reluctantly told Daddy what had happened that morning. "I told you he was crazy, and I told you what to do. You might not get thirty-five dollars for him now. He's beyond crazy, he's scary," Daddy snorted.

"Now, Daddy, you know I can't turn that man in like that. The state already knows he's mentally deficient. They are paying him, and through him, us, to take care of him."

"God. It's worse than I ever thought," Daddy sighed. "Sounds like he's so bad off that the state turned him in to you." They both had to stop and have a good laugh. "You want to know what your problem really is, Betsy?"

"My problem?"

"Yes," Daddy said, "Your problem. Your problem is that Harold is crazy."

"Oh, Daddy," Betsy complained, what does that have to do with anything?"

"Everything," Daddy replied. "You sit and sit and talk and talk with Harold and where does it get you? More crazy talk. You go on and on with Harold trying to have a sensible conversation, when Harold doesn't have a single sensible thought in his head. Harold doesn't make you talk to him, you make that choice. He's unreasonable, sure, because he is, and no amount of your trying to reason with him will make him otherwise. So, it's your problem," Daddy said. "Let him say whatever he wants. No matter how outrageous it may be, agree with it. Forget about logic. Don't try and talk sense to nonsense. If you do, then you are acting as crazy as he is."

"Betsy," Harold said, "You see those people outside?"

"I sure do," Betsy affirmed.

"Can you take me?" Harold started, and before he could even say where he wanted her to take him, Betsy interrupted him with a quick "Yes."

"Can you get William to take me to see the president's planes?"

"Yes. But, if he can't, I'll take you sometime," she said.

"Good night Betsy. You look good."

"Good night, Harold. You look good too."

"Good night,Betsy."

I shall not die, but live, and
declare the works of the Lord.
The Lord hath chastened me sore:
but, he has not given me over to death.

PSALMS 118:17, 18

A Game of Life

JUNE 30, 2002, WAS a day punctuated by miracles of God. There is
no other way to explain it. It started at a small breakfast fundraiser
for my re-election. I ate my usual healthy way—oatmeal, a bran
muffin and fruit. For half an hour, my host and the other three
of us talked prescription drug policy around issues that were to
come up later that evening for a floor vote in the context of a new
prescription drug benefit for seniors. It was a controversial matter. There were also complicated questions surrounding the right
of seniors to use their collective buying power to reduce the cost
of drugs and whether drugs should be permitted to be imported
from Canada. We were caught up in some of its nuances when
my host's phone rang. Somebody playfully said, "No phones," so
she looked at the number of the person calling and put the phone
away. Momentarily, it rang again. "I'm sorry," she said, "Looks like
I must take this one. It's family." She stepped a few feet away from
the table. "Oh, no!" my host exclaimed. "Oh, no!" she whispered
into the phone. She turned to us, suddenly tearful. Realizing that
we were staring at her, she whispered softly, "I'll have to call you
back in a minute. No, I'll come over in about fifteen minutes." She
sat looking stunned. We wanted to ask her what had happened.

But no one said a thing. It felt so awkward sitting there watching her try to control her sobbing, so intrusive, that I offered that we should leave and let her attend to her affairs. She didn't respond to that suggestion. She was trying to compose herself, fighting back tears. We gave her another moment. "They just found my brother-in-law's body in a park. He was out jogging and dropped dead. No one understands it. He was the picture of fitness, the picture of health." We didn't ask any questions. We expressed our grief and our condolences. Then, my host and I and all the others went our separate ways. I was to revisit this development later in the day in a most dramatic fashion. For now, however, except for the ephemeral thought that every man's death diminishes another, it appeared unconnected to me.

It was now four o'clock and I was waiting in Representative Carrie Meek's office to meet with her. She had called the meeting with me to talk about how her son, Kendrick, might succeed her in Congress, were she to retire. Ordinarily, four o'clock with me was not available to anyone. It was the time that I set aside every day that we were in session to go to the House gym to play basketball and work out. But Carrie was special and the topic of discussion so important to her that I didn't know how to say no. But, uncharacteristically, she didn't show up for her own meeting. After waiting in her office until about twenty-five after four, I started to feel the call of the gym, which was just below her office in the Rayburn building. I told her receptionist that I would have to reschedule, and I gave in to the familiar tug of my four o'clock workout routine. As it later turned out, it was good that Carrie was late. Her tardiness led me to the gym, and the gym to an unusually vigorous work out. This combination, this confluence of events, are two of the major reasons that I am alive today—or at least that I did not die that day or soon after.

"Hey, Mr. Jefferson," young Harold Ford Jr. called out, "come on, and let's play two on two." For some reason, there were only three guys waiting to play basketball that day, not the usual ten or fifteen that forced us to wait turns, or even sometimes to play a crowded five on five on the House's undersized basketball court. Because of the size of the guys on the court, I could see how we would match up if I were to play. Harold and I were about the same height, and the two other fellas on the court were clearly taller. Were I to play, I knew I would end up defending Harold, one of the youngest members of Congress. More importantly, Harold was the kind of player who was never discouraged from working to get open for a shot and never discouraged from taking a shot, no matter how bad a shooting day he was having. So I hesitated for a moment, contemplating whether I felt like chasing Harold all over. To any thinking person, it should be clear that when the guy you are supposed to guard in a basketball game calls you mister, that it is probably a game you should not be taking part in. Harold was polite, sure, but he always tried to bring his "A" game when I guarded him, so as not to be shown up by an "old man." I was usually especially motivated too, but on the other side of the coin. Besides, I prided myself on my defense, an art lost on most young players. But, a two-on-two game? This meant I would have no help from anyone else on the court, no switching, and no running him into double teams. "Come on, Mr. Jefferson," young Harold egged. "Let's get this thing going before votes are called."

Against good judgment, I decided to take up the challenge. "Okay. Let me get my stuff on. Let me get ready," I reluctantly agreed.

Having baited me into the game, Harold shot back with a smile, "Get as ready as you can, sir."

There is an arrogance that comes naturally with youth. I call it an innocent arrogance, because there is usually nothing sinister about it. Fundamentally, it is just a belief held by a young person that merely because he is young he has a natural advantage in some things over an older person. I don't envy this belief. I find it a strangely attractive quality. I even sometimes find it amusing. But I do enjoy testing it and deflating it when and where I can to kind of even the playing field of life as my years pile on. There are concessions in life that must be made to aging, but, I feel, only as necessity dictates. So I went to the locker room to get ready for my game that day with the firm intention of doing everything I could in this friendly pickup game to wipe the smirk from young Harold's face.

Our game was on. Harold didn't disappoint and neither did I. He was all over the half court, running and gunning, asking for the ball to take me on. But I didn't make it easy for him to get the ball or to get a good shot off. I was all over him like a cheap suit. I cut him off on his drives to the basket. I blocked one of his shots and kept a hand in his face as he became an all-too-predictable jump shooter after the lane was clogged. Fouls in our game are called on the honor system, but a frustrated player will sometimes call a foul to avoid embarrassment. That's what Harold did. Foul after foul he'd call, "My ball, Mr. Jeff," giving himself a chance to set up and reload and at the same time a chance to act as if a good defensive play shouldn't be credited.

After a grueling struggle, my team won by three points. Neither our win nor my successful defense on him was something Harold was willing to accept. "Let's go again," he exhorted, as soon as our last points trickled through the net. "We've got time." He looked over at me and saw that I was totally exhausted. But he knew I had given him a very tough game. He wanted another shot at me, so he said slyly, "Don't worry. I'll take it easy on you this time."

I was dog tired. Besides, I thought I'd been able to take away his feeling of natural advantage by mostly shutting him down. *Why give that back?* I asked myself. I smiled at him, and I waved him off. I went over to get a sip from the cooler and to get a towel to work on the streams of sweat that were running down my face. "I've had enough," I panted. My thought was to go to the weight room and take it easy for a few minutes, maybe tone my muscles a little at my own pace.

In the short time it took me to gather myself and to start to walk away from courtside, however, a conspiracy had developed. Harold and the other two players starting chanting my name, "Jeff, Jeff, Jeff, Jeff," and I seemed to have heard Harold chanting, "Mr.

Jeff, Mr. Jeff, Mr. Jeff." I knew it was just out of necessity that they were shouting out my name, but I got caught up in the fun and let myself get drawn into a second game. With the benefit of hindsight, it was a good thing that I did. One game, at least for me, did not disclose what two games did.

Harold played better this time. I was not as effective a defender on him as in game one, and progressively less so as the game wore on. Hype, enthusiasm, even an iron will, can carry a body only so far. For the rest of the job, it takes muscles, lungs and other important parts working harmoniously together. Every part I had was giving out, including the hype and enthusiasm pieces. The arrogance of youth, the advantage of simply having the capacity to endure over someone older in a game of chase and skill, emerged and Harold was truly again enjoying himself. Thankfully, at the tenth point of our game of fifteen, the voting bells sounded, and I was able to quit the game with something close to dignity, if not grace. "Good game, Mr. Jefferson," Harold intoned, I thought with a certain playful sarcasm, walking briskly past me, as I was bent over gripping the legs of my shorts to keep from toppling over.

I plodded my way to my locker and sat down in a chair that was just in front of it. I needed to sit for a minute, but I reminded myself that I had only about twelve minutes to run through the shower, get dressed and get to the floor. I had to get going, I was urging myself. I reached for the latch on my locker and at the same time tried to stand up, but I just could not move. I felt more tired than at any time in my life. With the most unusual second effort, I dragged myself across the room to the shower. I was thinking how stupid I was to spend myself as I had in a two-on-two game, and guarding Harold on top of that. How could I ignore my obvious gut instinct that clearly told me not to play? But, somehow, I was able to get moving, make it to the floor and vote.

When the voting ended, I felt fine, almost refreshed, like nothing unusual had happened. I went back to my office, kept an appointment with a senator on the Senate side of the Capitol, and, after meeting with him, raced back over to the House for another series of votes. Through all of that, I felt perfectly fine. I had a hot dog in the cloakroom and a carbonated drink along with it, the kind of food that usually upsets my stomach and that I never eat for health reasons, but even then, I felt great, nothing out of the ordinary. When I had finished my work on the floor, I went back to my office. Votes were coming up in a few hours, the last votes of the session prior to our July Fourth break. I sat at my desk and answered letters and returned calls for a while waiting for the next floor action, thinking no more of how I had felt earlier. I attributed my odd tiredness earlier to my overexertion during the games.

At around ten thirty at night, two bells sounded, signaling the long-awaited vote on the Medicare prescription drug benefit. I had the usual fifteen minutes to get to the floor, so I took my time finishing the last touches on a letter. I signed it and started to get up to go to the floor. Out of the blue, it was back. I felt the same overwhelming tiredness that had overtaken me just after the second game—as if I couldn't move, couldn't get started. It was a mammoth struggle to lift myself from my chair, again. But I got up and managed to put one foot before the other as I made my way to the floor. At the door of the Cannon building, where my office was located, I gripped the railing of the stairs and ambled down to Independence Avenue, then across it, and to the Capitol. Ordinarily, I would sprint up the steps on the east side of the Capitol to the second floor where voting takes place. I always thought of myself as in extraordinarily good shape. I usually passed up escalators in our buildings for stairways, and eschewed elevators for the stairs behind the exit doors—all a part of my daily exercise regimen. But that night I entered the Capitol on the ground floor, after a painstakingly slow walk there, and waited, leaning against the wall, for the elevator to take me up to the second floor to vote. I was more than exhausted as I took my seat and cast a vote on one of the issues we'd talked about early that morning. That breakfast now seemed a long, long time ago. Why was I feeling so tired? Was it the hot dog and carbonated drink that was making me feel faint and robbing me of my energy? This thinking might not seem to make sense, but I was searching for anything that might be out of the ordinary that I had done that day that could begin to explain this change in the operation of my body. Unlike when I had reached the floor and voted earlier in the day, the voting did not seem to cure me. I still felt drained. I finally had to open up to the possibility that something might be wrong. Then, I remembered. As long as the House was in session, the House physician's office was open. I decided it was time to ask for a professional opinion.

As I made my way toward the doctor's office, ironically, I passed Carrie Meek, who was emerging from the Lindy Boggs room on her way to vote. "Wake up, Jeff," she called out. "Let's get together when we come back."

I guess I was moving so slowly that she thought I was sleepy and tired. I was tired all right, but it had nothing to do with sleep deprivation. "Okay," I waved back to her. As we passed each other, Carrie was unaware of the role she had unwittingly played in bringing about the circumstances that had led to my walk to see a doctor that night.

"Do you smoke?"

"No," I answered.

"Drink?"

"Only red wine occasionally with dinner."

"Exercise?"

I smiled. "Every day."

"Sisters, brothers who have had heart attacks?"

"No!" *Heart attacks?* I asked myself, getting the drift of the doctor's questions. "My mother died at seventy-eight of a heart disease," I offered. "My father is ninety," I hurriedly added, feeling I needed to clear our family of heart diseases, "and he has had no heart problems." The battery of questions went on about my medical history, eating habits, personal routines, social practices, and the day's events.

"On a scale of one to ten, describe the pain in your chest," the doctor asked.

"No pain," I said. "Just a dull, full feeling."

"Any pain in your left arm?"

"No."

"How about your arm or neck on the left side?"

"No, none," I answered.

Another physician was called into the office. They conferred briefly. I was asked to go into an adjoining room, take off my shirt and lie down on an examining table for an EKG. Now I knew exactly where they were headed. But it made no sense. I had done everything right to avoid such a thing—a good diet, regular exercise, no smoking, watched the stress. "Could you slip this nitroglycerin tablet under your tongue? Just a precaution," one of the doctors said. There was little doubt now as to what their suspicions were. The nurse announced my blood pressure was much too high. Now I was thinking back to the morning's breakfast, and starting to feel personally connected to the call my host had taken. I was repeating to myself the very words of shock and disbelief she had whispered into the telephone then, when her sister had called her to tell her of her husband's death. "No one understands it," she'd said so softly and tearfully. "He was the picture of fitness, the picture of health."

The EKG was inconclusive, but the doctors thought they observed a slight irregularity compared to my last test just a few months earlier. This, taken together with my elevated blood pressure, that my initial tiredness came about during and after exercise, and my admission to something like pain in my chest, convinced the doctors that I should go to Bethesda Naval Hospital for more detailed testing. "But I have one more vote to take tonight," I protested. "It's a very important vote on prescription drugs for seniors within the Medicare program. I have got to take it," I insisted.

"With all due respect, sir," the doctor told me somberly, "nothing is more important right now to you and your family than to find out as quickly as we can what may be happening to you. You have to miss this vote. Please, come with us now!" For the first time in my life, in spite of all of my efforts at avoiding it, I had to face the fact that I might be dealing with a big health problem. They brought in an oxygen tank. They fitted the plastic tubing that comes with it into my nostrils. I took a seat in the wheelchair that was offered. They rolled me out of the Capitol onto the backseat of a waiting sedan. As we pulled off, I started to wonder if their suspicions were right. When would I be able to get back to work? Would I die of a heart attack in the backseat of the car on the way to Bethesda like that fit jogger had that morning in the park? I started to think about my wife and children and the rest of my family—how would they handle things if the worst happened? But my overwhelming thought was how happy I had been with them and how blessed I was to have them all. Then I just started to think about God, and I felt that I was all right with Him. Then, suddenly, I stopped worrying. I knew I should leave it in His will. I was ready for whatever was to come, and I knew for sure that my family would be too. Remembering the reaction of my host at breakfast that morning, my only prayer was for their comfort and peace. Anyway, I told myself, I should think positive things. There'd been no diagnosis yet. There wasn't anything yet to share with my family. I just relaxed and went along for the ride to Bethesda.

Thursday nights are special at Bethesda. That's when all of the cardio experts gather—nurses, doctors and the rest—because heart-related surgeries are conducted in the wee hours of Friday mornings. I would be arriving at Bethesda at the best time possible for one who had to be thoroughly checked out for, maybe, a heart-related problem. It was still hard to think about this as real. But here I was. As our car pulled into Bethesda, it looked as if I were meeting a welcoming party at a medical convention—all of the lights, orderlies, doctors and emergency personal were there to greet me. Someone had trumpeted the news that I might have a serious health problem and that I needed to be checked out thoroughly. By now, however, in just the short time that it took to make the trip from the Capitol to Bethesda, I was feeling good again. In contrast to the large but grim reception I received from the army of caregivers, my body was feeling, well, happy. It was ready to get back in the gym and chase around after young Harold Ford again—at least for that first one of our two-on-two games. Once more, the tiredness was completely gone. I didn't know whether to attribute it to the oxygen I had taken in or just the whacky on-again-off-again exhaustion I was experiencing. So I was back to starting to think that there really wasn't anything wrong with me. Maybe all of those early, worrisome tests taken back at the Capitol were false negatives, missing the real case. I'd get on with this, I was now thinking, get these other tests over as quickly as possible and get back home and rest.

To my delight, the tests bore out this view. "On a scale of one to ten, describe the pain," a new heart specialist asked—repeating the question of one of the doctors at the Capitol.

"None," I said eagerly, "none at all." The sonogram was equally unrevealing. My heart was beating powerfully, nothing irregular. I was able to watch its perfect pulsations on a monitor screen. There, I witnessed each chamber and each exterior surface being carefully reviewed. "Your heart beats beautifully, looks beautiful," the technician repeated to me with satisfaction.

After a review of the technician's report, a physician agreed. "It definitely does not look as if you had a heart attack. There is no evidence of any damage to your heart muscle." My confidence in my good health soared. I was sure everything my gut was telling me about my physical condition was right. Another EKG was ordered. Normal. My blood pressure was marginally high, not dangerously high as the nurse reported earlier at the Capitol.

"Have you had a treadmill test in the recent past?"

"Yes, six months ago," I replied. "I completed it with flying colors. I went through all the levels." Blood was drawn. Everything looked okay—electrolyte counts and all.

It was now near one o'clock and I had endured every test as happily and as good naturedly as I could. But with every negative result, I was feeling more and more like I was wasting my time. I was now sleepy and tired, as Carrie had supposed when I had last seen her in the Capitol, not just tired from some supposed malady. "Congressman, things look pretty good. But we remain troubled by the history of your case, especially what happened today. If you will permit us, there is one more thing I recommend that we do. It is called an angiogram, and it is the gold standard for determining whether oxygen is getting to your heart in the right proportions," a doctor I had not seen earlier explained to me.

I didn't know what to say. I was ready to go home. I didn't feel like being cut into when nothing had been found; I didn't want to take a test I'd never heard of. "What do you mean, invasive?" I inquired, somewhat disgustedly.

"It means we make a tiny incision in the big vein in your right groin, snake a very tiny camera inside of it and take pictures of the insides of your veins and arteries leading to and from your heart," he stated in a plaintive voice.

"I'm definitely not going to be put to sleep for this," I insisted, as if I were asserting some control over a situation that I really had no capacity to manage.

"Oh, no; you won't need to have general anesthesia," he said, "just something local."

"Well, I want to stay completely awake," I demanded. "I'd like you to do it without any anesthesia. Can you do that?"

"Yes, I believe I can just pluck it lightly, pat against the spot in the artery where we enter for the examination, and then quickly make a very small cut, maybe apply something topical."

It felt as if I had cut myself shaving, except for a little pressure in the area from the insertions. It was over in a few minutes. I lay there waiting for the doctor to return and send me home.

A slim man stood at my bedside when I awoke. He had a saintly demeanor, and the warm, friendly smile that a kind minister wears on his face. He held a Bible in his hands. Bright lights were all around me, blinding me. Was I in heaven? Coming out of an operation, awakening for the first time, can be fraught with illusions. So it took me some time to adjust my thinking and my eyes enough to make out the face of the man at my bedside. He was a soldier. I was able to tell that after looking hard at him. He was not adorned in glistening white angelic apparel, but in a drab, tan-colored Navy officer uniform. I wasn't in heaven after all, but at least the soldier turned out to be close to God. He was a chaplain. "I prayed for you," he said softly, leaning close to me.

"Why?" I asked, a little disoriented.

"It is not proper to ask why. These things are in God's divine determination," he answered.

"Oh, I believe that," I said. "My real question is not why this is happening to me, but rather why I am spared, why what I had didn't kill me, without warning, as it had so many others." It quickly became apparent to me that whatever "why" question I had, no matter what I intended by it, the chaplain provided the same response. I knew he was right, but the question would not let go of me.

From the moment the angiogram results had been pushed at me—a handful of X-ray looking pictures appearing to show a number of lines with small bulbs or chalk lines here and there—I had felt I was an unwilling participant in a supernatural experience. "Are these my pictures?" I'd asked incredulously.

"They certainly are," the doctor said, taking charge. "Look, sir, these little bulbs or chalk line images here are blockages of significant arteries and veins. There are six of them. One is in a small blood vessel, and is in a bad spot besides, so it is presently inoperable. But the other five are cabbage candidates.

"You are not a candidate for angioplasty because your blockages are far too severe, eighty percent to ninety percent occluded. You must have carotid arterial bypass operations in at least five different spots," he concluded. "You are very lucky, sir, very lucky." I smiled. *Blessed, I thought. Very blessed.*

It had all come together. The missed appointment with Carrie; the super-stress test Harold had put me through; the late working hours that had prevented me from going home and to perhaps a final sleep; the convenient, regular Thursday night gathering of heart care professionals; and that last revealing exam after all seemed normal—this was were more than natural good fortune. And I was meant to compare my outcome with that of my host's in-law----it was God's way of emphasizing his goodness and continued personal, unmerited favor toward me. My "why" question, was, in reality, a "what" question—having been spared, what does God have for me to do? What do I owe him now more than ever? I remembered Mrs. Mary Shorter. There had to be more to do for Him and for me through Him—to glorify Him. I would have to fight for the chance to do it. But I didn't realize then how hard.

Miss Southern and Her Court

IT WAS THE MOST important election of my life, up to that point, and the woman I was to marry voted for someone else. She confided that she did not vote for me. She said she felt sorry for the other guy—said I was going to win anyway. *But that's a poor excuse,* I thought, *for not voting her convictions.* When she told me this early on in our relationship, I was seriously wounded—stunned, not amused. My opponent didn't get many votes. I crushed him. I was sure that a girl like her, intelligent and beautiful, would see the same qualities in me, at least since almost everyone else had. She was the favorite in her race for Miss Southern, on the same ballot, on the same date as my election for the office of student body president. I'd voted for her, despite her widely anticipated win. And, when the votes were tallied, she had carried the day handily with my vote added to her huge stack. But with me, she'd chosen pity over promise. "You were the best, Jeff. You didn't need my vote. I can't help feeling for the underdog, that's all. Let it go. It was a long time ago. You won. Be magnanimous," she'd laughed at me, some months after she had disclosed what she'd done. But, for the longest time, I was not amused.

She was the sweetheart of a rival fraternity when I met her—Kappa Alpha Psi. I was an Omega man. Kappas were supposedly cool. We Omega men had more of a reputation for leadership and scholarship. That should have been enough for me. But when I met her in our junior year, wearing a beautiful white gown trimmed in red Kappa colors, in a picture book for the Kappas, I craved cool on top of everything else. I watched her after that. She claims she hardly noticed me, except in my role as junior class president, but "not as a special interest and certainly not as a love interest," she insisted. This I have also found profoundly unamusing—and, frankly, unbelievable. I wasn't cool, I concede, but everything else about me, I was sure, and not based only on my own assessment, oozed, well, things that I was certain were irresistible to the opposite sex. Anyway, I have always largely disregarded this claim, because, after all, she did leave the Kappas for an Omega man—me—and has now been my girl for the last thirty-eight years. Well, to be truthful, she has not been my only girl for all that time. There have been, still are, others.

Given that I triumphed over the Kappas, I am not worried by her early betrayal there. This exercise in bad judgment is largely attributable, I feel, to her having met me later in life than she met the Kappas. This makes the whole Kappa affair one that I can easily understand and accept. But we were thrust together out of the necessity of protocol and ceremony. And, almost before we got going with my first official escort of her to our first football game—Miss Southern and the student body president had to go together to such events—I was floored by her saying to me sprightly, "I'm looking forward to our being involved with student activities together. But, before you get the big head, and so that you may remain humble, and before you start thinking that I am thinking how lucky I am to have you as my escort, I want you to know that not everyone on campus voted for you." I was speechless. *Where did this come from?* I was thinking. I just looked at her. All right, I sort of glared at her a little. But she didn't back off. "I didn't. I didn't vote for you." She swallowed a little after that, I guess looking at my reaction and thinking I was in need of a little of her pity at that point. "I didn't vote for you for student body president." I gave her an incredulous look, waiting for the punch line to this joke. "Don't look at me like that. I didn't," she smiled. I felt what I detected to be a chill in the air, a chill between us. Then she reached for my hand. She tucked my hand inside of my coat, between my chest and my belly button, so that my arm assumed the escort ready position, and then slipped her dainty wrist into that small triangle created inside of my elbow. The ice melted. She tugged me forward. It would not be the last time that she would do so.

The chill was gone, but the disappointment arising out of what she had said lingered. She never knew how much that night, as we both stood cheering for a Southern victory. She could not know that I would not have been upset, wouldn't have cared, if anyone else had told me that. But since I had earlier noticed her, found her interesting and attractive, I suppose I was deflated in a way that I did not know that I could be. She did not know that I had her in mind in any special way at the time. She was just being herself, "honest and up front," she said, and handling me like she handled boys she thought might think themselves to be big men on campus, or hot stuff or something. I didn't necessarily think these things, not exactly anyhow, and not in a bad way. Sure, I was confident; after all, I was a winner of three student government elections, president of my Omega line, a battalion commander in the ROTC, a high honors student—sure, I was confident, but I wasn't cocky and I tried hard not to appear that way. I felt there must be more to what she was saying and doing. I thought it was more than her making sure to let me know that if I were feeling full of myself, that at least in her case, she was not impressed. Years later, I found out, as I again brought up for the umpteenth time her slight of not voting for me and her misunderstanding of my attitude, that there was indeed even more reason for her taking over that first night with me, more than I could have imagined. It wasn't just me with whom she was making her point. "It really didn't have anything much to do with you. Well, not everything," she said, holding back. "It was the whole system that galled me. I was proud to be Miss Southern. I still am. But when I walked into the waiting room to meet you that night, and saw all the boys as class officers and all the girls as class queens, at that moment, I just felt like protesting some kind of way and I guess you just became the target." I heard this some years after we were married. What rose up in her that night as she readied herself to grace our stadium as our shining queen was not an overwhelming feeling of pride in that accomplishment. Instead, she was thinking, *I should have had a chance to be student body president—just like you.* Putting it that way, well, I could begin to understand. Still, I could have avoided years of pain and years of second-guessing her stewardship of her student body vote if only she had explained herself to me much sooner.

Andrea served gracefully and effectively as Miss Southern. She was beloved by Southern's entire community—its faculty, the administration, and of course, and especially, her fellow students. We attended all the events we were required to go to together. Out of these formal outings, we got to know and to like each other. We became good friends. We spent a great deal of time studying, and I came to really appreciate her commitment to scholarship.

She was an excellent student teacher as well. I saw her once in that elementary school classroom set up at the Southern Laboratory School. The little children didn't want to see her leave when the bell rang to end class. They gathered around her skirt, hugging her legs, until she promised them profusely that she was returning soon. In her class with them, she drew them in, reading in character voices to them, and excitedly praising them for their efforts, making them feel special and successful at the same time. But when I took some time to extol her wonderful teaching skills, tears welled up in her eyes. It turned out that in high school, she coupled good writing and oratory proficiencies. She thought these capacities gave her the aptitude to pursue a career in law. When she sat down with her high school counselor to talk about her college major and her interest in law, he'd told her to forget about it. "Girls can't be lawyers," he'd said, dismissing her. "Now, what you can do is to become a teacher. Focus on that, something you can be successful with. Women make good teachers, especially in elementary school." Not knowing any better and not aware of any examples in her experience that she could draw from otherwise, she took her counselor's advice and majored in elementary education. So she undertook teaching about the same way she did her role as Miss Southern, doing both jobs exceptionally well, but feeling that she had not been able to freely choose her path. The legal profession, and probably student governing too, were robbed of her special competencies. It was a sign of the times. She, and later, I with her, were to make sure this didn't happen to the next generation.

Black boys had their dreams cut short too. I was one of them, early on. Southern boys, Black and white back in our day, looked forward to military service. I wanted to be a soldier, I thought, so I dreamed of going to West Point. I went to our colored library, found the address of the U.S. Military Academy, and sent off for the catalog and admission materials. I cannot begin to tell you how often I checked the mailbox out on the highway, half a mile away, for my return mail from the Academy. When I could not go to the mailbox myself, I asked any and everyone headed in that direction to look for it. Every day coming home from school, I looked in the mailbox just to see if perhaps someone gathering the midday mail had missed picking it up. When my West Point package finally arrived, I felt like doing cartwheels all the way home. That evening I devoured every word of the information. In sum, to qualify, you had to have physical skills of a high level, and grades to match. With this, I was in great shape. But it was the third requirement that took my chance away to go to West Point. The problem was that I had to get a nomination from my U.S. congressman or my U.S. senator to be considered. I didn't know how to go about doing this, which was obstacle enough. But even after I found out where and how to contact those officials, I learned that my lack of sophistication was not my real problem. When I finally fully investigated it all, and after I got the polite turndowns at the congressional offices, I was down to the real deal. The sad but unadulterated truth was that in 1964 no Black person had ever been nominated by any member of our congressional delegation to any of the military academies. So when it became clear that I was not going to be the one who would break that color barrier, I took the Academy's books and its papers, which I had already filled out as completely as I could without a congressional recommendation, and put them on a small shelf in the bedroom I shared with my brothers. Then I did as Andrea's counselor had advised her—I forgot about it. Nine years later, as a member of the staff of a U.S. senator, I would be able to goad my senator into nominating the first African American to a military academy, the U.S. Naval Academy. But this was a virtual lifetime away, as I dealt with my rejection for consideration for West Point.

Andrea's problem was even more devastating. She was at an all-Black school. Black boys and Black girls could dream within that environment and live out their dreams to achieve and exercise leadership more there than any place else. But Black girls, even at a Black high school or on a Black college campus, were taught, unlike Black boys, that they could not try to do whatever they might want to do, even there. Black girls were limited, even in our segregated schools, and instructed by word and deed, not just to defer their dreams but to give them up as impossibilities—sometimes in favor of Black boys. I felt ashamed all those years later not to have seen this in our college life. Somehow I'd always thought that there, unlike in the wider, real world, where discrimination was and was expected to be all around us, that you could compete and win just because you showed yourself to be better or more trustworthy than your competitor. But, sadly, this was only half true.

Two years later, in spite of the way she mishandled me starting out, she married me. Okay, I asked her to. And, somewhere near my hometown on a country road, the city girl said yes. I went away for my ROTC commission training after that and I got enough money together to send her a ring by mail, which she accepted as if I were presenting it to her on bended knee. It was 1970 and we were both twenty-three. The Black newspaper that reported on our wedding stated that we honeymooned in Montgomery, Alabama, and Washington DC. Facts are, though, that we departed New Orleans around seven at night, and after our noon wedding and mid-afternoon reception at the church hall, we were able to drive only as far as Montgomery, Alabama, before falling asleep. The next day we drove all the way to DC, where we made our next rest stop. The morning after that, we went on to Cambridge, Massachusetts, where we were to live for the summer while I worked at Boston Legal Aid. But since none of our friends who married ever had a honeymoon, and since the newspaper reported that we had, it engendered a certain undeserved envy among our contemporaries who were sure that we had had a glorious one. I'm sorry to say that we did nothing to disabuse them of that impression.

"Jeff, do you have air?" her father asked me as we started out.

"No, sir," I answered sheepishly. His eyes dropped, and I knew he felt sorry for his daughter. And I felt sorry for letting him down. But we drove happily the seventeen hundred miles to Cambridge with the windows of our 1963 Chevy Impala rolled down. The wind roared in our ears through our open windows and the beats of our hearts quickened as we pushed our humble marriage carriage to the limits of its speed. The June heat still stuck the old car's plastic seat covers to our backs and bottoms, and the wind sometimes made our eyes water, but that our spirits were riding high and dry was really all that mattered. Somewhere on the other side of Atlanta, our muffler suffered a slight separation from our exhaust pipe, converting our Chevy into a kind of nose and noise pollutant, burning the eyes and ears of some of our fellow travelers. Only our "Just Married" signs saved us from more obscene gestures than we endured. But we smiled right through that, too.

When we got to Cambridge, however, things started to go a little downhill. Andrea didn't have a summer job when we first arrived, and it killed her to stay home while I worked. What bothered her wasn't that she felt that she should be pulling her own weight, but that I should be home more We had our first argument about my not wanting to come home for lunch each day to break her monotony. I couldn't see the point, and she couldn't see the point more clearly. So she volunteered in a church school program.

It happened again when I started back to law school in the fall, and she began work as a newly minted master's degree holder in guidance and counseling from Rutgers University. "Why can't you study at home at night?" she wondered—very loudly. But I insisted on going to the library, as I had done in my first year when I wasn't hitched. When she exiled me to the floor of our efficiency apartment, and out of the pullout sofa bed that we shared, it gave me time to rethink and fine-tune my position. I was not in the least amused. I admit, though, that studying at home a night or two and taking her with me to the library on occasion proved a tonic for restoring some good health to our early marital ailing, and, more than that, restored me to my rightful side of our sofa bed. It was the first in a lifetime of imperfect, but commonsense, compromises that helped us to stick together through better and worse. I include better, too, because sometimes it was even hard to stand prosperity in the right respect. But let me quickly make clear, lest I mislead, that Andrea has compromised a whole lot more than I ever have over our years together, and she deserves most of the credit for the adult relationship, for the most part anyway, that we have shared.

"You've got a boy in there, definitely," my mother's friend, Miss Mary Mershon, assured us as she rubbed Andrea's stomach. "Look how high she's carrying that baby." I didn't put much stock in what she said. After all, she was Miss, not Mrs., Mershon, and had not mothered a child in any of her sixty years.

But she gained some credibility in our eyes when my mother, having given birth to ten children, and a farm neighbor, Mrs. Janie Henderson, the mother of twelve, seemed to rally around her. "Looks like a boy carry to me, too," Mama had said, to which Mrs. Henderson nodded agreement. In a day before all of the advanced medical devices that could detect the sex of the unborn with precision, we were put to rely on this sort of folk knowledge to get a jump on whether our little bundle was pink or blue. So later, at Miss Mershon's baby shower for Andrea, with so many other older ladies there accepting her assessment, we fairly well started picking out baby boy names, clothes, crib toys, and room colors. It is not that we prayed for or preferred a boy—we only prayed for a healthy baby. But with all the concrete, confident prophesying that it was a boy, we, naturally, were expecting it to turn out that way.

So when I stood at Andrea's head coaching her through delivery of our baby, and the nurse cried out, "Look at those gorgeous eyes," I naturally looked down at Andrea's eyes, which had been described in that way many times before. But her eyes looked more wide-eyed than gorgeous, as she was trying to peer beyond the sheets that covered her legs to get a glimpse of her first offspring. "It's a beautiful little girl," the nurse exclaimed, as the doctor raised her by her heels and slapped her bottom. She took it like a big girl; she didn't cry out, she whimpered, just a little. But she did bat those dazzling, stunningly lovely eyes, and we sensed she was just fine. In that instant, everything about "us" changed. We would never be able to talk about ourselves as the two of us ever again. It was the three of "us." And we would never listen to some old maids' and old wives' tales about the sex of the baby—and we would never again let anyone think that we cared. We named her Jamila Efuru, a name we gleaned from a book of African names, meaning "beautiful daughter of heaven."

There was something else that changed that night that I did not tell my wife about. Perhaps it was because I could not explain it to myself. Perhaps it was because I wasn't sure it was something that I should share with her on this, the night of her supreme joy. Perhaps it was because the thought itself was frightening. Perhaps because it made me feel a sense of disloyalty toward this woman who had just suffered through eight hours of childbirth to deliver to me my, our, new baby. I found my thoughts drifting away from Andrea. I didn't know whether it was natural or right. But I was thinking that I was feeling this keen affection, this irresistible devotion, this love for this new little person, who I had met just a few seconds ago and about whom I knew absolutely nothing, that was seeming to, in an instant, overwhelm the love I had for my wife and everybody else. I didn't know in that moment whether it threatened the love I had for Andrea and the rest of my family, and it disturbed me that I could even think that this was at stake. A few hours later, as I watched over her napping in the nursery from outside of its glass enclosure, I remember thinking that if I had to offer up my life or anybody else's to save her, I would happily do so, and I felt that I would be able to justify it to God. Watching a child come into the world, as I did with Jamila, is to bear witness to a miracle—as a baby moves from its mother's womb, a weightless environment, to at once being thrust into a totally different one, straight away subject to the pulls of gravity and the other weights of the world. The child is moved from a place in which it receives every nutrient, every breath of air and every perception in common with the mother, to one where it cries and struggles for its own sustenance and its own air and space. But it was not this miracle only, when the cord is cut, demanding that this brand new person immediately make its own connections, that so mystified me at Jamila's birth. I know that there is nothing like a mother's all-forgiving, all-encompassing and long-suffering love. And, I am sure beyond any doubt, because it would later happen with me, that a mother would put her child's welfare ahead of that of her own husband, so I was feeling nothing different from what Andrea would feel in this regard. But I just think that from the start, a father simply knows that his daughter will need him more, and a daughter will gravitate to him for that reason. Yes, I've read and lived all the stuff about the need of a young boy to have a role model, and I had one in my wonderful father. But it is what we are taught about "being a man"—that men don't cry; that a man should be in charge in every situation even if a woman may be more able to lead in one case or another; that men and boys have personal and social freedoms that women or girls do not, cannot have—that justifies a big part of the reason why a father knows that his daughter will need him more. Sometimes a father can explain away such foolish notions of male dominance like no one else and establish a foundation of confidence for his daughter to build on. A true knowledge of the inbred notions, learned and natural tendencies, and even more the tactics of men, only another caring man can convey. And a father, if he is any good, will impart this inside information to his daughter, as a shield and a sword to ward off and fight against, where necessary, the torrents of the unfair wiles, passions, and outright tricks that she may otherwise suffer at the hands of the men she will encounter. When she and our other girls who followed grew into their dating years, I would tell them so. "Look, Jam," I'd said to her when she was sixteen and I was taking her on her first date—a date with Dad, as I did with all the rest. "You will be better educated than am I, and there will be lots of things you will know that I will not know. And, for sure, as you grow into womanhood, you will know more about women than I ever will. But, no matter what you learn in school and from and about other women or men, there is one thing you will never know more about than me—and that is about men. I will always know more. I know everything—either I've done it as a man, or I have been a part of it with other men, or heard from some male friend of mine, things that never get shared with women, or not shared enough that it makes much difference. So, whatever you want to know about a man, don't go to your girlfriend, because they will only know a small part, if that, of what you need to know. Come and see me, your dad, about it. I know all and I will tell all, if you let me." In this, I know I have incurred a large debt with the men of the world, whose secrets I have liberally shared with my daughters. But this could not be helped. What father would deny his daughter whatever she might ask, if the thing asked about was within his power to give? Trouble is, I invited their questions. But how else would they know to ask? When it comes to a daughter, it's hard to be one of the guys.

So, on the night of Jamila's birth, I was thinking, you might say, way ahead. A girl child's psyche is safe and intact in her mother's womb, and among all the confusing thoughts and feelings I was having in these early hours of her life, I was thinking that a big part of my new job as Jamila's father was to make sure her psychic value was never written down. I would just have to try to insure a fair competition between Jamila and my wife for affection and time from me to do this. I was sure that the feelings I was experiencing for Jamila would never change; whether it would ever be fair or not to someone else I didn't know.

What is she thinking? I wondered as I held her inside the nursery. She opened those big, pretty eyes, and as I smiled in admiration of her, I felt a warm trickle from her cloth diaper onto my wrists. My high-minded musings were brought down to this bare-bottom. I quickly passed her back to the nurse. I was not amused. I wasn't quite ready for the kind of change she needed right now.

Jamila was dangerously curious and inconveniently independent from the start. To take an eye off of her for a minute was to risk an episode of her tasting flower pot mulch, newspaper print, sand and gravel, pencil erasers, rubber bands, and ballpoint pens. We did, and she tasted all those things. We double-covered every electrical socket in the house because she was intent on uncovering them and kissing them. I believe the first word she ever spoke was "no," the second one was "why," and her first phrase was "I can do it by myself." Her incessant insistence that "I can button my own coat" and "I can put my own shoe on" led to delays in our morning routines so severe that the only way to solve them was to just start earlier in the morning, as our two-year-old tried to establish her own ground. I didn't exactly call this giving in to her, but her mother did. Somehow her stubbornness was my problem. Andrea would call out to me at Jamila's every objection to things, and there were many, "Jeff, do something with your daughter."

I did something. I held her and I read to her and I told silly stories to her that made her laugh and look forward to more. She would fall asleep on my chest, and stay there until her mother took her to feed her or tuck her into bed. In between, I tried to talk with her about our helping each other out, she by bringing my shoes to me and me by helping her to button her coat, for example. This set of ploys, this desperate effort to get Jamila and me to share responsibilities was only moderately successful in redirecting her misguided shows of independence. But the success was in this other area. I discovered that she loved my stories and that she wanted me to explain and describe every character. But, more surprisingly, she wanted me to tell her why characters did what they did and said what they said in the stories. My stories were punctuated with "what" and "why" inquiries, as were the rest of our encounters with the world outside of books. "Mommy, what are memories?" she asked as that word popped out of a radio tune. This was a pretty heavy question for a two-year-old, we thought.

Jamila spoke very early, but, oddly, she didn't want to part with her pacifier. Once, when we were traveling home for a holiday, we tried to take advantage of an airline rule that permitted children under two years old to fly for free. Jamila was in fact slightly beyond her second birthday, but we thought, liberally rounded off, she was a lot closer to two than three. But when a clever ticket agent asked her, "Hey, little girl, what is that in your mouth?" and Jamila expertly removed it and spoke as plainly as if she were in the tenth grade, "This is a pacifier," we knew the jig was up. We were not amused. This was not the last time we would be undone by her precocious behavior.

When we were married, my mother had given me a tapestry, crocheted by ladies who worked with her at a senior citizens' center, which bore the message "Don't hurry; don't worry; and don't forget to smell the flowers." She told me it was to remind me that now that I had a wife, and possibly soon a whole family to be responsible for, that they were the flowers of my life and that I should not hurry in pursuit of any other objective without treating them as most important. In Jamila's first year, I hung this tapestry in my office and I have not taken it down since. My mother's life went beyond the words she passed on to me through her knitting, but was instructive by example—completely self-sacrificing and totally committed to the education of her children. It was a constant reminder of how much I was required to give to our children in this regard. Andrea's father's vision for the education of his children mirrored that of my mother and we drew from their experiences and advice as we tried to help Jamila to learn. Besides, with a child so interested in learning and appearing to be adept at it, we were highly motivated.

So my storytelling, inspired by my father, who was a master at it, although he had only a fifth-grade education, became not just a one-sided affair with me reading or dictating to her, but one in which she participated and added to the characters and expanded the story line. "So, what happened next?" I might ask her after delivering a passage from one of our books. This would result in an endless flow of add-ons from her that I would guide and encourage to the lengths of our imaginations. We made poems this way too, in which I would start with a verse and invite her to provide the next one. She would try hard, and sometimes succeed at the moment of my invitation, but were she to fail at that moment, she would not give up on it. At first I encouraged her not to give up, but later, she simply refused to give up on her own. As she was approaching three, if we would leave a stanza or a story undone, and were to leave it for another day, she would catch me when I came in from work to tell me that she had thought of something that might finish our story or poem. She wouldn't exactly say it like that; it would be more like, "Let's play some more with the story." But we knew it meant that she was not going to quit, and that she was having fun learning.

My mother, who was one of five daughters, had to perform all of the chores around the house, even those that would have ordinarily been reserved for boys, including chopping wood. I remembered her telling me she had learned counting and her multiplication tables, which Mama called "times tables," from the rhythm of her wood chopping—"Two times two is four, whack! Eight plus six is fourteen, whack!" Jamila learned to add, subtract and multiply this way from the time she was three. No, I don't mean we had our little girl wielding an axe, but it was this rhythm method, this learning by keeping in time, coupled with making it fun through games, that kept her interest in numbers and that blossomed into her early success in math. In our first apartment, Jamila would run around our coffee table, reciting the times tables and the alphabet until we were sure that she was getting dizzy and make her stop. We'd make her wait for a few minutes and then she would want to run around the table again, chasing words and numbers, laughing and having fun. When we got a place with a second story, she kept up the same thing running up and down the stairs. We were sure that she was a genius, a child prodigy, a candidate for the university ahead of even kindergarten.

"I'm sorry if you folks think your daughter is going to be a great student. Look, everybody thinks their child has some super potential based on assessments that are not done by professionals." This was the evaluation offered up by a Catholic nun, with a great reputation for early childhood education. As we sat dazed and bewildered, she poured it on even more. "Please, I think you need to hear my frank judgment so that you can plan properly for your child's education. She is just going to be an average student. There! I am not saying she will fail as a student, she does have some ability. But she will not be an A-type student." She smiled nicely. She wasn't trying to be unkind. This is how she truly felt, but it didn't ring true to us. We looked at this educator, so self-assured, so clear in her judgment, that if we had not come from backgrounds in which we had been told that we would not succeed in some academic or at some other endeavor, we might have doubted our own experience with Jamila and taken her word for it. We might have even thought that we were needlessly pressuring her beyond her capacities, unwittingly hurting her. We might have thought that she would be happier and healthier if we planned a path for her that included more standard playtime and less time playing with books. But we'd seen this sort of thing limit children before, and we had already decided that we would make our own decisions and trust our own judgments about our children's potential, as honestly as we could. So we went home, surprised by how Jamila's abilities had been gauged, but undeterred in our expectations for or opinions about her. When we asked Jam about her school, she said she liked it, but, "Daddy, it is boring me." She raised and dropped her arms and hands at her side as she said this, showing exasperation. The next day, we sat down and wrote a letter to the school administrator, withdrawing Jamila from the school.

A year before this drama played out at what would become Jamila's former school, we were blessed with a second daughter. I don't think the doctor had to slap her behind for a sign of life; she seemed to come out smiling. Jamila had been a bit lethargic at birth, because, in spite of our best efforts to prepare for a natural childbirth—no anesthesia—the umbilical cord had wrapped around her neck, creating an emergency. Jalila didn't give the cord a chance to entangle her and didn't wait for any pain medication for her mother, either. She burst forth like a sunflower. Before I could park the car and come into the hospital, she was born; before her mother made it to the labor room, there she was—a pretty, happy, chubby bundle full of joy. We got out our book of West African names. She became Jalila Eshe, "splendid gift of life."

The first year of her life turned out to be a struggle, however. She encountered one respiratory complication after the other. Finally, at eight months of age, with our whole family holding vigil in shifts around the clock, we prayed her through a tussle with pneumonia that almost took her away. During this serious illness, she lost her smile, the one that seemed always there from the start. She could always be coaxed into smiling through a game of peek-a-boo, where I would dip out of sight at the foot of her baby bed, and pop up making some silly smile or noise. But even that didn't work when I did it at the foot of her hospital bed. One more series of treatments was left, the doctor announced to us, and after that he didn't know what to do. As I watched the IV drip her life-saving medicine slowly through her tiny veins, none of us knew if we would see her open her eyes again. She drifted off about eight in the evening. She seemed to sleep forever, hardly moving, like a little enchanted African princess, with her hair done up in tiny Afro-puffs and ribbons, and a pretty, pinkish cotton print gown with lace around the collar. She awoke, however, with the first rays of sunlight. As they streamed into her room, she stretched and yawned—and smiled. She was herself again. Since there were so many of us keeping watch over her that night, a loud roar of a cheer went up in her room, like when the home team scores the winning touchdown, when she came back to us. We realized we had named her perfectly—it was if she had been reborn to us, a gift to us all over again, as of the moment of her birth. She would grow into the splendid part of her name in short order.

Jalila had a big sister who welcomed her with open arms and with her usual inquisitiveness. "How did she get out of Mommy's tummy?" It wasn't just enough to tell her that that was where she had come from; she wanted every question answered that naturally followed or that preceded that answer. She wanted to hold her and, of course, she wanted to and thought that she could take care of her little sister by herself. It was a struggle to keep her safe from some unintended accident by Jam, who was trying her best to attend to Jalila's every apparent need. As Jalila grew into her second year, Jam was busy teaching her everything she knew—the ABC's, some counting, how to say words. It was wonderful to watch. But Jalila and Jamila were different people. Jam loved to be pushed; Jalila required a more relaxed approach. Jamila would walk in the mud outside after a rain. Jalila walked around it. Jamila kept a million things going on at one time, and she kept them in perfect order, and had a plan for everything. Jalila, while neater than Jam, was a mess at both organizing and, at the other extreme, improvising. Jalila was smart, and if she could work without pressure, could learn as well as Jamila. As new parents, these differences seemed bizarre. How could children from the same parents have such a fundamentally different approach to learning and to responding to their environment? We couldn't answer the question, but the important thing was that we recognized that the question in fact did exist. It was this fundamental realization that was the single most important reason why we had success with teaching the lessons of life to our children, whether from books or otherwise. Each one demanded an examination by us to figure out as best we could how to deal with their needs individually. It was a blessing that Jamila and Jalila were so different in so many ways. Had we been able to approach them both in the same way and had they, in fact, been more the same, we might have thought that our third child and the ones to come later should have conformed to the styles of the earlier two. Instead, for the most part, we took all of them as we found them, which led us to know how they and we could get the most out of our interactions.

"I can't learn to read, Daddy," a frustrated Jalila told me when she was about four. "I'm just too stupid!" she cried in frustration. Jamila would never have said this, as she would have just kept on attacking the problem. So instead of pushing her on, we started to take her for rides and read from building signs and put together alphabet sounds from the words we saw posted somewhere, anywhere along the roadside. We matched things that we saw to things in some of her beginning reading books. The stories gained more meaning, and reading would become more interesting to her. When we got back to the books at bedtime several weeks later, the girl who had declared herself too dumb to read, had, in a less pressurized atmosphere, become a reading whiz. "I can read!" she blurted out joyfully, turning page after page, as she genuinely seemed to surprise herself with this newfound capacity. Of course, Jam sat there wondering what all the fuss, all the drama was about. After all, she had been reading before she could remember. She laughed at Jalila's early theatrics. But they would weigh on Jam later in life. She would not always find them amusing.

If Jalila led us into a revelation that was extraordinarily useful to us in winning with our children, Jamila led us into the one that was absolutely essential. Jamila, as early as the first grade, treated academic pursuits as one might an athletic challenge. "It was the last seconds of the game, and the score was tied and I dribbled across half-court and lofted a forty-foot jumper, and—swish—nothing but net," some young baller might exclaim, falling back on his bed and thrusting his hands skyward, screaming "Yes!" Jam would say, "I was sitting in the back of the room, and the teacher was going around asking everyone for the answer to the question, and they all blew it. I was sitting there with the answer waiting for her to call on me and she finally did and I nailed it." Then she would say, "Yes!" while falling on her back onto her bed. We loved it, but there was an unseen danger in such celebration and, well, bragging, on her part and such indulgence of it on ours. One day, she came home and said, "Daddy, there is this boy in our class who is so dumb. He can't get anything right."

This was a signal not to be ignored. "Baby, come here and sit with me. Daddy wants to talk to you about what you just said. Remember when I told you that when you were inside your mommy before you were born and you were attached to her by a cord through which you got food and air from her? Remember that?" She meekly said yes, not knowing where I was going, but not liking the feel of the conversation. "It's okay," I reassured her, "But here is what I want to say: That cord was actually wrapped around your neck as you were being born, and the doctor told us that it was choking you, and that if you were not born right away that the air needed for you to breathe would be cut off so long that it would hurt your brain. If this had happened, instead of being able to answer questions at school the way you do, you might be unable to learn like that little boy you were talking about. So, what you have, God just decided to let you keep it, and you should always use it just like you are doing. But, never, ever look down on someone who doesn't have your ability. The difference between you and him may just be that you were born a little bit faster than he was."

She looked at me with those big eyes that were now welling up with tears. "I'm sorry, Daddy," she said softly.

"You don't need to be sorry," I said. "It was just something you had to learn. You're a good girl. You are a very good person. Now that we know better, we can do better." She hugged my neck, and she bussed me.

We taught them all this same lesson, and like Jam, they grew up never, ever forgetting it. Jamila stayed competitive, but she always kept her wins in perspective. It's a wonderful thing to have someone say that your kids are smart and industrious. But we've always taken the greatest pride when people say that our kids are really nice.

Jalila thrived with the same basic methodology, with some

tweaking, of making up stories and the rhythmic counting and multiplying, up and down the stairway. She was breezing through things with a passion for learning that matched Jamila's and with equally strong results. Jamila, ever aggressive, was forced to look over her shoulder every now and then to see if Jalila was gaining on her in one area or the other, when Jalila was a little past four. Jamila wasn't pulling against her to do well; she just wanted to make sure she didn't give any ground.

They ended up taking a test to see whether they should be placed in gifted classes when Jam was seven and Jalila was four. Jalila took her test first. The tester announced that Jalila had indeed achieved the gifted designation. Naturally, at that point, the tester congratulated her and so did we, with small hugs and kisses. The pressure was on. Jamila went in and rushed through her test as spiritedly and as confidently as she could. But she was so anxious to see her results that she asked the tester immediately after she finished, "Did I pass?" The tester looked shocked at what she might have considered an improper question. Fearful that we might see the outcome of the test compromised if Jam asked any more questions or insisted on an answer to the first one, we had to promptly apologize to the tester, and, as quietly and as quickly as we could, we moved our little gung-ho person from the testing room. When the tester emerged, despite our best effort to settle her, Jamila raced to meet her, reaching for the test results. "I passed, didn't I?" she exclaimed.

"With flying colors," the tester answered softly, shaking her head, "with flying colors." I don't think she was amused—not in the least.

Jalila seemed to be in sync with the rhythms that permeated New Orleans. She especially liked church, or, I should say, she liked church music. When the "church ladies" would rise to their feet and sway and clap and shout, Jalila would leap up and join in with them, chanting and yelling out "Hallelujah". Jamila had the superior talent to sing, but Jalila had such a higher spirit, and a natural timing with the beat of music that her celebration was contagious.

At these times, her big smile turned into a loud laugh, expressing a joy that touched the hearts of the people sitting around us. They started to look for her every Sunday. She was younger than two when she started these exhibitions, these interactions with all these church folk. At around four, she became a little self-conscious of all the attention she was generating. But it was already too late. We had already seen what was inside of her—this warm, exciting spirit on the inside that showed in the form of a radiant smile on the outside.

Jalila's affectionate smile and warmhearted friendliness would later lead her to follow me into politics. During her childhood, through high school and even through college, she showed no sign that she had the least interest in public service. She, in fact, denied any interest, decrying the snooping of the press into every private corner of our lives as a principal reason.

As she came into the final semester of her senior year in law school, I got a call from her that was so ominous sounding that it was very unsettling. "Daddy, I need to talk to you, face-to-face."

This is not the kind of call a father wants to get from his adult daughter. I thought it could only mean trouble. "Jalila," I said firmly, "what is it? If it's something bad, tell me now. I don't want to wait to see you in person. If it isn't good, it can only get worse by not talking about it. So, talk to me, please."

She paused for a moment that seemed like forever. Was she in some trouble with some guy? I didn't know that she had a boyfriend, But was she pregnant? Did she have some dread disease? Had she failed a course, or had some other bad outcome in law school? She sighed after a long pause. "Stop worrying, Daddy. Really, it's nothing bad. But I do want to talk to you face-to-face. Can you please get me a plane ticket to Washington?"

I arrived at our agreed-upon dinner spot before she did. I waited uncomfortably, wanting to believe her assurances, but still, I had to admit, I was slightly worried. "Hey, Daddy," she yelled out to me, grinning and beaming. My heart was instantly relieved, for if there is one of our children who has the hardest time not telling the truth with a straight face, it is Jalila. Still, what was it?

We relaxed and talked. It is quite pleasant to have a grown-up discussion with any of my grown daughters. When we are talking, I always find myself staring at them as my mind usually drifts to thoughts of some fond experience I had with them as little children and thinking of how much they have changed.

Finally, she laughed and said, "I guess you may want to know why I called this meeting?" I nodded yes, yes! "Well, I wanted to tell you that I have decided what I want to do with my life. I want to do what you are doing. I want to go into public service, into elective politics. I wanted to talk to you face-to-face because I have never told you this before and I didn't think you would believe me, at least not believe how serious I am about it, unless I could talk with you in person, look you in the eye and answer your questions."

She was right. She was the last one I expected this kind of interest and resolve from about going into politics, because while some of our other daughters had held elective office in high school, Jalila had never even run for any position whatsoever, anywhere. She said she had prayed about it, not satisfied with the prospect of going into traditional legal practice. In the end, she had concluded that, after all, public service was a good thing, and that there was no better use she could make of time and talents than to help people.

It was flattering and rewarding. At first, I was totally surprised. As I thought about it, though, I figured we should have seen something of it coming, even in the beginning moments in the life of this, our most amiable and demonstrative descendant.

It was a month out from my state senate win, in my first try for real elective office, and a few months after Andrea earned her doctorate degree in education, when daughter number three showed up. My wife was insistent that I be there for the birth, campaigning aside. The truth is, I felt the same way, especially since I had missed witnessing Jalila's birth, but I was under strict orders anyway. So we had it all planned out: From the first sign of a labor pain or any other indication that the baby was on the way, I was to be contacted by my office and campaign workers, and I was to immediately rush home to accompany Andrea to the hospital. It was our third baby, after all, and we were pros at all the things that might happen. We were right to plan, but it was foolhardy to expect a plan, depending on the cooperation of an unborn child, to come anywhere near predicting what might actually happen. The baby was due to come in a week from the morning that I left home to do some street campaigning. Andrea started having terrible labor pains about ten minutes after I had departed for the streets. She knew I was campaigning somewhere, but didn't know at which particular street corner. Since it was about seven thirty in the morning, neither my campaign office nor my law office was open. No one had a cell phone back then. So Andrea had to do the unthinkable—she drove herself to the hospital.

It was impossible to please her at the hospital. And even though we had both made the plans in which there were such obvious gaps, it was as if I had pronounced them in a decree from atop Mount Olympus all by myself. Naturally, at a time like that, with my wife upset, mostly, but incorrectly at me, and about to have a baby, putting off explanations and defenses to a time to be determined later appeared the prudent course. So I sucked it up and sat down next to the bedside, and just listened—and listened, until my presence became a source of support instead of irritation.

A few hours passed, and things seemed to be moving really slowly. Andrea's doctor came in and confirmed it. "You are nowhere near ten centimeters dilated," he announced. It was high noon.

Andrea looked over at me. I had been chastised enough, she probably thought, and I had made up for not being around to activate our plan to drive her by sitting with her and patiently listening to her, mostly complaining, for the better part of four hours. "Jeff," she sweetly called out to me, "why don't you go and get some lunch?"

I looked at the doctor. "It should be a while," he assured me, "I'd go on if I were you."

Now, you may not believe this, as well you may, given how things were running that day, but I decided to take their, and I remind you, *their* advice, and drove the ten blocks home for lunch. When I walked into the house, the phone was ringing. It was a worrisome tone. I could tell it was not good. "Mr. Jefferson! You've got to return immediately! Your wife is giving birth."

When I got to the hospital, the apologetic doctor told me that moments, literally moments, after I walked out of the hospital room, Jelani made her dash onto the world stage without warning. He sent someone to catch up with me, thinking they could stop me before I left the hospital grounds, but missed me by seconds and inches. "They decide when they want to come," the doctor now said, sounding helpless. I wanted to ask him, "How long have you known this about babies?" But there was little else that could be exacted from him by way of contrition. He seemed as sad as was I. My wife just threw up her hands when I walked into her room. I took our squirming little girl from her arms. She was asleep, as if she bore no responsibility for all of the emergencies she had created and the missteps she had caused on my part throughout that day. A nurse promptly took her from me, saying she had a jaundice condition and would have to be placed in a special place in the nursery, under a special set of lamps.

It was a whirlwind of weird experiences, not necessarily driven by my campaign. But as we sat there in the hospital room, Andrea and I, without our precious, unpredictable newborn, we were thinking about how much more certain we were now about the campaign, the outcome of which we had thought we couldn't begin to figure out, than about getting a hold of this childbirth thing. So we decided to just make an affirmative statement surrounding her birth that would be predictive of the result we would have in our campaign and in her life. We called her Jelani Faizah, meaning "mighty victorious."

Jelani is a boy's name. But this was just another way of ignoring one more superficial distinction between boys and girls that we hoped would insure her strength. When she was old enough to flex a bicep muscle and coordinate it with the idea of might or mighty, she would curl her skinny little arm to show off a nonexistent muscle, and say, "I'm a mighty child." She was, and she had already shown, in just a few hours of life, that we might as well get out of her way. She was not going to do things in the conventional fashion.

After having come a little early in the hospital, she didn't seem to want to leave with us. She was under this lamp to combat yellow jaundice that had her skin color looking, I'm afraid, yellow, and from the rays of the lamp, a bit sunburned too. I had never really seen her eyes after three days, since when the nurses whisked her away from me in her mother's hospital room, her eyes were closed, and under the lamp she was wearing covers for her eyes to prevent damage to her sight. Andrea wouldn't go home without her, so we stayed around for five days past her birth, and I slacked up on my campaigning to make sure I was close—well, close enough, in any event. We took her home with the areas around her eyes, now patchless, much lighter than the rest of her face. Still, she looked remarkably like a little yellow and tan Jamila. The same stunning eyes. Would we have two of these Jamilas? We both hoped so and hoped not. I trust you understand.

To know Jelani now as a person who's careful, under control, and easy to get along with, is in super-sharp contrast to how things began with her. When she was a tiny baby, were she to become upset, she would redden in anger and flail and cry hard, as if she would not stop. It took patience to endure one of her many tantrums. We didn't know what to do, so we just held her and talked to her, bumped her on our knees, sang to her, petted her, anything to calm her down. We talked to doctors, counselors, everyone we thought should know how to handle a baby with a severely bad temper. No one had answers that worked beyond the ones with which we were already experimenting. My mother had told us that when we had children, we should do three things consistently: take them to church, send them to school and send them for the switch. Jamila had already driven us to the last option, rather repeatedly, not for temper flare-ups that were matching Jelani's, although she certainly had a temper too, but mostly when she was going through her terrible-twos stage. Jamila's run-ins with the switch were largely because of her intransigence, though. Jelani was already in a terrible cycle, and she was not even six months old yet. "Mama, have you ever seen a baby carry on like this?" I asked her when she was with me to witness one of Jelani's outbursts.

"She may be little," Mama said, "but, believe me, she knows what she's doing. This is the time to check her. It will only get worse."

I looked at her. "No, she's too little to spank," I gasped.

"Have it your way, then. If she were mine, I'd tap her little legs sharply a time or two. It'll surprise her, shock her and she will get the message. You can't talk to her right now about her conduct. She is acting out her emotions and she's getting away with it."

Well, we didn't do what Mama said. It just seemed too harsh too early. We were sure we were right.

We had moved into our first house just before Jelani was born. It was a big old house that needed lots of repairs, but it had wonderful hardwood floors and, in the kitchen and breakfast room areas, Spanish tile mosaic floors fastened onto cement. Both floors were very, very hard. Jelani was going on seven months and she was sitting up. Instead of simply flailing or tossing violently when she became cross, now she could and would just throw herself backward, banging her back and head onto the bed or even the floor. As I was in the kitchen one day, Jelani followed me in, crawling and crying for something. I apparently wasn't paying enough attention to her soon enough, because she sat up and started bawling. I reached to pick her up and before I could get her, she threw herself backward, and her head slammed—*smack*—against the floor. It scared the living daylights out of me. Without thinking, I hoisted her up and slapped her little thighs sharply. "Don't ever do that!" I yelled at her. "Don't ever do that again!" And she stopped crying. She looked at me, and I said it again, "Don't ever do that. You understand me." She looked at me with a weird expression that was a mix between amazement and confusion. But she was quiet and she was still. I hugged her and put her back down on the floor. She crawled away from me, stopped and sat up and looked back at me, then crawled away some more over to her toys that were spread onto the floor. She'd gotten it. Mama was right. Whenever she became infuriated about something after that, she would catch herself and look at me or at her mother to see our reaction.

Every child is different, and each responds to different stimuli. We had to keep re-learning the same adages and working practices that our parents already knew. That's really not a smart way to go. I think babies expect us to take charge of them—not to hurt them—but to straighten them out. They act out how they feel, but I don't really think they necessarily want to keep down that path. Their actions are a mix of instinct and consciousness, but consciousness at their level. We have to meet them at both places and intervene there if we are to do our best by them. This was not the last time that we had to "intervene" with Jelani in this way, but it was the best time, despite our earlier misgivings. As far as she can remember now, she never got a spanking in her entire life. Every corrective step was taken so early and she responded so well, that when she was of an age to remember a spanking, the outbursts were gone and she was as sweet and as temperate as a warm slice of pecan pie on a balmy day.

As Mama had seen, Jelani was very smart. She learned everything so quickly and so eagerly that it surprised even us, who by this time were already dealing with two truly intellectually gifted children. We put her through the same paces as her sisters, with stories and counting and the like. She grew to love reading and stories and poetry. She showed a dry wit, and a proclivity for funniness that was born of her braininess. And this formerly out-of-control baby was, at three, a composed, mature-acting mediator of childish disputes between her elder siblings.

Once, when we were on a family vacation to Canada, I won a large teddy bear in a dart-throwing game. Since Jelani was the baby, I gave her the prize. Subsequent to that, I won a medium-sized stuffed animal, and one slightly under medium-sized. According to my thinking pattern, I gave the smallest one to the eldest, Jamila. This didn't sit well with Jamila, and a squabble ensued, Jamila wondering aloud why she had come up on the short end of this gift-giving. Without any prompting from us, Jelani went over to them and said to Jamila, "Here, take mine. This settles it." And she handed Jam her big bear and took the smallest prize.

This was to be a pattern for Jelani—seeing both sides of a problem and trying to fix it to the satisfaction of those involved. Sometimes she would do this to a fault, and her standing in the middle to get a resolution may have led her to make unnecessary excuses for her friends' conduct from time to time. But she was imbued early on with a special spirit of service to others that was often self-sacrificing.

Jalila developed this spirit later in life. Jelani had it from the start. Jamila leads by openly, unmistakably taking charge and by having a plan. Jelani leads by quiet strength and empathy. Maybe that is because Jamila had the whole family of girls to take care of, and Jelani just had to be the leader of the three little girls. Maybe. But in any event, that's what Jelani, Nailah and Akilah came to be called by our family—the three little girls, the three little ones. Jam and Jalila were three years apart; Jalila and Jelani are four years apart; and, Lani, Nai-Nai and Kilah have just two years between them.

By the time Nailah Anan came in December of 1981, we had run out of names beginning with the letter "J" that we liked. She says we were in a rush, maybe a little less creative in our thinking when it came to naming her, or maybe just a little more tired. On the surface she has an arguable point, at least about her middle name, since Anan means simply "fourth-born daughter." But we liked the sound of it. The Nailah part of her name, however, was more reassuring, we think, of our hope for her and our belief in her future, for Nailah means "one who succeeds." She started out right. To the month, to the week, to the day, nearly to the hour, she met every expectation as to the time and timing of her birth. We had long ago abandoned the natural childbirth romanticism in favor of medication that permitted Andrea to be awake and relatively pain-free during childbirth. So we both saw her as she arrived, carefree, hardly blinking and without tears. She had the most perfect birth and was the most perfect of all of our babies at birth. She would have me say that she was our prettiest baby, too, and I might agree with her, except that is something a parent, especially a father, can never do—single out one of his daughters as prettier than the others. When my sisters asked this question of my mother, she was the ultimate diplomat—"each in your own way," she'd said. And this was a mother talking. Imagine the greater risks a father takes, one who is to be more studied in paying attention to and judging female beauty, in giving a straight answer on this issue. But I will say that she was a strikingly beautiful baby, with soft round features, and plump arms and legs, like those of a baby doll. And she did have a facial feature that none of the others had. Just below her left eye, just at her nice high, Indian-like cheek bone, there was affixed a dark brown mark that draws you to her face. Her grandmother on Andrea's side called her "chocolate chip," and it caught on for a while with others in the family. But it was dropped over the years, without notice or ceremony, I think because the phrase didn't begin to describe how special the mark was. It wasn't just a birth mark. It was an authentic beauty mark!

I don't want to give the impression that Nai-Nai was obsessed with her good looks, because as a little kid, how could she even be aware of such a thing? But she was obsessed with how she looked as early as she was able to start adorning herself with things. She wanted her mother's beaded necklace, not to put into her mouth as most babies would, but, rather, she wanted to take them from her mother and put them around her own neck. She tried on her hats, her shoes, her purse, as soon as she could walk. She primped before the mirror, and added to and changed her look as she modeled her clothes for us and for herself. Jelani provided leadership in the plays, songs and dance presentations that they performed at home, but it was Nailah who was most responsible for creating them. She liked stories, but she didn't like reading as much as a two-year-old as the others had. She preferred more visual things—like "decorating" hats and clothing—and she liked to make things—such as doll clothing and scarves. To hold her interest, we had to surround our efforts to get her to learn letters, reading, and even counting in a visual context, with things walking and talking on these subjects or presented in big, larger-than-life examples or in a way that allowed her to imagine them Busy as we were trying to fit her into a round peg/round hole pattern, she was really a square peg that could not, should not, be forced into any set pattern. We could not see it then, but in years to come this unusual way that she dealt with learning things blossomed into notions of producing film and television programs and in creative marketing. But then, we were rolling with the rhythm the child produced, trying to keep our objectives clear, and finding a comfort level for the three of us. With her, we had to learn to tolerate a great deal of ambiguity.

Nai-Nai's flair was not accompanied by a smile for some time. When people would get in her face, talking baby talk to her and trying to get her to interact, she would lash out at them with a well-aimed scratch to each face. She didn't express herself in temper tantrums like Jelani; instead she sat like a cobra, quiet and seeming uninterested. But if you were to come close enough to threaten her space, she would let you know that she did not want to be bothered. My brother dismissed her intemperate habit on the basis that she had nothing to smile with, since her teeth didn't come in until she was nearly eighteen months old. Her toddler toothlessness was a source of many a family joke, with all sorts of remedies offered, from supplements to pills to tot dentures. Of course we waited this problem out, and what showed up was worth waiting for—wonderfully lovely baby teeth, followed a few years later with large shining enamels that showed off her other attractive features. I wouldn't go so far as to agree with my brother that her bad temper was due to not having teeth to smile with, but it is true that her disposition sweetened, inexplicably, by the time her teeth came in somewhere near two years of age. Hmm!

Nai-Nai is our optimist and caregiver. She brings you soup when you get sick and she encourages the belief in you that you will get well soon. You tend to believe it, because you can see that she does. She has cheered her sisters on through hard times, cheered them on to good times, and has often exhibited wisdom beyond her years. When Jamila had a rather bad breakup with a guy she thought she had some future with, for some reason his brother kept coming by as if he were still on a friendly basis—even though Jam's former beau took up with another girl immediately after abandoning Jamila. Jamila was twenty-five, and Nai was fifteen. But she saw through the phoniness of the brother's relationship with Jam. "I don't have any business," she said to Jam, after questioning her about why this guy was still coming around, "but, if I did, Akilah would know it." Jam quickly figured out that the brother must have known of his brother's unfaithfulness to her.

Nailah's performance in school, while outstanding, and in most households would have been considered excellent, often fell short of that of her sisters. She became more successful academically as her schooling narrowed more and more to the disciplines she adopted as her specialties. The most special thing about Nai-Nai, though, was that she pulled very hard for and cheered for the success of each of her sisters. "Watch when they call the name of the top student today, Daddy," she excitedly told me as we waited for that announcement at the summer science program's closing exercises. "It's going to be Akilah. She's the smartest one. I bet you!" In her own right, she showed better judgment than the rest at an earlier age, worked harder than anyone on the things that interested her most and looked forward to every tomorrow with hopefulness centered in faith. She always had more friends, and the most genuine and longest-lasting friendships of any of our children. This is largely because she gave more attention to cultivating them, tolerated shallow relationships less well than her sisters, and was able to have more exuberance and enjoyment with her friends because of it. With her caring heart, Nai-Nai has the spirit to see things both as they are and as she would like them to be. These traits are the cornerstones of her success.

Boys beware. She listened better than her sisters when it came to the guys. I told them all not to be flattered if some boy should come up to them and say something like, "You're so cute," or "You're so beautiful." "All they're doing is stating a fact, for which you owe them nothing—a fact that neither he nor you had anything to do with. If he wants to give credit for your looks, tell him to see Mom and me," I'd said. She took it to heart. I overheard her on the phone once saying to her friend, "My daddy said that if a guy says ..." Music to a father's ears! And when she didn't particularly like a certain fellow who had been around for such a while that she felt bad cutting him loose, I'd advised that she shouldn't be afraid to make the best choices for herself, especially early on in her life when no one else was implicated except her and this guy. She later told me that she had not realized that fear of hurting him and of leaving a certain comfort zone was in the way of her true feelings and that our talk had helped her have a conversation with him to break things off.

All of my daughters were good listeners, but some of them had trouble disengaging from situations with boys who they knew weren't the best for them. Nai-Nai has been helpful to herself and to them on this issue from time to time. The young men of hers, and the young men of my other daughters and her girlfriends who have been cut off by Nailah's special powers of insight, have found it, I am sure, well, not amusing. But she is. This same eye that has proven critical in the discernment of foolishness and phoniness has given rise to a sense of humor, that is, well, a little sarcastic. It is relentless and biting. It backs people off and keeps them off guard. And it is really funny. It sometimes upsets. But it always bespeaks intolerance for nonsense and a conviction to stand her ground—maybe the way her baby scratches did from the start. This chocolate chip does not crumble, and anyone who knows her rather doubts that she will.

"Jeff, this is the last one, right?" This is the question Andrea's father had asked me after our fifth daughter, Akilah, had come onto the scene. This was a question only a father could ask. As young people having children, we gave thought only to the health of the baby, never really thinking about the risk Andrea might face to her own good health. But her father did. And, as I would learn later when my daughters started having children, as much as you might look forward to grandchildren, your thoughts turn first to your daughter's well being and then to that of the unborn child. If this were a matter that I should feel guilty about, then, I was thinking that I should feel only nearly half as guilty as Mr. Green himself, for he was the father of eleven. But I understood his point. Akilah's birth had not been easy. You would think that after number four had gone so smoothly, number five would be a breeze. The epidurals Andrea had taken to see her painlessly through the births of Jelani and Nailah she decided to trade for an intravenous drip medication. It didn't work nearly as well for her, neither as a painkiller nor as a way to keep her alert during the birthing of the baby. She was dull and, worse, the baby was too, and neither one was able to do her part fully to move things along. The labor took a very long time—both Andrea and the baby working much too hard. Finally, near the end, it seemed they both gave out at about the same time. Akilah's crown showed, and after six hours her full head slowly emerged, but nothing else. The doctor was alarmed. I heard him talking things over with another doc about his worry of shoulder dystocia, possible nerve damage to her arms and shoulder, and potential paralysis of one or more of her upper limbs if she were not hurriedly extracted. I prayed as hard as I could. It was at once unsettling and reassuring to see the doctor praying too. Then, he stepped up to my wife, took Akilah's head into his hands, and with a grip that appeared firm and loose at the same time, engaged in a sustained tug until she literally popped out, popping sound and all, into his arms. Poor thing, she was hardly awake and very listless. Andrea, too, was limp and lethargic. We gave her the first name of her mother as a middle name and Akilah—meaning "intelligent one"—as a first moniker. She was the smallest and skinniest of our babies—the runt of the litter. I alone may call her "runt." That is my pet name for her.

Akilah took a little something from everyone, it seemed: Jamila's and Jelani's eyes, Jalila's smile, Nai's interest in artsy things, her mother's interest in flowers, and, she says, my upper lip. In any event, for one arriving so late—indeed, as Mr. Green had prayed, last on the immediate family tree—comparisons were inevitable. Cutting her own path was hard. Every leftover book and hand-me-down piece of clothing was hers. Jelani had gotten a new baby bed, because there was such a spread between Jalila and her, and Nailah had gotten a new one because she and Jelani were born so close together that Lani had not given hers up when Nai-Nai came. Kilah got Lani's baby bed.

Orders were handed down the line, too. If Jamila was told that I wanted something from the kitchen, she'd asked Jalila to get it, were she of a mind to do so, and Jalila would routinely comply. And so the chain of non-responsibility passed from one higher-up in the hierarchy to one who had come into the picture later. Of course, Akilah got orders from every one of her sisters. I did not know it, but this bothered her to no end. As number six in my family of ten, I had routinely engaged in this practice, that I believe, more or less, goes on in every family with siblings of childhood ages. My older brother and sisters told me what to do, and when I could, I passed it down to a younger brother or sister. I took it in stride, either way. By the time Akilah was five, she was fed up with this practice, since she had no one to hand off to.

I had taken the responsibility to talk to each one of our children individually at least every week or so. My question of them was always the same: "How are things going? Are they better or worse than the last time we talked?" I knew to do this because I noticed earlier in our group talks that the older children naturally dominated the conversation, so I could not get much discussion out of the younger ones. At one such one-on-one meeting with Akilah, I asked her the standard questions, to which she replied,

"Things are horrible. I hate my house. I have to do everything everyone wants!" Then she explained her problem as I have just set it out. I was shocked at her reaction, because I had not felt as put-upon when I had been given assignments by a higher-up. But she was not finished. "I'm going to run away from home!" I thought this was totally amusing—a five-year-old running away?

"Where will you go?" I asked.

"I don't know." She started to cry. "But I have already packed my things." Indeed, she had. She was serious. In her Barbie Doll suitcase, she had packed a few pairs of shorts, and some shirts, and some dolls. I had to quickly sit everyone down and plead with them to take care of their own assignments and not give them to Kilah, because she couldn't deal with it anymore.

But Akilah also learned from this bottom treatment to fight for herself. Once, while at the dinner table, Jamila was making fun of Akilah's ears, which, I must admit, were rather large for her small face when she was about five and a half. I was about to intervene to stop Jamila's teasing when Akilah said to her, "Jamila, do you remember the story of the mouse and the lion?" I sat back in my chair, satisfied that the runt was developing mettle enough to handle her sisters, at least enough to get by. And I knew also that she was learning from my stories to her, for it had been just a week earlier that I had told her the mouse and lion story. It involved a mouse that was caught by a lion and was reduced to begging for his life. He promised the mighty lion that if he would spare him that he might help him in time of trouble. To this, of course, the lion roared in laughter. "How could a tiny mouse help the king of the jungle?" he laughed. Weeks later, the story goes, the mouse was foraging for food when he came upon the lion trapped in a rope trap set by lion hunters. The little mouse gnawed the lion free, establishing the notion that sometimes big guys need little guys.

Indeed, going back to when she was really small, somewhere around three, we took Akilah to a learning center for the summer. She had shown great interest in books and numbers and appeared to be learning as fast and as well as any of her sisters had. But now she was in a "formal school" and we would see what she would be able to do. A counseling session was set up for us three weeks into the program. But we got the picture of her performance before the time of the session.

One night, Akilah came and got in our bed, lay on my pillow, and put her hands behind her head as one does when relaxing. "You know what?" she said, with kind of a whimsical, quirky look on her face, or maybe with just a look of surprised satisfaction.

"No, what, baby?" I asked in reply.

"At school," she started, "at school, I get everything right." And the "intelligent one," as we had named her, went on from there to higher academic heights. Sometimes things came so easily to Akilah that she might often not try hard enough, or even be willing to settle for less than she could do, because she was confident that she had nothing to prove.

"Daddy, what's wrong with a B?" she inquired of me as I chastised her for not getting an A in a subject that I knew she understood.

"Nothing is wrong with a B," I said, "if that is the best you can do. But, if God has given you the ability to make an A and you won't do it, then everything is wrong with it."

After a few of these exchanges, and a few withdrawn incentives, she got the message. We were shocked at this question, because none of our other children had ever asked this of either of us. It was a reminder that you never know enough as parents to stop learning about your children, and that you can never get comfortable as a parent whose other children have been successful, or become so complacent or so tired as to let the baby go without applying the same attention and guidance, as needed, as with the earlier children. Each one is different—for real!

Jamila says that Akilah is the "biggest girl" of them all. This is certainly not because she is the neatest of them all, because after my living with five daughters, if there are any such things as "girl traits or tendencies," I doubt that neatness is one of them. Our girls tended to have a lot more things than most guys I know and therefore a lot fewer places to put them. On vacations from school, they brought a lot of stuff that they never fully unpacked, and they lived out of their suitcases. Akilah kept the same mess as the rest in this regard. What Jam means, though, is that Akilah orders all the beauty and makeup magazines, knows how to use makeup in ways most girls don't take the time with, and is the family "professional" when it comes to hairstyling, plaiting, and fixing. She takes the most time with the "pretty things" that girls deal with than the others, at least according to Jam. This is another area in which a prudent father cannot take a position, and so I point out again—these are Jam's observations, not mine.

Akilah has a definite creative side. It expressed itself early in her life in her artwork; her drawings and colorings were detailed and plain good for a little child. She joined Nai-Nai in decorating dolls and making pretty things. She loved cameras, having her picture taken, and pretending to take pictures. Later, she took to making jewelry, which she now displays, and sometimes sells in the stores of her friends. But unlike the others of her close kin, who merchandised in words, Akilah had a keen interest in science. She wanted to know about rocks and twigs—how they grew and where they came from. She cared about dinosaurs and insects, and planets and stars. She loved science projects and making poster boards showing acids and bases. She was interested in the insides of frogs, and horses and people. As a little girl, she wanted a doctor's kit and bag, and to lift up your shirt and examine you and to try to make you feel better. It was a sign of things to come.

Akilah's sense of humor is not like Jelani's. Lani's is dry and with a definite, although not always instantly obvious, punch line. Akilah's humor is slapstick, accompanied by irrepressible, surround-sound laughter, and mostly coming from poking fun at anything and everything with which she comes in contact. Nai-Nai's humor often sends a message or is retaliatory. But with Akilah, nothing is provoked and nothing and no one is off-limits as objects of her humorous ridicule—old people, fat people, skinny people, smelly people, and family people, even herself. She laughs out loud at everything. Her jokes, if you can call them that, aren't necessarily funny, but she is. Even if they don't have a punch line, obvious or not, you laugh because she does. Sometimes she doesn't say anything at all, she just starts laughing for no apparent reason, and then so do you. If you can handle running the risk of being laughed at, she can be one of the most pleasant and outrageously entertaining and flat funny people you can be around.

But she is and always will be the baby. This means that she gets away with more and is required to do less, at least according to her sisters. Part of all the laughter, they will sometimes say, is because she hasn't engaged life seriously enough because she hasn't been made to by her two suddenly lenient parents—us. But we beg to differ, Kilah, Andrea, and I. Sure, she will miss plane schedules, which we shrug off as understanding that she slept late. And when she blows her allowance for the month about halfway through, instead of telling her to get a job and to get her budget right, we just make up the difference. And, of course, when she wanted to try for still another degree while she waited for medical school applications to be processed—we would have told the others, "No way!"— "Instead, you let her do it and happily pay for a degree she might not have needed," the others say. They wonder if we have gone soft. But the way we see it—Kilah, Andrea, and I—is not that we are putting our heads together on this or working together against the other children, but that we haven't changed, things simply have. Researchers have now discovered that a child needs sleep more in the morning than the rest of us, up to age twenty-five. We simply didn't have this information available to us when the others were coming along. And we have known for a long time that allowances were too low, but we couldn't afford to pay a higher one earlier. We really think it is exceptional that Kilah makes it as far in a month as she does without going broke. We have no idea how the others managed on so little, but that is no reason, it seems to us—Kilah, Andrea, and I—to stay stuck in the past and not do better by Akilah than we did by them. Fair is fair, we feel. And, as for the extra degree—the world is a lot more competitive than a few years back.

One has to adjust, doesn't one? Sure, she may not need it, but, but, she's the baby. Oops!

However all that may be, Akilah has turned out really well, as have the others before her. She's in her first year of medical school, now, soon to be the doctor she always dreamed and prayed she would be. We think her stint in the hospital in Botswana, Africa, sealed and made real her early ambition for medicine. She became ill on our family trip to Botswana, and had to be treated there. She saw, firsthand, how far medicine has to go to reach the underserved of the world. More than that, she saw what she might contribute to help to fill this gap. After getting the Golden Griffin Award at her elementary school, like her sisters had, she went on to become an A student in high school, then on to Brown University, to Harvard for post baccalaureate work for course requirements for medical school, to the master's degree in biomedical advocacy from Georgetown, and now to Tulane Medical School.

Nailah fulfilled her creative interest by getting degrees in film and television and in creative marketing from Boston University and Emerson College, respectively. She's headed to success in the world of visual arts, game and movie production, as the Good Lord cut her out to do.

When Jelani was in the fifth grade, she was walking with me, holding my hand, and said, "Daddy, know what I am going to do?"

"No, what, baby?"

"I'm going to get the Golden Griffin Award, as the top student in sixth grade next year, and then I am going to make a four-point average in high school, and I am going to go to Harvard College and to Harvard Law School." That's exactly what she did. I am not sure, though, whether this was an original thought, or maybe a course suggested to her by the path her older sisters were already carving. Indeed, up to that point, Jamila had already accomplished three of Lani's stated objectives, and Jalila, one of them. In a few short years to follow they each would indeed have accomplished all four goals—all three of them. Jalila, the kid who thought she would never learn to read, and Jamila, who was told earlier by an early childhood "expert" that she would be only an average student, graduated from Harvard College and Harvard Law School.

This is the court that our Miss Southern, with a little help from a cool Omega man—me—has raised up. What has happened with our girl children may have had its genesis on that cool night in September when we stood waiting to go to our first college football game together, when their mother swore, and later made me swear, that the girls of our future, whether ours or someone else's, would not have to stand for one election or selection when she would rather stand for or make another.

Well, having said what I've said here, and Andrea having expressed herself pointedly on the subject of girls thinking and being thought about in nontraditional terms, I should probably drop the beauty-queen metaphor, and say these are wonderful young women, not a wonderful queen's court, that we have, through the grace of God, raised. But, bear with me. Perhaps, if I keep referring to her as Miss Southern, she will take my hand, as she did on that night in a room outside of the Southern University football stadium, now long years past, tuck it inside my coat, somewhere between my chest and my belly button, so that my elbow naturally forms the escort-ready position, slip her still-dainty wrist through that small triangle-shaped space thus created, and tug me forward once again. Amuse me!

Miss Southern and Her Court, Circa 1991.
Back: Jelani, Jalila, and Jamila.
Front: Akilah, Miss Southern, and Nailah.